PRAISE FOR DICK FRANCIS . . .

(continued on next page)

THE *NEW YORK TIMES* BESTSELLER...

10 Lb. Penalty ... A politician recruits his son to help him win an election—but a long-ago danger returns to threaten their very lives ...

"ANOTHER WINNER."
—*Orlando Sentinel*

THE *NEW YORK TIMES* BESTSELLER...

To the Hilt ... Living in a remote part of Scotland, Alexander Kinloch was an artist and the black sheep of his family. Until his desperate clan requested his urgent help ...

"*TO THE HILT* DELIVERS THE PLEASURES PEOPLE PAY FOR."
—*The New York Times Book Review*

"DELIGHTFUL ... The Mystery Writers of America honored Francis as a Grand Master; this novel again shows why."
—*Publishers Weekly*

WINNER OF THE EDGAR AWARD FOR BEST NOVEL...

Come to Grief ... Ex-jockey Sid Halley can't help but suspect his dear friend Ellis Quint is behind a shocking series of violent acts. But no one wants to believe him ...

"A SURE BET."
—*Booklist*

A *NEW YORK TIMES* NOTABLE BOOK OF THE YEAR . . .

Wild Horses . . . Director Thomas Lyon finally has the chance to direct a blockbuster, based on a twenty-six-year-old unsolved crime. But a cryptic confession and a frightening assault lead him to pick up the thread of this unfinished tale—and follow it to its perilous end . . .

"THE BOOK'S PAGES SEEM TO TURN BY THEMSELVES."
—San Francisco Chronicle

A *NEW YORK TIMES* BESTSELLER . . .

Decider . . . An architect becomes involved with a warring upper-class family battling over a once-grand racecourse—and finds himself in a race to save himself—and his own family—from deadly peril . . .

"AND THE WINNER IS . . . THE READER."
—Indianapolis Star

A *NEW YORK TIMES* BESTSELLER . . .

Proof . . . A wine merchant is catering a society soiree when a team of hit men crashes the party—literally . . .

"A VINTAGE BLEND . . . *Proof* can be savored with pleasure."
—Chicago Tribune

"GREAT FUN!"
—People

DEAD CERT

DICK FRANCIS

JOVE BOOKS, NEW YORK

DEAD CERT

A Jove Book / published by arrangement with
HarperCollins Publishers, Inc.

PRINTING HISTORY
Previously published by Ballantine Books
Jove edition / January 2000

The Penguin Putnam Inc. World Wide Web site address is
http://www.penguinputnam.com

ISBN: 0-515-12726–4

A JOVE BOOK®
Jove Books are published by The Berkley Publishing Group,
a division of Penguin Putnam Inc.,
375 Hudson Street, New York, New York 10014.
JOVE and the "J" design
are trademarks belonging to Penguin Putnam Inc.

PRINTED IN THE UNITED STATES OF AMERICA

10 9 8 7 6 5 4 3 2 1

chapter 1

THE MINGLED SMELLS of hot horse and cold river mist filled my nostrils. I could hear only the swish and thud of galloping hooves and the occasional sharp click of horseshoes striking against each other. Behind me, strung out, rode a group of men dressed like myself in white silk breeches and harlequin jerseys, and in front, his body vividly red and green against the pale curtain of fog, one solitary rider steadied his horse to jump the birch fence stretching blackly across his path.

All, in fact, was going as expected. Bill Davidson was about to win his ninety-seventh steeplechase. Admiral, his chestnut horse, was amply proving he was still the best hunter 'chaser in the kingdom, and I, as often before, had been admiring their combined back view of several minutes.

Ahead of me the powerful chestnut hind-quarters bunched, tensed, sprang: Admiral cleared the fence with the effortlessness of the really great performer. And he'd gained another two lengths, I saw, as I followed him over. We were down at the far end of Maidenhead racecourse with more than half a mile to go to the winning post. I hadn't a hope of catching him.

The February fog was getting denser. It was now impossible to see much farther than from one fence to the next, and the silent surrounding whiteness seemed to shut us, and isolated string of riders, into a private lonely limbo. Speed was the only reality. Winning post, crowds, stands and stewards, left behind in the mist, lay again invisibly ahead, but on the long deserted mile and a half circuit it was quite difficult to believe they were really there.

It was an eerie, severed world in which anything might happen. And something did.

We rounded the first part of the bend at the bottom of the racecourse and straightened to jump the next fence. Bill was a good ten lengths in front of me and the other horses, and hadn't exerted himself. He seldom needed to.

The attendant at the next fence strolled across the course from the outside to the inside, patting the top of the birch as he went, and ducked under the rails. Bill glanced back over his shoulder and I saw the flash of his teeth as he smiled with satisfaction to see me so far behind. Then he turned his head towards the fence and measured his distance.

Admiral met the fence perfectly. He rose to it as if flight were not only for birds.

And he fell.

Aghast, I saw the flurry of chestnut legs threshing the air as the horse pitched over in a somersault I had a glimpse of Bill's bright-clad figure hurtling head downwards from the highest point of his trajectory, and I heard the crash of Admiral landing upside down after him.

Automatically I swerved over to the right and kicked my horse into the fence. In mid-air, as I crossed it, I looked down at Bill. He lay loosely on the ground with one arm outstretched. His eyes were shut. Admiral had fallen solidly, back downwards, across Bill's unprotected abdomen, and he was rolling backward and forward in a frantic effort to stand up again.

I had a brief impression that something lay beneath them. Something incongruous, which ought not to be there. But I was going too fast to see properly.

As my horse pressed on away from the fence, I felt as sick as if I'd been kicked in the stomach myself. There had been a quality about that fall which put it straight into the killing class.

I looked over my shoulder. Admiral succeeded in getting to his feet and cantered off loose, and the attendant stepped forward and bent over Bill, who still lay motionless on the ground. I turned back to attend to the race. I had been left in front and I ought to stay there. At the side of the course a black-suited, white-sashed First-Aid man was running towards and past me. He had been standing at the fence I was now approaching, and was on his way to help Bill.

I booted my horse into the next three fences, but my heart was no longer in it, and when I emerged as the winner into the full view of the crowded stands, the mixed gasp and groan which greeted me seemed an apt enough welcome. I passed the winning post, patted my mount's neck, and looked at the stands. Most heads were still turned towards the last fence, searching in the impenetrable mist for Admiral, the odds-on certainty who had lost his first race in two years.

Even the pleasant middle-aged woman whose horse I was riding met me with the question, "What happened to Admiral?"

"He fell," I said.

"How lucky," said Mrs. Mervyn, laughing happily.

She took hold of the bridle and led her horse into the winner's unsaddling enclosure. I slid off and undid the girth buckles with fingers clumsy from shock. She patted the horse and chattered on about how delighted she was to have won, and how unexpected it was, and how fortunate that Admiral had tripped up for a change, though a great pity in another way, of course.

I nodded and smiled at her and didn't answer, because what I would have said would have been savage and unkind. Let her enjoy her win, I thought. They come seldom enough. And Bill might, after all, be all right.

I tugged the saddle off the horse and, leaving a beaming Mrs. Mervyn receiving congratulations from all around, pressed through the crowd into the weighing room. I sat on the scales, was passed as correct, walked into the changing room, and put my gear down on the bench.

Clem, the racecourse valet who looked after my stuff, came over. He was a small elderly man, very spry, and tidy, with a weatherbeaten face and wrists whose tendons stood out like tight strung cords.

He picked up my saddle and ran his hand caressingly over the leather. It was a habit he had grown into, I imagine, from long years of caring for fine-grained skins. He stroked a saddle as another man would a pretty girl's cheek, savouring the suppleness, the bloom.

"Well done, sir," he said; but he didn't look overjoyed.

I didn't want to be congratulated. I said abruptly, "Admiral should have won."

"Did he fall?" asked Clem anxiously.

"Yes," I said. I couldn't understand it, thinking about it.

"Is Major Davidson all right, sir?" asked Clem. He valeted Bill too and, I knew, looked upon him as a sort of minor god.

"I don't know," I said. But the hard saddle-tree had hit him plumb in the belly with the weight of a big horse falling at thirty miles an hour behind it. What chance has he got, poor beggar, I thought.

I shrugged my arms into my sheepskin coat and went along to the First-Aid room. Bill's wife, Scilla, was standing outside the door there, pale and shaking and doing her best not to be frightened. Her small neat figure was dressed gaily in scarlet, and a mink hat sat provocatively on top of her cloudy dark curls. They were clothes for success, not sorrow.

"Alan," she said, with relief, when she saw me. "The doctor's looking at him and asked me to wait here. What do you think? Is he bad?" She was pleading, and I hadn't much comfort to give her. I put my arm round her shoulders.

She asked me if I had seen Bill fall, and I told her he had dived on to his head and might be slightly concussed.

The door opened, and a tall slim well-groomed man came out. The doctor.

"Are you Mrs. Davidson?" he said to Scilla. She nodded.

"I'm afraid your husband will have to go along to the hospital," he said. "It wouldn't be sensible to send him home without an X-ray." He smiled reassuringly, and I felt some of the tension go out of Scilla's body.

"Can I go in and see him?" she said.

The doctor hesitated. "Yes," he said finally, "but he's almost unconscious. He had a bit of a bang on the head. Don't try to wake him."

When I started to follow Scilla into the First-Aid room the doctor put his hand on my arm to stop me.

"You're Mr. York, aren't you?" he asked. He had given me a regulation check after an easy fall I'd had the day before.

"Yes."

"Do you know these people well?"

"Yes. I live with them most of the time."

The doctor closed his lips tight, thinking. Then he said, "It's not good. The concussion's not much, but he's bleeding internally, possibly from a ruptured spleen. I've telephoned the hospital to take him in as an emergency case as soon as we can get him there."

As he spoke, one of the racecourse ambulances backed up towards us. The men jumped out, opened the rear doors, took out a big stretcher and carried it into the First-Aid room. The doctor went in after them. Soon they all reappeared with Bill on the stretcher. Scilla followed, the anxiety plain on her face, deep and well-founded.

Bill's firm brown humourous face now lolled flaccid, bluish-white, and covered with fine beads of sweat. He was gasping slightly through his open mouth, and his hands were restlessly pulling at the blanket which covered him. He was still wearing his green and red checked racing colours, the most ominous sign of all.

Scilla said to me, "I'm going with him in the ambulance. Can you come?"

"I've a ride in the last race," I said. "I'll come along to the hospital straight after that. Don't worry, he'll be all right." But I didn't believe it, and nor did she.

After they had gone I walked along beside the weighing room building and down through the car park until I came to the bank of the river. Swollen from recently melted snow, the Thames was flowing fast, sandy brown and grey with froths of white. The water swirled out of the mist a hundred yards to my right, churned round the bend where I stood, and disappeared again into the fog. Troubled, confused, not seeing a clear course ahead. Just like me.

For there was something wrong about Bill's accident.

Back in Bulawayo where I got my schooling, the mathematics master spent hours (too many, I thought in my youth) teaching us to draw correct inferences from a few known facts. But deduction was his hobby as well as his job, and occasionally we had been able to side-track him from problems of geometry or algebra to those of Sherlock Holmes. He produced class after class of boys keenly observant of well-worn toe-caps on char-women and vicars and calluses on the finger tips of harpists; and the mathematics standard of the school was exceptionally high.

Now, thousands of miles and seven years away from the sun-baked schoolroom, standing in an English fog and growing very cold, I remembered my master and took out my facts, and had a look at them.

Known facts . . . Admiral, a superb jumper, had fallen abruptly in full flight for no apparent reason. The race-course attendant had walked across the course behind the fence as Bill and I rode towards it, but this was not at all unusual. And as I had cleared the fence, and while I was looking down at Bill, somewhere on the edge of my vision there had been a dull damp gleam from some-thing grey and metallic. I thought about these things for a long time.

The inference was there all right, but unbelievable I had to find out if it was the correct one.

I went back into the weighing room to collect my kit and weigh out for the last race, but as I packed the flat lead pieces into my weight cloth to bring my weight up to that set by the handicapper, the loudspeakers were turned on and it was announced that owing to the thick-ening fog the last race had been abandoned.

There was a rush then in the changing room and the tea and fruitcake disappeared at a quickened tempo. It was a long time since breakfast, and I stuffed a couple of beef sandwiches into my mouth while I changed. I arranged with Clem for my kit to go to Plumpton, where I was due to ride four days later, and set off on an un-inviting walk. I wanted to have a close look at the place where Bill had fallen.

It is a long way on foot from the stands to the far end of Maidenhead racecourse, and by the time I got there my shoes, socks, and trouser legs were wet through from the long sodden grass. It was very cold, very foggy. There was no one about.

I reached the fence, the harmless, softish, easy-to-jump fence, made of black birch twigs standing upright. Three feet thick at the bottom slanting to half that size at the top, four feet six inches tall, about ten yards wide. Ordinary, easy.

I looked carefully along the landing side of the fence. There was nothing unusual. Round I went to the take-off side. Nothing. I poked around the wing which guides the horses into the fence, the one on the inside of the course, the side Bill had been when he fell. Still nothing.

It was down underneath the wing on the outside of the course that I found what I was looking for. There it lay in the long grass, half hidden, beaded with drops of mist, coiled and deadly.

Wire.

There was a good deal of it, a pale silver grey, wound into a ring about a foot across, and weighted down with a piece of wood. One end of it led up the main side post of the wing and was fastened round it two feet above the level of the top of the birch. Fastened, I saw, very securely indeed. I could not untwist it with my fingers.

I went back to the inside wing and had a look at the post. Two feet above the fence there was a groove in the wood. This post had once been painted white, and the mark showed clearly.

It was clear to me that only one person could have fixed the wire in place. The attendant. The man whom I myself had seen walk across from one side of the course to the other. The man, I thought bitterly, whom I had left to *help* Bill.

In a three mile 'chase at Maidenhead one rode twice round the course. On the first circuit there had been no trouble at this fence. Nine horses had jumped it safely, with Admiral lying third and biding his time, and me riding alongside telling Bill I didn't think much of the English climate.

Second time around, Admiral was lengths out in front. As soon as the attendant had seen him land over the fence before this one, he must have walked over holding the free end of wire and wound it round the opposite post so that it stretched there taut in the air, almost invisible, two feet above the birch. At that height it would catch the high-leaping Admiral straight across the shoulders.

The callousness of it awoke a slow deep anger which, though I did not then know it, was to remain with me as a spur for many weeks to come.

Whether the horse had snapped the wire when he hit it, or pulled it off the post, I could not be sure. But as I could find no separate pieces, and the coil by the outer wing was all one length, I thought it likely that the falling horse had jerked the less secure end down with him. None of the seven horses following me had been brought down. Like me, they must have jumped clear over the remains of the trap.

Unless the attendant was a lunatic, which could by no means be ruled out, it was a deliberate attack on a particular horse and rider. Bill on Admiral had normally reached the front by this stage in a race, often having opened up a lead of twenty lengths, and his red and green colours, even on a misty day, were easy to see.

At this point, greatly disturbed, I began the walk back. It was already growing dark. I had been longer at the fence than I had realised, and when I at length reached the weighing room, intending to tell the Clerk of the Course about the wire, I found everyone except the caretaker had gone.

The caretaker, who was old and bad-tempered and incessantly sucked his teeth, told me he did not know where the Clerk of the Course could be found. He said the racecourse manager had driven off towards the town five minutes earlier. He did not know where the manager had been going, nor when he would be back; and with a grumbling tale that he had five separate stoves besides the central boiler to see to, and that the fog was bad for his bronchitis, the caretaker shuffled purposefully off towards the dim murky bulk of the grandstand.

Undecided, I watched him go. I ought, I knew, to tell someone in authority about the wire. But who? The Stewards who had been at the meeting were all on their way home, creeping wearily through the fog, unreachable. The manager had gone; the Clerk of the Course's office, I discovered, was locked. It would take me a long time to locate any of them, persuade them to return to the racecourse and get them to drive down the course over the rough ground in the dark; and after that there would be discussion, repetition, statements. It after that there would be discussion, repetition, statements. It would be hours before I could get away.

Meanwhile Bill was fighting for his life in Maidenhead hospital, and I wanted profoundly to know if he were winning. Scilla faced racking hours of anxiety and I had promised to be with her as soon as I could. Already I had delayed too long. The wire, fog-bound and firmly twisted round the post, would keep until tomorrow, I thought; but Bill might not.

Bill's Jaguar was alone in the car park. I climbed in, switched on the side lights and the fog lights, and drove off. I turned left at the gates, went gingerly along the road for two miles, turning left again over the river, twisted through Maidenhead's one-way streets, and finally arrived at the hospital

There was no sign of Scilla in the brightly lit busy hall. I asked the porter.

"Mrs. Davidson? Husband a jockey? That's right, she's down there in the waiting room. Fourth door on the left."

I found her. Her dark eyes looked enormous, shadowed with grey smudges beneath them. All other colour had gone from her sad strained face, and she had taken off her frivolous hat.

"How is he?" I asked.

"I don't know. They just tell me not to worry." She was very close to tears.

I sat down beside her and held her hand.

"You're a comfort, Alan," she said.

Presently the door opened and a fair young doctor came in, stethoscope dangling.

"Mrs. Davidson, I think . . ." he paused, "I think you should come and sit with your husband."

"How is he?"

"Not . . . very well. We are doing all we can." Turning to me he said, "Are you a relative?"

"A friend. I am going to drive Mrs. Davidson home."

"I see," he said. "Will you wait, or come back for her? Later this evening." There was meaning in his careful voice, his neutral words. I looked closely into his face, and I knew that Bill was dying.

"I'll wait."

"Good."

I waited for four hours, getting to know intimately the pattern of the curtains and the cracks in the brown linoleum. Mostly, I thought about wire.

At last a nurse came, serious, young, pretty.

"I am so sorry . . . Major Davidson is dead."

Mrs. Davidson would like me to go and see him, she said, if I would follow her. She took me down the long corridors, and into a white room, not very big, where Scilla sat beside the single bed.

Scilla looked up at me. She couldn't speak.

Bill lay there, grey and quiet, finished. The best friend a man could wish for.

chapter 2

EARLY NEXT MORNING I drove Scilla, worn out from the vigil she had insisted on keeping all night beside Bill's body, and heavily drugged now with sedatives, home to the Cotswolds. The children came out and met her on the doorstep, their three faces solemn and round-eyed. Behind them stood Joan, the briskly competent girl who looked after them, and to whom I had telephoned the news the evening before.

There on the step Scilla sat down and wept. The children knelt and sat beside her, putting their arms round her, doing their best to comfort a grief they could only dimly understand.

Presently Scilla went upstairs to bed. I drew the curtains for her and tucked her in, and kissed her cheek. She was exhausted and very sleepy, and I hoped it would be many hours before she woke again.

I went along to my own room and changed my clothes. Downstairs I found Joan putting coffee, bacon and eggs, and hot rolls for me on the kitchen table. I gave the children the chocolate bars I had bought for them the previous morning (how very long ago it seemed) and they sat with me, munching, while I ate my breakfast. Joan poured herself some coffee.

"Alan?" said William. He was five, the youngest, and he would never go on speaking until you said "Yes?" to show you were listening.

"Yes?" I said.

"What happened to Daddy?"

So I told them about it, all of it except the wire.

They were unusually silent for a while. Then Henry, just eight, asked calmly, "Is he going to be buried or burnt?"

Before I could answer, he and his elder sister, Polly, launched into a heated and astonishingly well-informed discussion about the respective merits of burial and cremation. I was horrified, but relieved, too, and Joan, catching my eye, was hard put to it not to laugh.

The innocent toughness of their conversation started me on my way back to Maidenhead in a more cheerful frame of mind. I put Bill's big car in the garage and set off in my own little dark blue Lotus. The fog had completely gone, but I drove slowly (for me), working out what was best to do.

First I called at the hospital. I collected Bill's clothes, signed forms, made arrangements. There was to be a routine post mortem examination the next day.

It was Sunday. I drove to the racecourse, but the gates were locked. Back in the town the Clerk of the Course's office was shut and empty. I telephoned his home, but there was no answer.

After some hesitation I rang up the Senior Steward of the National Hunt Committee, going straight to the top steeplechase authority. Sir Creswell Stampe's butler said he would see if Sir Creswell was available. I said it was very important that I should speak with him. Presently he came on the line.

"I certainly hope what you have to say *is* very important, Mr. York. I am in the middle of luncheon with my guests."

"Have you heard, sir, that Major Davidson died yesterday evening?"

"Yes. I'm very sorry about it, very sorry indeed." He waited. I took a deep breath.

"His fall wasn't an accident," I said.

"What do you mean?"

"Major Davidson's horse was brought down by wire," I said.

I told him about my search in the fence, and what I had found there.

"You have let Mr. Dace know about this?" he asked. Mr. Dace was the Clerk of the Course.

I explained that I had been unable to find him.

"So you rang me. I see." He paused. "Well, Mr. York, if you are right, this is too serious to be dealt with entirely by the National Hunt Committee. I think you should inform the police in Maidenhead without delay. Let me know this evening, without fail, what is happening. I will try to get in touch with Mr. Dace."

I put down the receiver. The buck had been passed, I thought. I could imagine the Stampe roast beef congealing on the plate while Sir Creswell set the wires humming.

The police station in the deserted Sunday street was dark, dusty-looking, and uninviting. I went in. There were three desks behind the counter, and at one of them sat a young constable reading a newspaper of the juicier sort. Keeping up with his crime, I reflected.

"Can I help you, sir?" he said, getting up.

"Is there anyone else here?" I asked. "I mean, someone senior? It's about a . . . a death."

"Just a minute, sir." He went out of a door at the back, and returned to say, "Will you come in here, please?"

He stood aside to let me into a little inner office, and shut the door behind me.

The man who rose to his feet was small for a policeman, thickset, dark, and in his late thirties. He looked more of a fighter than a thinker, but I found later that his brain matched his physique. His desk was littered with papers and heavy-looking law books. The gas fire had made a comfortable warm fug, and his ashtray was overflowing. He, too, was spending his Sunday afternoon reading up crime.

"Good afternoon. I am Inspector Lodge," he said. He gestured to a chair facing his desk, asking me to sit down. He sat down again himself, and began to shape his papers into neat piles.

"You have come about a death?" My own words, repeated, sounded foolish, but his tone was matter-of-fact.

"It's about a Major Davidson . . ." I began.

"Oh yes. We had a report. He died in the hospital last night after a fall at the races." He waited politely for me to go on.

"That fall was engineered," I said bluntly.

Inspector Lodge looked at me steadily, then drew a sheet of paper out of a drawer, unscrewed his fountain pen, and wrote, I could see, the date and the time. A methodical man.

"I think we had better start at the beginning," he said. "What is your name?"

"Alan York."

"Age?"

"Twenty-four."

"Address?"

I gave Davidsons' address, explaining whose it was, and that I lived there a good deal.

"Where is your own home?"

"In Southern Rhodesia," I said. "On a cattle station near a village called Induna, about fifteen miles from Bulawayo."

"And you are a professional jockey?"

"No, an amateur. I work in London three days or so a week."

"Occupation?"

"I represent my father in his London office."

"And your father's business?"

"The Bailey York Trading Company."

"What do you trade on?" asked Lodge.

"Copper, lead, cattle. Anything and everything. We're transporters mainly," I said.

He wrote it all down, in quick distinctive script.

"Now then," he put down the pen, "what is it all about?"

"I don't know what it's about," I said, "but this is what happened." I told him the whole thing. He listened without interrupting, then he said, "What made you even begin to suspect that this was not a normal fall?"

"Admiral is the safest jumper there is. He's sure-footed, like a cat. He doesn't make mistakes."

But I could see from his politely surprised expression that he knew little, if anything, about steeplechasing, and thought that one horse was as likely to fall as another.

I tried again. "Admiral is brilliant over fences. He would never fall like that, going into an easy fence in his own time, not being pressed. He took off perfectly. I saw him. That fall was unnatural. It looked to me as though something had been used to bring him down. I thought it might be wire, and I went back to look, and it was. That's all."

"Hm. Was the horse likely to win?" asked Lodge.

"Certain," I said.

"And who did win?"

"I did," I said.

Lodge paused, and bit the end of his pen.

"How do the racecourse attendants get their jobs?" he asked.

"I don't really know. They are casual staff, taken on for the meeting, I think," I said.

"Why would a racecourse attendant wish to harm Major Davidson?" He said this naively, and I looked at him sharply.

"Do you think I have made it all up?" I asked.

"No." He sighed. "I suppose I don't. Perhaps I should have said, how difficult would it be for someone who wished to harm Major Davidson to get taken on as a racecourse attendant?"

"Easy," I said.

"We'll have to find out." He reflected. "It's a very chancy way to murder a man."

"Whoever planned it can't have meant to kill him," I said flatly.

"Why not?"

"Because it was so unlikely that he would die. I should think it was simply meant to stop him winning."

"Why was such a fall unlikely to result in death?" said Lodge. "It sounds highly dangerous to me."

I said: "It could have been meant to injure him, I suppose. Usually, when a horse is going fast and hits a fence hard when you're not expecting it, you get catapulted out of the saddle. You fly through the air and hit the ground way out in front of where your horse falls. That may do a lot of damage, but it doesn't often kill. But Bill Davidson wasn't flung off forwards. His toe may have stuck in his stirrup, though that's not very likely. Perhaps the wire caught round his leg and pulled him back. Anyway, he fell straight down and his horse crashed on top of him. Even then it was sheer bad luck that the saddle tree hit him in the stomach. You couldn't even hope to kill a man like that on purpose."

"I see. You seem to have given it some thought."

"Yes." The pattern of the hospital waiting room curtains, the brown linoleum, came back into my mind in association.

"Can you think of anyone who might wish to hurt Major Davidson?" asked Lodge.

"No," I said. "He was very well liked."

Lodge got up and stretched. "We'll go and have a look at your wire," he said. He put his head out into the big office. "Wright, go and see if Hawkins is there, and tell him I want a car if there's one available."

There was a car. Hawkins (I presumed) drove, I sat in the back with Lodge. The main gates of the racecourse were still locked, but there were ways and means, I found. A police key opened another, inconspicuous, gate in the wooden fence.

"In case of fire," said Lodge, seeing my sideways look.

There was no one about in the racecourse buildings: the manager was out. Hawkins drove over the course into the centre and headed down towards the farthest fence. We bumped a good deal on the uneven ground. The car drew up just short of the inside wing, and Lodge and I climbed out.

I led the way past the fence to the outer wing.

"The wire is over here," I said.

But I was wrong.

There was the post, the wing, the long grass, the birch fence. And no coil of wire.

"Are you sure this is the right fence?" said Lodge.

"Yes," I said. We stood looking at the course set out in front of us. We were at the very far end, the stands a blurred massive block in the distance. The fence by which we stood was alone on a short straight between two curves, and the nearest fence to us was three hundred yards to the left, round a shallow bend.

"You jump that fence," I said, pointing away to it. "Then there's quite a long run, as you can see, to this one." I patted the fence beside us. "Then twenty yards after we land over this one there is that sharpish left turn into the straight. The next fence is some way up the straight, to allow the horses to balance themselves properly after coming round the bend, before they have to jump. It's a good course."

"You couldn't have made a mistake in the mist?"

"No. This is the fence," I said.

Lodge sighed. "Well, we'll take a closer look."

But all there was to be seen was a shallow groove on the once white inner post, and a deeper groove on the outer post, where the wire had bitten into the wood. Both grooves needed looking for and would ordinarily have been unnoticed. Both were at the same level, six feet, six inches from the ground.

"Very inconclusive indeed," said Lodge.

We went back to Maidenhead in silence. Glum and feeling foolish, I knew now that even though I could reach no one in authority, I should have found someone, anyone, even the caretaker, the day before, to go back to the fence with me, after I had found the wire, to see it in its place. A witness who had seen wire fastened to a fence, even though it would have been dark and foggy, even though perhaps he could not swear at which fence he had seen it, would definitely have been better than no witness at all. I tried to console myself with the possibility that the attendant had been returning to the fence with his wire clippers at the same time that I was walking back to the stands, and that even if I had returned at once with a witness, it would already have been too late.

From Maidenhead police station I called Sir Creswell Stampe. I had parted him this time, he said, from his toasted muffins. The news that the wire had disappeared didn't please him, either.

"You should have got someone else to see it at once. Photographed it. Removed it. We can't proceed without evidence. I can't think why you didn't have sense enough to act more quickly, either. You have been very irresponsible, Mr. York." And with these few kind words he put down his receiver.

Depressed, I drove home.

I put my head quietly round Scilla's door. Her room was dark, but I could hear her even breathing. She was still sound asleep.

Downstairs, Joan and the children were sitting on the floor in front of the welcoming log fire playing poker. I had introduced them to the game one rainy day when the children were tired of snap and rummy and had been behaving very badly, quarrelling and shouting and raising tempers all round. Poker, the hitherto mysterious game of the cowboys in Westerns, had worked a miracle.

Henry developed in a few weeks into the sort of player you wouldn't sit down with twice without careful thought. His razor-sharp mathematical mind knew the odds to a fraction against any particular card turning up: his visual memory was formidable; and his air of slight bewilderment, calculated to be misleading, led many an unsuspecting adult straight into his traps. I admired Henry. He could out-bluff an angel.

Polly played well enough for me to be sure she would never lose continually in ordinary company, and even William knew a running flush from a full house.

They had been at it for some time. Henry's pile of poker chips was, as usual, three times as big as anyone else's.

Polly said, "Henry won all the chips a little while ago, so we had to share them out and start all over again."

Henry grinned. Cards were an open book to him and he couldn't help reading.

I took ten of Henry's chips and sat in with them. Joan dealt. She gave me a pair of fives and I drew another one. Henry discarded and drew two cards only, and looked satisfied.

The others threw in during the first two rounds. Then I boldly advanced two more chips to join the two on the table. "Raise you two, Henry," I said.

Henry glanced at me to make sure I was looking at him, then made a great show of indecision, drumming his fingers on the table and sighing. Knowing his habit of bluffing, I suspected he had a whopper of a hand and was scheming how to get me to disgorge the largest possible number of chips.

"Raise you one," he said at last.

I was just about to put another two chips firmly out, but I stopped and said, "Oh no you don't, Henry. Not this time," and I threw in my hand I pushed the four chips across to him. "This time you get four, and no more."

"What did you have, Alan?" Polly turned my cards over, showing the three fives.

Henry grinned. He made no attempt to stop Polly looking at his cards, too. He had a pair of kings. Just one pair.

"Got you that time, Alan," he said happily.

William and Polly groaned heavily.

We played until I had won back my reputation and a respectable number of Henry's chips. Then it was the children's bedtime, and I went up to see Scilla.

She was awake, lying in the dark.

"Come in, Alan."

I went over and switched on the bedside lamp. The first shock was over. She looked calm, peaceful.

"Hungry?" I asked. She had not eaten since lunch the day before.

"Do you know, Alan, I am," she said as if surprised.

I went downstairs and with Joan rustled up some supper. I carried the tray up and ate with Scilla. Sitting propped up with pillows, alone in the big bed, she began to tell me about how she had met Bill, the things they had done together, the fun they had had. Her eyes shone with remembered happiness. She talked for a long time, all about Bill, and I did not stop her until her lips began to tremble. Then I told her about Henry and his pair of kings, and she smiled and grew calm again.

I wanted very much to ask her whether Bill had been in any trouble or had been threatened in any way during the last few weeks, but it wasn't the right time to do it.

So I got her to take another of the sedatives the hospital had given me for her, turned off her light, and said good night.

As I undressed in my own room the tiredness hit me. I had been awake for over forty hours, few of which could be called restful. I flopped into bed. It was one of those times when the act of falling asleep is a conscious, delicious luxury.

Half an hour later Joan shook me awake again. She was in her dressing-gown.

"Alan, wake up for goodness sake. I've been knocking on your door for ages."

"What's the matter?"

"You're wanted on the telephone. Personal call," she said.

"Oh no," I groaned. It felt like the middle of the night. I looked at my watch. Eleven o'clock.

I staggered downstairs, eyes bleary with sleep.

"Hello?"

"Mr. Alan York?"

"Yes."

"Hold on, please." Some clicks on the line. I yawned.

"Mr. York? I have a message for you from Inspector Lodge, Maidenhead police. He would like you to come here to the police station tomorrow afternoon, at four o'clock."

"I'll be there," I said. I rang off, went back to bed, and slept and slept.

LODGE WAS WAITING for me. He rose, shook hands, pointed to a chair. I sat down. The desk was clear now of everything except a neat, quarto-sized folder placed squarely in front of him. Slightly behind me, at a small table in the corner, sat a constable in uniform, pencil in hand, shorthand notebook at the ready.

"I have some statements here," Lodge tapped the file,

"which I will tell you about. Then I have some questions to ask." He opened the file and took out two sheets of paper clipped together.

"This is a statement from Mr. J. L. Dace, Clerk of the Course of Maidenhead racecourse. In it he says nine of the attendants, the men who stand by to make temporary repairs to the fences during the races, are regularly employed in that capacity. Three of them were new this meeting."

Lodge laid down this statement, and took out the next.

"This is a statement from George Watkins, one of the regular attendants. He says they draw lots among themselves to decide which fence each of them shall stand by. There are two at some fences. On Friday they drew lots as usual, but on Saturday one of the new men volunteered to go down to the farthest fence. None of them likes having to go right down there, Watkins says, because it is too far to walk back between races to 'have a bit' on a horse. So they were glad enough to let the stranger take that fence, and they drew lots for the rest."

"What did this attendant look like?" I asked.

"You saw him yourself," said Lodge.

"No, not really," I said. "All he was to me was a man. I didn't look at him. There's at least one attendant at every fence. I wouldn't know any of them again."

"Watkins says he thinks he'd know the man again, but he can't describe him. Ordinary, he says. Not tall, not short. Middle-aged, he thinks. Wore a cap, old grey suit, loose mackintosh."

"They all do," I said gloomily.

Lodge said, "He gave his name as Thomas Cook. Said he was out of work, had a job to go to next week and was filling in time. Very plausible, nothing odd about him at all, Watkins says. He spoke like a Londoner though, not with a Berkshire accent."

Lodge laid the paper down and took out another.

"This is a statement from John Russell of the St. John

Ambulance Brigade. He says he was standing beside the first fence in the straight watching the horses go round the bottom of the course. Because of the mist he says he could see only three fences: the one he was standing beside, the next fence up the straight, and the farthest fence, where Major Davidson fell. The fence before that, which was opposite him on the far side of the course, was an indistinct blur.

"He saw Major Davidson race out of the mist after he had jumped that fence. Then he saw him fall at the next. Major Davidson did not reappear, though his horse got up and galloped off riderless. Russell began to walk towards the fence where he had seen Major Davidson fall; then when you, Mr. York, passed him looking over your shoulder, he began to run. He found Major Davidson lying on the ground."

"Did he see the wire?" I asked eagerly.

"No. I asked him if he had seen anything at all unusual. I didn't mention wire specifically. He said there was nothing."

"Didn't he see the attendant roll up the wire while he was running towards him?"

"I asked him if he could see either Major Davidson or the attendants as he ran towards them. He says that owing to the sharp bend and the rails round it he could not see them until he was quite close. I gather he ran round the course instead of cutting across the corner through the long rough grass because it was too wet."

"I see," I said despondently. "And what was the attendant doing when he got there?"

"Standing beside Major Davidson looking down at him. He says the attendant looked frightened. This surprised Russell, because although he was knocked out Major Davidson did not appear to him to be badly injured. He waved his white flag, the next First-Aid man saw it and waved his, and the message was thus relayed through the fog all the way up the course to the ambulance."

"What did the attendant do then?"

"Nothing particular. He stayed beside the fence after the ambulance had taken Major Davidson away, and Russell says he was there until the abandonment of the last race was announced."

Clutching at straws, I said, "Did he go back with the other attendants and collect his pay?"

Lodge looked at me with interest. "No," he said, "he didn't."

He took out another paper.

"This is a statement from Peter Smith, head travelling lad for the Gregory stables, where Admiral is trained. He says that after Admiral got loose at Maidenhead he tried to jump a blackthorn hedge. He stuck in it and was caught beside it, scared and bleeding. There are cuts and scratches all over the horse's shoulders, chest, and forelegs." He looked up. "If the wire left any mark on him at all, it is impossible to distinguish it now."

"You have been thorough," I said, "and quick."

"Yes. We were lucky, for once, to find everyone we wanted without delay."

There was only one paper left. Lodge picked it up, spoke slowly.

"This is the report of the post mortem of Major Davidson. Cause of death was multiple internal injuries. Liver and spleen were both ruptured."

He sat back in his chair and looked at his hands.

"Now, Mr. York, I have been directed to ask you some questions which ... " his dark eyes came up to mine suddenly, " ... which I do not think you will like. Just answer them." His half smile was friendly.

"Fire away," I said.

"Are you in love with Mrs. Davidson?"

I sat up straight, surprised.

"No," I said.

"But you live with her?"

"I live with the whole family," I said.

"Why?"

"I have no home in England. When I first got to know Bill Davidson he asked me to his house for a weekend. I liked it there, and I suppose they liked me. Anyway, they asked me often. Gradually the weekends got longer and longer, until Bill and Scilla suggested I should make their house my headquarters. I spend a night or two every week in London."

"How long have you lived at the Davidsons'?" asked Lodge.

"About seven months."

"Were your relations with Major Davidson friendly?"

"Yes, very."

"And with Mrs. Davidson?"

"Yes."

"But you do not love her?"

"I am extremely fond of her. As an elder sister," I said, sitting tight on my anger. "She is ten years older than I am."

Lodge's expression said quite plainly that age had nothing to do with it. I was aware, just then, that the constable in the corner was writing down my replies.

I relaxed. I said, tranquilly, "She was very much in love with her husband, and he with her."

Lodge's mouth twitched at the corners. He looked, of all things, amused. Then he began again.

"I understand," he said, "that Major Davidson was the leading amateur steeplechase jockey in this country?"

"Yes."

"And you yourself finished second to him, a year ago, after your first season's racing in England?"

I stared at him. I said, "For someone who hardly knew steeplechasing existed twenty-four hours ago, you've wasted no time."

"Were you second to Major Davidson on the amateur

riders' list last year? And were you not likely to be second to him again? Is it not also likely that now, in his absence, you will head the list?"

"Yes, yes, and I hope so," I said. The accusation was as plain as could be, but I was not going to rush unasked into protestations of my innocence. I waited. If he wanted the suggestion made that I had sought to injure or kill Bill in order to acquire either his wife or his racing prestige, or both, Lodge would have to make it himself.

But he didn't. A full minute ticked by, during which I sat still. Finally Lodge grinned.

"Well, I think that's all, then, Mr. York. The information you gave us yesterday and your answers today will be typed together as one statement, and I shall be glad if you will read and sign it."

The policeman with the notebook stood up and walked into the outer office. Lodge said, "The coroner's inquest on Major Davidson is to be held on Thursday. You will be needed as a witness; and Mrs. Davidson, too, for evidence of identification. We'll be getting in touch with her."

He asked me questions about steeplechasing, ordinary conversational questions, until the statement was ready. I read it carefully and signed it. It was accurate and perfectly fair. I could imagine these pages joining the others in Lodge's tidy file. How fat would it grow before he found the accidental murderer of Bill Davidson?

If he ever did.

He stood up and held out his hand, and I shook it. I liked him. I wondered who had "directed" him to find out if I might have arranged the crime I had myself reported.

chapter 3

I RODE AT Plumpton two days later.

The police had been very discreet in their enquiries, and Sir Creswell also, for there was no speculation in the weighing room about Bill's death. The grapevine was silent.

I plunged into the bustle of a normal racing day, the minor frustration of a lot of jockeys changing in a smallish space, the unprintable jokes, the laughter, the cluster of cold half-undressed men round the red-hot coke stove.

Clem gave me my clean breeches, some pants, a thin fawn under-jersey, a fresh white stock for my neck, and a pair of nylon stockings. I stripped and put on the racing things. On top of the nylon stockings (laddered, as always) my soft, light, close-fitting racing boots slid on easily. Clem handed me my racing colours, the thick woolen sweater of coffee and cream checks, and the brown satin cap. He tied my stock for me. I pulled on the jersey, and slid the cap on to my crash helmet, ready to put on later.

Clem said, "Only the one ride today, sir?" He pulled two thick rubber bands from his large apron pocket and slipped them over my wrists. They were to anchor the sleeves of my jersey and prevent the wind blowing them up my arms.

"Yes," I said. "So far, anyway." I was always hopeful.

"Will you be wanting to borrow a light saddle? The weight's near your limit, I should think."

"No," I said, "I'd rather use my own saddle if I can. I'll get on the trial scales with that first, and see how much over-weight I am."

"Right you are, sir."

I went over with Clem, picked up my six pound racing saddle with its girths and stirrup leathers wound round it, and weighed myself with it, my crash helmet perched temporarily and insecurely on the back of my head. The total came to ten stone, nine pounds, which was four pounds more than the handicapper thought my horse deserved.

Clem took back the saddle, and I put my helmet on the bench again.

"I think I'll carry the overweight, Clem," I said.

"Right." He turned off to attend to someone else.

I could have got down to the proper weight—just— by using a three pound "postage stamp" saddle and changing into silk colours and "paper" boots. But as I was riding my own horse I could please myself, and he was an angular animal whose ribs would probably have been rubbed raw by too small a saddle.

He, Forlorn Hope, my newest acquisition, was a strongly built brown gelding only five years old. He looked as though he would develop into a 'chaser in a year or two, but meanwhile I was riding him in novice hurdle races to give him some sorely needed experience.

His unreliability as a jumper had made Scilla, the evening before, beg me not to ride him at Plumpton, a course full of snares for the unwary.

Unbearably strung up, and facing her loss for the first time without the help of drugs, she was angry and pleading by turns.

"Don't, Alan. Not a novice hurdle at Plumpton. You know your wretched Forlorn Hope isn't safe. You haven't got to do it, so why do you?"

"I like it."

"There never was a horse more aptly named," she said, miserably.

"He'll learn," I said. "But not if I don't give him the opportunity."

"Put someone else up. Please."

"There isn't any point in my having a horse if I don't ride it myself. That's really why I came to England at all, to race. You know that."

"You'll be killed, like Bill." She began to cry, help-lessly, worn out. I tried to reason with her.

"No, I won't. If Bill had been killed in a motor crash you wouldn't expect me to stop driving a car. Steeple-chasing's just as safe and unsafe as motoring." I paused, but she went on crying. "There are thousands more peo-ple killed on the roads than on the race-track," I said.

At this outrageous statement she recovered enough to point out acidly the difference in the number of people engaged in the two pursuits.

"Very few people are killed by steeplechasing," I tried again.

"Bill was . . ."

"Only about one year, out of hundreds," I went on.

"Bill was the second since Christmas."

"Yes." I looked at her warily. There were still tears in her eyes.

"Scilla, was Bill in any sort of trouble recently?"

"Why ever do you ask?" She was astounded by my question.

"Was he?"

"Of course not."

"Not worried about anything?" I persisted.

"No. Did he seem worried to you?"

"No," I said. It was quite true. Until the moment of

his fall Bill had been the same as I had always known him, cheerful, poised, reliable. He had had, and enjoyed, a pretty wife, three attractive children, a grey stone manor house, a considerable fortune, and the best hunter 'chaser in England. A happy man. And rack my memory as I would, I could not recall the slightest ruffling of the pattern.

"Then why do you ask?" said Scilla, again.

I told her as gradually, as gently as I could, that Bill's fall had not been an ordinary accident. I told her about the wire and about Lodge's investigations.

She sat like stone, absolutely stunned.

"Oh no," she said. "Oh, no. Oh, no."

As I stood now outside the weighing room at Plumpton I could still see her stricken face. She had raised no more objections to my racing. What I had told her had driven every other thought out of her head.

A firm hand came down on my shoulder. I knew it well. It belonged to Pete Gregory, racehorse trainer, a burly man nearly six feet tall, running to fat, growing bald, but in his day, I had been told, the toughest man ever to put his foot in a racing stirrup.

"Hello, Alan me lad. I'm glad to see you're here. I've already declared you for your horse in the second race."

"How is he?" I asked.

"All right. A bit thin, still." Forlorn Hope had only been in his stable for a month. "I should give him an 'easy,' coming up the hill the first time, or he'll blow up before the finish. He needs more time before we can hope for much."

"O.K." I said.

"Come out and see what the going is like," said Pete. "I want to talk to you." He hitched the strap of his binoculars higher on his shoulder.

We walked down through the gate on to the course and dug our heels experimentally into the turf. They sank in an inch.

"Not bad, considering all the snow that melted into it a fortnight ago," I said.

"Nice and soft for you to fall on," said Pete with elementary humour.

We went up the rise to the nearest hurdle. The landing side had a little too much give in it, but we knew the ground at the other end of the course was better drained. It was all right.

Pete said abruptly, "Did you see Admiral fall at Maidenhead?" He had been in Ireland buying a horse when it happened and had only just returned.

"Yes. I was about ten lengths behind him," I said, looking down the course, concentrating on the hurdle track.

"Well?"

"Well, what?" I said.

"What happened? Why did he fall?" There was some sort of urgency in his voice, more than one would expect, even in the circumstances. I looked at him. His eyes were grey, unsmiling, intent. Moved by an instinct I didn't understand, I retreated into vagueness.

"He just fell," I said. "When I went over the fence he was on the ground with Bill underneath him."

"Did Admiral meet the fence all wrong, then?" he probed.

"Not as far as I could see. He must have hit the top of it." This was near enough to the truth.

"There wasn't . . . anything else?" Pete's eyes were fierce, as if they would look into my brain.

"What do you mean?" I avoided the direct answer.

"Nothing." His anxious expression relaxed. "If you didn't see anything . . ." We began to walk back. It troubled me that I hadn't told Pete the truth. He had been too searching, too aware I was certain he was not the man to risk destroying a great horse like Admiral, let alone a friend, but why was he so relieved now he believed I had noticed nothing?

I had just decided to ask him to explain his attitude, and to tell him what had really happened, when he began to speak.

"Have you got a ride in the Amateur 'Chase, Alan?" He was back to normal, bluff and smiling.

"No, I haven't," I said. "Pete, look . . ."

But he interrupted, "I had a horse arrive in my yard five or six days ago, with an engagement in today's Amateur 'Chase. A chestnut. Good sort of animal. I should say. He seems to be fit enough—he's come from a small stable in the West country—and his new owner is very keen to run him. I tried to ring you this morning about it, but you'd already left."

"What's his name?" I asked, for all this preamble of Pete's was, I knew, his way of cajoling me into something I might not be too delighted to do.

"Heavens Above."

"Never heard of him. What's he done?" I asked.

"Well, not much. He's young, of course . . ."

I interrupted. "What *exactly* has he done?"

Pete sighed and gave in. "He's only had two runs, both down in Devon last autumn. He didn't fall, but—er—he got rid of his jockey both times. But he jumped well enough over my schooling fences this morning. I don't think you'd have any difficulty in getting him round safely, and that's the main thing at this stage."

"Pete, I don't like to say no, but . . ." I began.

"His owner is so hoping you'll ride him. It's her first horse, and it's running for the first time in her brand new colours. I brought her to the races with me. She's very excited. I said I'd ask you . . ."

"I don't think . . ." I tried again.

"Well at least meet her," said Pete.

"If I meet her, you know it'll be far more difficult for me to refuse to ride her horse."

Pete didn't deny it.

I went on, "I suppose she's another of your dear old

ladies about to go into a nursing home from which she is unlikely to return, and wants a final thrill before she meets her fate?"

This was the sad tale which Pete had used not long before to inveigle me on to a bad horse against my better judgement. And I often saw the old lady at the races afterwards. The nursing home and her fate were still presumably awaiting her.

"This one is not," said Pete, "a dear old lady."

We came to a stop in the paddock, and Pete looked around him and beckoned to someone. Out of the corner of my eye I saw a woman begin to walk towards us. It was already, without unforgivable rudeness, too late to escape. I had time for one heart-felt oath in Pete's ear before I turned to be introduced to the new owner of the jockey-depositing Heavens Above.

"Miss Ellery-Penn, Alan York," said Pete.

I was lost before she spoke a word. The first thing I said was, "I'll be glad to ride your horse."

Pete was laughing openly at me.

She was beautiful. She had clear features, wonderful skin, smiling grey eyes, dark glossy hair falling almost to her shoulders. And she was used to the effect she had on men: but how could she help it?

Pete said, "Right, then I'll declare you for the amateurs'—it's the fourth race. I'll give the colours to Clem." He went off towards the weighing room.

"I am so glad you agreed to ride my horse," the girl said. Her voice was low-pitched and unhurried. "He's a birthday present. Rather a problem one, don't you think? My Uncle George, who is a dear fellow but just the slightest bit off the beat, *advertised* in *The Times* for a racehorse. My aunt says he received fifty replies and bought this horse without seeing it because he liked the name. He said it would be more amusing for me to have a horse for my birthday than the conventional string of pearls."

"Your Uncle George sounds fascinating," I said.

"But just a little devastating to live with." She had a trick of lifting the last two or three words in a sentence so that they sounded like a question. As if she had added. "Don't you agree?" to her remark.

"Do you in fact live with him?" I asked.

"Oh, yes. Parents divorced in the murky past. Scattered to the four winds, and all that."

"I'm sorry."

"Waste no sympathy. I can't remember either of them. They abandoned me on Uncle George's doorstep, figuratively speaking, at the tender age of two."

"Uncle George has done a good job," I said, looking at her with the frankest admiration.

She accepted this without gaucherie, almost as a matter of course.

"Aunt Deb, actually. She is faintly more on the ball than Uncle George. Absolute pets, the pair of them."

"Are they here today?" I asked.

"No, they aren't," said Miss Ellery-Penn. "Uncle George remarked that having given me a passport into a new world peopled entirely by brave and charming young men, it would defeat the object if my path were cluttered up with elderly relatives."

"I am getting fonder of Uncle George every minute," I said.

Miss Ellery-Penn gave me a heavenly smile which held no promises of any sort.

"Have you seen my horse? Isn't he a duck?" she said.

"I haven't seen him. I'm afraid I didn't know he existed until five minutes ago. How did Uncle George happen to send him to Pete Gregory? Did he pick the stable with a pin?"

She laughed. "No, I don't think so. He had the stable all planned. He said I could get a Major Davidson to ride for me if the horse went to Mr. Gregory's." She reflected, wrinkling her brow. "He was quite upset on

Monday when he read in the paper that Major Davidson
had been killed."

"Did he know him?" I asked idly, watching the delicious curves at the corner of her red mouth.

"No, I'm sure he didn't know him personally. Probably he knew his father. He seems to know most people's fathers. He just said 'Good God, Davidson's dead'
in a shocked sort of way and went on eating his toast.
But he didn't hear me or Aunt Deb until we had asked
him four times for the marmalade!"

"And that was all?"

"Yes. Why do you ask?" said Miss Ellery-Penn, curiously.

"Oh, nothing special," I said. "Bill Davidson and I
were good friends."

She nodded. "I see." She dismissed the subject. "Now
what do I have to do in my new role as racehorse owner?
I don't particularly want to make a frightful boob on my
first day. Any comments and instructions from you will
be welcome, Mr. York."

"My name is Alan," I said.

She gave me an appraising look. It told me plainer
than words that although she was young she was already
experienced at fending off unwelcome attentions and not
being rushed into relationships she was not prepared for.

But finally she smiled, and said, "Mine is Kate." She
bestowed her name like a gift; I was pleased to receive
it.

"How much do you know about racing?" I asked.

"Not a thing. Never set foot on the Turf before today."
She gave the capital letter its full value, ironically.

"Do you ride, yourself?"

"Positively not."

"Perhaps your Uncle George is fond of horses? Perhaps he hunts?" I suggested.

"Uncle George is the most un-addicted man to horses
I have ever met. He says one end kicks and the other

bites, and as for hunting, he says that he has cosier things to do than chase bushy-tailed vermin in the gravest discomfort over water-logged countryside in the depths of winter."

I laughed. "Perhaps he bets. Off the course?" I asked.

"Uncle George has been known to ask, on Cup Final day, what has won the Derby."

"Then why Heavens Above?"

"Wider horizons for me, Uncle George says. My education has been along the well-tramped lines of boarding school, finishing school, and an over-chaperoned tour of Europe. I needed to get the smell of museums out of my nose, Uncle George said."

"So he gave you a racehorse for your twenty-first birthday," I stated matter-of-factly.

"Yes," she said: then she looked at me sharply. I grinned. I had jumped her defences, that time.

"There's nothing special for you to do as an owner," I said, "except go along to those stalls over there," I pointed, "before the fourth race, to see your horse being saddled up. Then you'll go into the parade ring with Pete, and stand around making intelligent remarks about the weather until I arrive and mount and go out for the race."

"What do I do if he wins?"

"Do you expect him to win?" I asked. I was not sure how much she really knew about her horse.

"Mr. Gregory says he won't."

I was relieved. I did not want her to be disappointed.

"We'll all know much more about him after the race. But if he should come in the first three, he will be unsaddled down there opposite the weighing room. Otherwise, you'll find us up here on the grass."

It was nearly time for the first race. I took the delectable Miss Ellery-Penn on to the stands and fulfilled Uncle George's design by introducing to her several brave and charming young men. I unfortunately realized that by the time I came back from riding in the novice hurdle, I should probably be an "also ran" in the race for Miss Ellery-Penn's attentions.

I watched her captivating a group of my friends. She was a vivid, vital person. It seemed to me that she had an inexhaustible inner fire battened down tight under hatches, and only the warmth from it was allowed to escape into the amused, slow voice. Kate was going to be potently attractive even in middle age, I thought inconsequently, and it crossed my mind that had Scilla possessed this springing vitality instead of her retiring, serene passiveness, Inspector Lodge's implications might not have been very far off the mark.

After we had watched the first race I left Kate deciding which of her new acquaintances should have the honour of taking her to coffee, and went off to weigh out for the novice hurdle. Looking back, I saw her setting off to the refreshment room with a trail of admirers, rather like a comet with a tail. A flashing, bewitching comet.

For the first time in my life I regretted that I was going to ride in a race.

chapter 4

IN THE CHANGING room Sandy Mason stood with his hands on his hips and laid about him with his tongue. His red hair curled strongly, his legs, firmly planted with the feet apart, were as rigid as posts. From the top to toe he vibrated with life. He was a stocky man in his thirties, on the short side, very strong, with dark brown eyes fringed disconcertingly by pale, reddish lashes.

As a jockey, a professional, he was not among the top dozen, but he had had a good deal of success, mainly owing to his fighting spirit. Nothing ever frightened him. He would thrust his sometimes unwilling mounts into the smallest openings, even occasionally into openings which did not exist until he made them by sheer force. His aggressiveness in races had got him into hot water more than once with the Stewards, but he was not particularly unpopular with the other jockeys, owing to his irrepressible, infectious cheerfulness.

His sense of humour was as vigorous as the rest of him, and if I thought privately that some of his jokes were too unkindly practical or too revoltingly obscene, I appeared to be in a minority.

"Which of you sods has half-inched my balancing pole?" he roared in a voice which carried splendidly above the busy chatter to every corner of the room. To this enquiry into the whereabouts of his whip, he received no reply.

"Why don't you lot get up off your fannies and see if you're hatching it," he said to three or four jockeys who were sitting on a bench pulling on their boots. They looked up appreciatively and waited for the rest of the tirade. Sandy kept up a flow of invective without repeating himself until one of the valets produced the missing whip.

"Where did you find it?" demanded Sandy. "Who had it? I'll twist his bloody arm."

"It was on the floor under the bench, in your own place."

Sandy was never embarrassed by his mistakes. He roared with laughter and took the whip. "I'll forgive you all this time, then." He went out into the weighing room carrying his saddle and whacking the air with his whip as if to make sure it was as pliable as usual. He always used it a good deal in the course of a race.

As he passed me where I stood just inside the changing room door, his eyes lifted to mine with one of the darting, laughing glances which made him likeable in spite of his faults. I turned and watched him go over and sit on the scales, parking the whip on the table beside him. He said something I couldn't hear, and both the Clerk of the Scales and the Judge, who was sitting there learning the colours so that he could distinguish them at the finish, laughed as they checked him against their lists and passed him for the race.

There had been rumours, a while back, that Sandy had "stopped" a few horses and had been rewarded handsomely by bookmakers for the service. But nothing had been proved, and the official enquiry had lasted barely an hour. Those who had felt the rough edge of Sandy's practical jokes believed him capable of anything. Everyone else pointed out that stopping a horse was entirely out of character for one who had been in trouble for trying too ruthlessly to win.

Watching the free and easy way he handled the two racing officials, I could understand that in face of that friendly, open manner, the Stewards at the enquiry must have found it impossible, in the absence of solidly convincing evidence, to believe him guilty. The general opinion among the jockeys was that Sandy had "strangled" a couple at one stage, but not during the past few months.

"Stopping" a horse can be done by missing the start, setting off some lengths behind, and staying at the back. Then the crooked jockey can ride a fairly honest finish from the second last fence, when he is closely under the eyes of the crowd, secure in the knowledge that he has left his horse far too much to do and cannot possibly win. It is rare enough, because a jockey seen to do it regularly soon finds himself unemployed.

During my one and a half season's racing I had seen it happen only twice. It was the same man both times, a fair, round-faced youth called Joe Nantwich. On the second occasion, about two months ago, he had been lucky to escape with his licence, for he had been foolish enough to try it in a race where one of the jockeys was David Stampe, the tale-bearing younger son of the Senior Steward.

Joe, and, I was sure, Sandy, too, had both gone to the lengths of deliberately holding back horses which, without their interference, would have been certain to win. They had, in fact, been guilty of criminal fraud. But was I so very much better, I wondered, as I tied on my helmet and took my saddle over to the scales. For I proposed to take Forlorn Hope sensibly over the hurdles, concentrating on getting round the course, and I had no intention of riding him all out in the faint possibility that he might finish in the first three. He was not properly fit, and too hard a race would do him great harm. Of course, if by some unforeseen circumstances, such as a lot of falls among the other horses, I found myself placed with a winning chance, I intended to seize it. There is a world of difference between "stopping" and "not trying hard, but willing to win" but the result for disgruntled backers is the same. They lose their money.

I took my saddle out to the saddling boxes, where Pete was already waiting with Forlorn Hope. He saddled up, and Rupert, the tiny stable lad, led the horse out into the parade ring. Pete and I strolled in after him, discussing the other horses in the race. There was no sign of Kate.

When the time came I mounted and rode out on to the course. The familiar excitement was in my blood again. Not Bill's death nor Scilla's mourning, nor the thought of Kate making progress with someone else, could affect the gripping happiness I always felt when cantering down to the starting gate. The speed of racing, the quick decisions, the risks, these were what I badly needed to counteract the safeties of civilisation. One can be too secure. Adventure is good for the soul, especially for someone like me, whose father stopped counting after the fourth million.

And my father, with an understanding based on his own much wilder youth, had given me unconditionally a fast car and three good horses and turned me loose in a country five thousand miles from home. He said however, as he despatched me with his blessing, that he thought steeplechasing was rather mild for one who had been taken crocodile hunting on the Zambezi every year since he was ten. My father's annual month away from his trading empire usually meant for us a dash across the veldt and a plunge into the primeval forest, sometimes equipped with the absolute minimum of kit and no one but ourselves to carry it. And I, for whom the deep jungle was a familiar playground, found the challenge I needed in a tamed land, on friendly animals, in a sport hemmed all about with rules and regulations. It was very odd, when one came to consider it.

The starter called the roll to make sure everyone had arrived, while we circled round and checked the tightness of the girths. I found Joe Nantwich guiding his horse along beside me. He was wearing his usual unpleasant expression, half petulance, half swank.

"Are you going back to the Davidsons' after the races, Alan?" he asked. He always spoke to me with a familiarity I slightly resented, though I tried not to.

"Yes," I said. Then I thought of Kate. "I may not go at once, though."

"Will you give me a lift as far as Epsom?"

"I don't go that way," I said, very politely.

"But you go through Dorking. I could get a bus on from there if you don't want to go to Epsom. I came with someone who is going on to Kent, so I've got to find some transport home." He was persistent, and although I thought he could easily find someone going directly to Epsom if he tried hard enough, I agreed in the end to take him.

We lined up for the start. Joe was on one side of me and Sandy on the other, and from the looks they gave each other across me, there was no love lost between them. Sandy's smile was a nasty one: Joe's round baby face puckered up like a child trying not to cry. I imagined that Sandy had been puncturing Joe's inflated ego with one of those famous practical jokes, such as filling the feet of his racing boots with jam.

Then we were off, and I gave all my attention to getting Forlorn Hope round as neatly, quickly, and safely as I could. He was still very green and inclined to waver as he met the clattering hurdles, but the basic spring was there. He was going so well that for over half the race I lay in third place, staying slightly towards the outside, to give him a clear view of the obstacles. The last quarter mile coming up the hill was too much for him, though, and we finished sixth. I was satisfied, and Scilla would be reassured.

Sandy Mason finished ahead of me. Then Joe Nantwich's horse galloped past loose, reins dangling, and looking back to the far end of the course. I saw the tiny figure of Joe himself trudging back to the stands. No doubt I would be hearing a stride by stride account of the calamity all the way to Dorking.

I unsaddled; went back to the weighing room, changed into Kate's brand new colours, got Clem to pack me a weight cloth with ten pounds of flat lead pieces, the weight I needed for the Amateur 'Chase and went out to see what had become of Miss Ellery-Penn.

She was leaning on the parade ring rails, looking alternately at the horses and (with too much approval, I thought) at Dane Hillman, one of the brave and charming young men I had introduced to her.

"Mr. Hillman has been telling me," said Kate, "that that poor looking bag of bones over there—the one with his head down by his knees and those floppy ears—is the fastest horse in the race. Am I to believe it, or is the mickey being gently taken?"

"No mickey," I said. "That's the best horse. Not on looks, I grant you, but he's a certainty today, in this company."

Dane said, "Horses who go along with their heads down like that are nearly always good jumpers. They look where they're going."

"But I like this gorgeous creature coming round now," said Kate, looking at a bay with an arched neck and high head carriage. Most of his body was covered by a rug to keep out the February cold, but at the back his glossy rump swelled roundly.

"He's much too fat," said Dane. "He probably ate his head off during the snow and hasn't had enough exercise since. He'll blow up when he's asked to do anything."

Kate sighed. "Horses appear to be as full of paradoxes as G. K. Chesterton. The duds look good, and the good look duds."

"Not always," said Dane and I together.

"I shall be glad," said Dane, "to give you a prolonged course in racehorse recognition, Miss Ellery-Penn."

"I am a slow learner, Mr. Hillman."

"All the better," said Dane, cheerfully.

"Aren't you riding today, Dane?" I asked hopefully.

"In the last two, my lad. Don't worry, I shall be able to look after Miss Ellery-Penn for you while you ride her horse." He grinned.

"Are you a jockey too, Mr. Hillman?" asked Kate in a surprised voice.

"Yes," said Dane, and left it at that. He was the rising star of the profession, clearly heading straight to the top. Pete Gregory had first claim on him, which, apart from natural affinity, brought us together a good deal. Strangers often mistook us for each other. We were the same age, both dark, both of middle height and medium build. On horseback the difference was greater; he was a better jockey than I would ever be.

"I thought all jockeys were instantly recognisable as having come straight from Lilliput," said Kate, "but you two are quite a decent size." She had to look up to both of us, although she was tall enough herself.

We laughed. I said, "Steeplechasing jockeys are nearly all a decent size. It's easier to stick on over big fences if you have long legs to grip with."

"Several of the Flat chaps are as tall as us, too," said Dane. "But they are very skinny, of course."

"All my illusions are being shattered," said Kate.

Dane said, "I like your new horse, Alan. He'll make a good 'chaser next year."

"Are you riding your own horses today, too?" Kate asked Dane.

"No, I'm not. I haven't any," said Dane. "I'm a professional, so I'm not allowed to own racehorses."

"A professional?" Kate's eyebrows went up. She had clearly taken in the superlative tailoring of the suit under the short camel overcoat, the pleasant voice, the gentle manners. Another illusion was being shattered, I was amused to see.

"Yes. I ride for my life," said Dane, smiling. "Unlike Alan, I haven't a stinking rich father. But I get paid for doing what I like best in the world. It's a very satisfactory state of affairs."

Kate looked carefully from one to the other of us. "Perhaps in time I shall understand what makes you want to risk your elegant necks," she said.

"When you find out, please tell us," said Dane. "It's still a mystery to me."

We wandered back to the stands and watched the third race. The poor-looking horse won in a canter by twenty lengths. Kate's fancy was tailed-off after a mile and refused at the third last fence.

"Don't imagine that we always know what's going to win," said Dane. "Jockeys are bad tipsters. But that one was a cert, a dead cert."

A dead cert. The casual, everyday racing expression jabbed in my mind like a needle. Bill Davidson's attacker had relied on Admiral's being a certainty.

A dead cert. Dead . . .

KATE'S HORSE, FOR a pig in a poke, was not as bad as I feared. At the second fence he put in a short one and screwed in mid-air. I came clear out of the saddle and landed back in it more by luck than judgement. This was obviously the trick which had rid Heavens Above of his former jockey, who now had all my sympathy. He did it again at the third open ditch, but the rest of our journey was uneventful. The horse even found an unsuspected turn of foot up the hill and, passing several tired animals, ran on into fourth place.

Kate was delighted.

"Bless Uncle George for a brainwave," she said. "I've never had such a happy day in my life."

"I thought you were coming off at the second, Alan," said Pete Gregory, as I undid the girth buckles.

"So did I," I said, feelingly. "It was sheer luck I didn't."

Pete watched the way Heavens Above was breathing: the ribs were moving in and out a good deal, but not labouring. He said, "He's remarkably fit, considering everything. I think we'll win a race or two with him before the end of the season."

"Can't we all go and celebrate with the odd magnum?" asked Kate. Her eyes were shining with excitement.

Pete laughed. "Wait till you have a winner, for the magnum," he said. "I'd like to have drunk a more modest toast to the future with you, though, but I've a runner in the next. Alan will take you, no doubt." He looked at me sideways, very amused still at my complete surrender to the charm of Miss Ellery-Penn.

"Will you wait for me, Kate?" I asked. "I have to go and weigh in now, because we were fourth. I'll change and be out as quickly as I can."

"I'll come down outside the weighing room," promised Kate, nodding.

I weighed in, gave my saddle to Clem, washed and changed back into ordinary clothes. Kate was waiting outside the weighing room, looking at a group of girls standing near her chatting.

"Who are they?" asked Kate. "They have been here all the time I have, just doing nothing."

"Jockeys' wives, mostly," I said, grinning. "Waiting outside the weighing-room is their chief occupation."

"And jockeys' girlfriends too, I suppose," said Kate, wryly.

"Yes," I said. "And I've just found out how nice it is

to know there is someone waiting for you outside."

We went round to the bar, and settled for cups of coffee.

"Uncle George will be shattered to hear we drank to Heavens Above so non-alcoholically," said Kate. "Don't grain and grapes figure in your life?"

"Oh, yes, of course. But I've never got used to them at three o'clock in the afternoon. How about you?"

"Champers for breakfast is my passion," said Kate, with smiling eyes.

I asked her then if she would spend the evening with me, but she said she could not. Aunt Deb, it appeared, was having a dinner party, and Uncle George would be agog to hear how the birthday present had got on.

"Tomorrow, then?"

Kate hesitated and looked down at her glass. "I'm . . . er . . . going out with Dane, tomorrow."

"Blast him," I said, exploding.

Kate positively giggled.

"Friday?" I suggested.

"That will be lovely," said Kate.

We went up on to the stands and watched Dane win the fifth race by a short head. Kate cheered him home uninhibitedly.

chapter 5

A BATTLE WAS raging in the car park. I walked out of the gate to go home after the last race, and came to a dead stop. In the open space between the gate and the first rank of parked cars, at least twenty men were fighting, and fighting to hurt. Even at first glance there was a vicious quality about the strictly non-Queensberry type blows.

It was astounding. Scuffles between two or three men are common on racecourses, but a clash of this size and seriousness had to be caused by more than a disagreement over a bet.

I looked closer. There was no doubt about it. Some of the men were wearing brass knuckles. A length of bicycle chain swung briefly in the air. The two men nearest to me were lying on the ground, almost motionless, but rigid with exertion, as if locked in some strange native ritual. The fingers of one were clamped round the wrist of the other, whose hand held a knife with a sharp three-inch blade. Not long enough to be readily lethal, it was designed to rip and disfigure.

There seemed to be two fairly equally matched sides fighting each other, but one could not distinguish which was which. The man with the knife, who was slowly getting the worst of it, I saw to be little more than a boy, but most of the men were in their full strength. The only older-looking fighter was on his knees in the centre with his arms folded over his head, while the fight raged on around him.

They fought in uncanny silence. Only their heavy breathing and a few grunts were to be heard. The semicircle of open-mouthed homeward-bound racegoers watching them was growing larger, but no one felt inclined to walk into the mêlée and try to stop it.

I found one of the newspaper sellers at my elbow.

"What's it all about?" I asked. Nothing much to do with racing escapes the newsboys.

"It's the taxi-drivers," he said. "There's two rival gangs of 'em, one lot from London and one lot from Brighton. There's usually trouble when they meet."

"Why?"

"Couldn't tell you, Mr. York. But this isn't the first time they've been at it."

I looked back at the struggling mob. One or two of them still had peaked caps on. Some pairs were rolling about on the ground, some were straining and heaving against the sides of the taxis. There were two rows of taxis parked there. All the drivers were fighting.

The fists and what they held in the way of ironmongery were doing a lot of damage. Two of the men were bent over, clasping their bellies in agony. There was blood on nearly all their faces, and the clothes of some of them had been torn off to the skin.

They fought on with appalling fury, taking no notice at all of the swelling crowd around them.

"They'll kill each other," said a girl standing next to me, watching the scene in a mixture of horror and fascination.

I glanced up over her head at the man standing on the other side of her, a big man well over six feet tall, with a deeply tanned skin. He was watching the fight with grim disapproval, his strong profile bleak, his eyes narrowed. I could not remember his name, though I had a feeling I ought to know it.

The crowd was growing uneasy, and began looking round for the police. The girl's remark was not idle. Any of the men might die, if they were unlucky, from the murderous chopping, gouging, and slogging, which showed no signs of abating.

The fight had caused a traffic jam in the car park. A policeman came, took a look, and disappeared fast for reinforcements. He returned with four constables on foot and one on horseback, all armed with truncheons. They plunged into the battle, but it took them several minutes to stop it.

More police arrived. The taxi-drivers were dragged and herded into two groups. Both lots appeared to be equally battered, and neither side seemed to have won. The battlefield was strewn with caps and torn pieces of coats and shirts. Two shoes, one brown, one black, lay on their sides ten feet apart. Patches of blood stained the ground. The police began making a small pile of collected weapons.

The main excitement over, people began drifting away. The little knot of prospective customers for the taxis moved across to ask a policeman how long the drivers would be detained. The tall sunburned man who had been standing near me went over to join them.

One of the racing journalists paused beside me, scribbling busily in his notebook.

"Who is that very big man over there, John?" I asked him. He looked up and focused his eyes. He said, "His name's Tudor, I think. Owns a couple of horses. A newly arrived tycoon type. I don't know much about him. He doesn't look too pleased about the transport situation."

Tudor, in fact, looked heavily angry, his lower jaw

jutting forward obstinately. I was still sure there was something about this man which I ought to remember, but I did not know what. He was not having any success with the policeman, who was shaking his head. The taxis remained empty and driverless.

"What's it all about?" I asked the journalist.

"Gang warfare, my spies tell me," he said cheerfully.

Five of the taxi-drivers were now lying flat out on the cold damp ground. One of them groaned steadily.

The journalist said, "Hospital and police station in about equal proportions, I should say. What a story!"

The man who was groaning rolled over and vomited.

"I'm going back to phone this lot through to the office," said the journalist. "Are you off home now?"

"I'm waiting for that wretched Joe Nantwich," I said. "I promised him a lift to Dorking, but I haven't seen a sign of him since the fourth race. It would be just like him to get a lift right home with someone else and forget to let me know."

"The last I saw of him, he was having a few unfriendly words with Sandy in the gents, and getting the worst of it."

"Those two really hate each other," I said.

"Do you know why?"

"No idea. Have you?" I asked.

"No," said the journalist. He smiled good-bye and went back into the racecourse towards the telephone.

Two ambulances drove up to collect the injured drivers. A policeman climbed into the back of each ambulance with them, and another sat in front beside the driver. With full loads the ambulances trundled slowly up the road to the main gates.

The remaining drivers began to shiver as the heat of the battle died out of them and the raw February afternoon took over. They were stiff and bruised, but unrepentant. A man in one group stepped forward, gave the other group a sneer, and spat, insultingly, on the ground in their direction. His shirt was in ribbons and his face was swelling in lumps. The muscles of his forearm would have done credit to a blacksmith, and silky dark hair grew low on his forehead in a widow's peak. A dangerous-looking man. A policeman touched his arm to bring him back into the group and he jumped round and snarled at him. Two more policemen began to close in, and the dark-haired man subsided angrily.

I was just giving Joe up when he came out of the gate and hailed me with no apology for his lateness. But I was not the only person to notice his arrival.

The tall dark Mr. Tudor strode towards us.

"Nantwich, be so good as to give me a lift into Brighton, will you?" he said, authoritatively. "As you can see, the taxis are out of action, and I have an important appointment in Brighton in twenty minutes."

Joe looked at the taxi-drivers with vague eyes.

"What's happened?" he said.

"Never mind that now," said Tudor impatiently. "Where is your car?"

Joe looked at him blankly. His brain seemed to be working at half speed He said, "Oh—er—it isn't here, sir I've got a lift."

"With you?" said Tudor to me. I nodded. Joe, typically, had not introduced us.

"I'll be obliged if you will take me into Brighton," said Tudor, briskly. "I'll pay you the regular taxi fare."

He was forceful and in a hurry. It would have been difficult to refuse to do him a favour so small to me, so clearly important for him.

"I'll take you for nothing," I said, "but you'll find it a bit of a squeeze. I have a two-seater sports car."

"If it's too small for all of us, Nantwich can stay here and you can come back for him," said Tudor in a firm voice. Joe showed no surprise, but I thought that the dark Mr. Tudor was too practised at consulting no one's convenience but his own.

We skirted the groups of battered taxi-drivers, and threaded our way to my car. Tudor got in. He was so large that it was hopeless to try to wedge Joe in as well.

"I'll come back for you, Joe," I said, stifling my irritation. "Wait for me up on the main road."

I climbed into the car, nosed slowly out of the car park, up the racecourse road, and turned out towards Brighton. There was too much traffic for the Lotus to show off the power of the purring Climax engine, and going along at a steady forty gave me time to concentrate on my puzzling passenger.

Glancing down as I changed gear, I saw his hand resting on his knee, the fingers spread and tense. And suddenly I knew where I had seen him before. It was his hand, darkly tanned, with the faint bluish tint under the finger-nails, that I knew.

He had been standing in the bar at Sandown with his back towards me and his hand resting flat on the counter beside him, next to his glass. He had been talking to Bill; and I had waited there, behind him, not wanting to interrupt their conversation. Then Tudor finished his drink and left, and I had talked with Bill.

Now I glanced at his face.

"It's a great shame about Bill Davidson," I said.

The brown hand jumped slightly on his knee. He turned his head and looked at me while I drove.

"Yes, indeed it is." He spoke slowly. "I had been hoping he would ride a horse for me at Cheltenham."

"A great horseman," I said.

"Yes indeed."

"I was just behind him when he fell," I said, and on an impulse added, "There are a great many questions to be asked about it."

I felt Tudor's huge body shift beside me. I knew he was still looking at me, and I found his presence overpowering. "I suppose so," he said. He hesitated, but added nothing more. He looked at his watch.

"Take me to the Pavilion Plaza Hotel, if you please. I have to attend a business meeting there," he said.

"Is it near the Pavilion?" I asked.

"Fairly. I will direct you when we get there." His tone relegated me to the status of chauffeur.

We drove for some miles in silence. My passenger sat apparently deep in thought. When we reached Brighton he told me the way to the hotel.

"Thank you," he said, without warmth, as he lifted his bulk clumsily out of the low-slung car. He had an air of accepting considerable favours as merely his due, even when done him by complete strangers. He took two steps away from the car, then turned back and said, "What is your name?"

"Alan York," I said. "Good afternoon." I drove off without waiting for an answer. I could be brusque, too. Glancing in the mirror I saw him standing on the pavement looking after me.

I went back to the racecourse.

Joe was waiting for me, sitting on the bank at the side of the road. He had some difficulty opening the car door, and he stumbled into his seat, muttering. He lurched over against me, and I discovered that Joe Nantwich was drunk.

The daylight was almost gone. I turned on the lights. I could think of pleasanter things to do than drive the twisty roads to Dorking with Joe breathing alcohol all over me. I sighed, and let in the clutch.

Joe was nursing a grievance. He would be. Everything which went wrong for Joe was someone else's fault, according to him. Barely twenty, he was a chronic grumbler. It was hard to know which was worse to put up with, his grousing or his bragging, and that he was treated with tolerance by the other jockeys said much for their good nature. Joe's saving grace was his undoubted ability as a jockey, but he had put that to bad use already by his "stopping" activities, and now he was threatening it altogether by getting drunk in the middle of the afternoon.

"I would have won that race," he whined.

"You're a fool, Joe," I said.

"No, honestly, Alan, I would have won that race. I had him placed just right. I had the others beat, I had 'em stone cold. Just right." He made sawing motions with his hands.

"You're a fool to drink so much at the races," I said.

"Eh?" He couldn't focus.

"Drink," I said. "You've had too much to drink."

"No, no, no, no . . ." The words came dribbling out, as if once he had started to speak it was too much effort to stop.

"Owners won't put you on their horses if they see you getting drunk," I said, feeling it was no business of mine, after all.

"I can win any race, drunk or not," said Joe.

"Not many owners would believe it."

"They know I'm good."

"So you are, but you won't be if you go on like this," I said.

"I can drink and I can ride and I can ride and I can drink. If I want to." He belched.

I let it pass. What Joe needed was a firm hand applied ten years ago. He looked all set now on the road to ruin and he wasn't going to thank anyone for directions off it.

He was whining again. "That bloody Mason."

I didn't say anything. He tried again.

"That bloody Sandy, he tipped me off. He bloody well tipped me off over the bloody rails. I'd have won that race as easy as kiss your hand and he knew it and tipped me off over the bloody rails."

"Don't be silly, Joe."

"You can't say I wouldn't have won the race," said Joe argumentatively.

"And I can't say you would have won it," I said. "You fell at least a mile from home."

"I didn't fall. I'm telling you, aren't I? Sandy bloody Mason tipped me off over the rails."

"How?" I asked idly, concentrating on the road.

"He squeezed me against the rails. I shouted to him to give me more room. And do you know what he did? Do you know? He laughed. He bloody well laughed. Then he tipped me over. He stuck his knee into me and gave a heave and off I went over the bloody rails." His whining voice finished on a definite sob.

I looked at him. Two tears were rolling down his round cheeks. They glistened in the light from the dashboard, and fell with a tiny flash on to the furry collar of his sheepskin coat.

"Sandy wouldn't do a thing like that," I said mildly.

"Oh yes he would. He told me he'd get even with me. He said I'd be sorry. But I couldn't help it, Alan, I really couldn't." Two more tears rolled down.

I was out of my depth. I had no idea what he was talking about; but it began to look as though Sandy, if he had unseated him, had had his reasons.

Joe went on talking. "You're always decent to me, Alan, you're not like the others. You're my friend . . ." He put his hand heavily on my arm, pawing, leaning over towards me and giving me the benefit of the full force of his alcoholic breath. The delicate steering of the Lotus reacted to his sudden weight on my arm with a violent swerve towards the curb.

I shook him off. "For God's sake sit up, Joe, or you'll have us in the ditch," I said.

But he was too immersed in his own troubles to hear me. He pulled my arm again. There was a lay-by just ahead. I slowed, turned into it, and stopped the car.

"If you won't sit up and leave me alone you can get out and walk," I said, trying to get through to him with a rough tone.

But he was still on his own track, and weeping noisily now.

"You don't know what it's like to be in trouble," he sobbed.

I resigned myself to listen. The quicker he got his resentments off his chest, I thought, the quicker he would relax and go to sleep.

"What trouble?" I said, I was not in the least interested.

"Alan, I'll tell you because you're a pal, a decent pal." He put his hand on my knee. I pushed it off.

Amid a fresh burst of tears Joe blurted, "I was supposed to stop a horse and I didn't, and Sandy lost a lot of money and said he'd get even with me and he's been following me around saying that for days and days and I knew he'd do something awful and he has." He paused for breath. "Lucky for me I hit a soft patch or I might have broken my neck. It wasn't funny. And that bloody Sandy," he choked on the name, "was laughing. I'll make him laugh on the other side of his bloody face."

This last sentence made me smile. Joe with his baby face, strong of body perhaps, but weak of character, was no match for the tough, forceful Sandy, more than ten years older and incalculably more self-assured. Joe's bragging, like his whining, sprang from feelings of insecurity. But the beginning of his outburst was something different.

"What horse did you not stop?" I asked. "And how did Sandy know you were supposed to be going to stop one?"

For a second I thought caution would silence him, but after the smallest hesitation he babbled on. The drink was still at the flood. So were the tears.

From the self-pitying, hiccuping, half incoherent voice I learned a sorry enough story. Shorn of blasphemy and reduced to essentials, it was this. Joe had been paid well for stopping horses on several occasions, two of which

I had seen myself. But when David Stampe had told his father the Senior Steward about the last one, and Joe had nearly lost his licence, it gave him a steadying shock. The next time he was asked to stop a horse he said he would, but in the event, from understandable nerves, he had not done it thoroughly enough early in the race, and at the finish was faced with the plain knowledge that if he lost the race he would lose his licence as well. He won. This had happened ten days ago.

I was puzzled. "Is Sandy the only person who has harmed you?"

"He tipped me over the rails . . ." He was ready to start all over again.

I interrupted. "It wasn't Sandy, surely, who was paying you not to win?"

"No. I don't think so. I don't know," he snivelled.

"Do you mean you don't know who was paying you? Ever?"

"A man rang up and told me when he wanted me to stop one, and afterwards I got a packet full of money through the post."

"How many times have you done it?" I asked.

"Ten," said Joe, "all in the last six months." I stared at him.

"Often it was easy," said Joe defensively. "The ——s wouldn't have won anyway, even if I'd helped them."

"How much did you get for it?"

"A hundred. Twice it was two-fifty." Joe's tongue was still running away with him, and I believed him. It was big money, and anyone prepared to pay on that scale would surely want considerable revenge when Joe won against orders. But Sandy? I couldn't believe it.

"What did Sandy say to you after you won?" I asked.

Joe was still crying. "He said he'd backed the horse I beat and that he'd get even with me," said Joe. And it seemed that Sandy had done that.

"You didn't get your parcel of money, I suppose?"

"No," said Joe, sniffing.

"Haven't you any idea where they come from?" I asked.

"Some had London postmarks," said Joe. "I didn't take much notice." Too eager to count the contents to look closely at the wrappings, no doubt.

"Well," I said, "surely now that Sandy has had his little revenge, you are in the clear? Can't you possibly stop crying about it? It's all over. What are you in such a state about?"

For answer Joe took a paper from his jacket pocket and gave it to me.

"You might as well know it all. I don't know what to do. Help me, Alan. I'm frightened."

In the light from the dashboard I could see that this was true. And Joe was beginning to sober up.

I unfolded the paper and switched on the lights inside the car. It was a single sheet of thin, ordinary typing paper. In simple capital letters, written with a ball-point pen, were five words: BOLINGBROKE. YOU WILL BE PUN-ISHED.

"Bolingbroke is the horse you were supposed to stop and didn't?"

"Yes." The tears no longer welled in his eyes.

"When did you get this?" I asked.

"I found it in my pocket, today, when I put my jacket on after I'd changed. Just before the fifth race. It wasn't there when I took it off."

"And you spent the rest of the afternoon in the bar, in a blue funk, I suppose," I said.

"Yes . . . and I went back there while you took Mr. Tudor to Brighton. I didn't think anything was going to happen to me because of Bolingbroke, and I've been frightened ever since he won. And just as I was thinking it was all right Sandy pushed me over the rails and then I found this letter in my pocket. It isn't fair." The self-pity still whined in his voice.

I gave him back the paper.

"What am I to do?" said Joe.

I couldn't tell him, because I didn't know. He had got himself into a thorough mess, and he had good reason to be afraid. People who manipulated horses and jockeys to that extent were certain to play rough. The time lag of ten days between Bolingbroke's win and the arrival of the note could mean, I thought, that there was a cat-and-mouse, rather than a straightforward mentality at work. Which was little comfort to offer Joe.

Apart from some convulsive hiccups and sniffs, Joe seemed to have recovered from his tears, and the worst of the drunkenness was over. I switched off the inside lights, started the car up, and pulled back on to the road. As I had hoped, Joe soon went to sleep. He snored loudly.

Approaching Dorking, I woke him up. I had some questions to ask.

"Joe, who is that Mr. Tudor I took to Brighton? He knows you."

"He owns Bolingbroke," said Joe. "I often ride for him."

I was surprised. "Was he pleased when Bolingbroke won?" I asked.

"I suppose so. He wasn't there. He sent me ten-percent afterwards, though, and a letter thanking me. The usual thing."

"He hasn't been in racing long, has he?" I asked.

"Popped up about the same time you did," said Joe, with a distinct return to his old brash manner. "Both of you arrived with dark sun-tans in the middle of winter."

I had come by air from the burning African summer to the icy reception of October in England but after eighteen months my skin was as pale as an Englishman's. Tudor's, on the other hand, remained dark.

Joe was sniggering. "You know why Mr. Clifford bloody Tudor lives at Brighton? It gives him an excuse to be sunburnt all the year round. Touch of the old tar, really."

After that I had no compunction in turning Joe out at the bus stop for Epsom. Unloading his troubles on to me seemed, for the present at least, to have restored his ego.

I drove back to the Cotswolds. At first I thought about Sandy Mason and wondered how he had got wind of Joe's intention to stop Bolingbroke.

But for the last hour of the journey I thought about Kate.

chapter 6

SCILLA WAS LYING asleep on the sofa with a rug over her legs and a half-full glass on a low table beside her. I picked up the glass and sniffed. Brandy. She usually drank gin and Campari. Brandy was for bad days only.

She opened her eyes. "Alan I'm so glad you're back. What time is it?"

"Half past nine," I said.

"You must be starving," she said, pushing off the rug. "Why ever didn't you wake me? Dinner was ready hours ago."

"I've only just got here, and Joan is cooking now, so relax," I said.

We went in to eat. I sat in my usual place. Bill's chair, opposite Scilla, was empty. I made a mental note to move it back against the wall.

Halfway through the steaks, Scilla said, breaking a long silence, "Two policemen came to see me today."

"Did they? About the inquest tomorrow?"

"No, it was about Bill." She pushed her plate away. "They asked me if he was in any trouble, as you did. They asked me the same questions in different ways for over half an hour. One of them suggested that if I was as fond of my husband as I said I was and on excellent terms with him, I ought to know if something was wrong in his life. They were rather nasty, really."

She was not looking at me. She kept her eyes down, regarding her half-eaten, congealing steak, and there was a slight embarrassment in her manner, which was unusual.

"I can imagine," I said, realising what was the matter. "They asked you, I suppose, to explain your relationship with me, and why I was still living in your house?"

She glanced up in surprise and evident relief. "Yes, they did. I didn't know how to tell you. It seems so ordinary to me that you should be here, yet I couldn't seem to make them understand that."

"I'll go tomorrow, Scilla," I said. "I'm not letting you in for any more gossip. If the police can think that you were cheating on Bill with me, so can the village and the county. I've been exceedingly thoughtless, and I'm very very sorry." For I, too, had found it quite natural to stay on in Bill's house after his death.

"You will certainly not go tomorrow on my account, Alan," said Scilla with more resolution than I would have given her credit for. "I need you here. I shall do nothing but cry all the time if I don't have you to talk to, especially in the evenings. I can get through the days, with the children and the house to think about. But the nights . . ." And in her suddenly ravaged face I could read all the tearing, savage pain of a loss four days old.

"I don't care what anyone says," she said through starting tears, "I need you here. Please, please, don't go away."

"I'll stay," I said. "Don't worry. I'll stay as long as you want me to. But you must promise to tell me when you are ready for me to go."

She dried her eyes and raised a smile. "When I begin to worry about my reputation, you mean? I promise."

I had driven the better part of three hundred miles besides riding in two races, and I was tired. We went to our beds early, Scilla promising to take her sleeping pills.

But at two o'clock in the morning she opened my bedroom door. I woke at once. She came over and switched on my bedside light, and sat down on my bed.

She looked ridiculously young and defenceless. She was wearing a pale blue knee-length chiffon nightdress which flowed transparently about her slender body and fell like mist over the small round breasts.

I propped myself up on my elbow and ran my fingers through my hair.

"I can't sleep," she said.

"Did you take the pills?" I asked.

But I could answer my own question. Her eyes looked drugged, and in her right mind she would not have come into my room so revealingly undressed.

"Yes, I took them. They've made me a bit groggy, but I'm still awake. I took an extra one." Her voice was slurred and dopey. "Will you talk for a bit?" she said. "Then perhaps I'll feel more sleepy. When I'm on my own I just lie and think about Bill . . . Tell me more about Plumpton . . . You said you rode another horse. Tell me about it. Please . . ."

So I sat up in bed and wrapped my eiderdown round her shoulders, and told her about Kate's birthday present and Uncle George, thinking how often I had told Polly and Henry and William bedside stories to send them to sleep. But after a while I saw she was not listening, and presently the slow heavy tears were falling from her bent head on to her hands.

"You must think me a terrible fool to cry so much," she said, "but I just can't help it." She lay down weakly beside me, her head on my pillow. She took hold of my hand and closed her eyes. I looked down at her sweet, pretty face with the tears trickling past her ears into her cloudy dark hair, and gently kissed her forehead. Her body shook with two heavy sobs. I lay down and slid my arm under her neck. She turned towards me and clung to me, holding me fiercely, sobbing slowly with her deep terrible grief.

And at last, gradually, the sleeping pills did their job. She relaxed, breathing audibly, her hand twisted into the jacket of my pyjamas. She was lying half on top of my bedclothes, and the February night was cold. I tugged the sheet and blankets gently from underneath her with my free hand and spread them over her, and pulled the eiderdown up over our shoulders. I switched off the light and lay in the dark, gently cradling her until her breath grew soft and she was soundly asleep.

I smiled to think of Inspector Lodge's face if he could have seen us. And I reflected that I should not have been content to be so passive a bedfellow had I held Kate in my arms instead.

During the night Scilla twisted uneasily several times, murmuring jumbled words that made no sense, seeming to be calmed each time by my hand stroking her hair. Towards morning she was quiet. I got up, wrapped her in the eiderdown, and carried her back to her own bed. I knew that if she woke in my room, with the drugs worn off, she would be unnecessarily ashamed and up- set.

She was still sleeping peacefully when I left her.

A FEW HOURS later, after a hurried breakfast, I drove her to Maidenhead to attend the inquest. She slept most of the way and did not refer to what had happened in the night. I was not sure she even remembered.

Lodge must have been waiting for us, for he met us as soon as we went in. He was carrying a sheaf of pa- pers, and looked businesslike and solid. I introduced him to Scilla, and his eyes sharpened appreciatively at the sight of her pale prettiness. But what he said was a surprise.

"I'd like to apologise," he began, "for the rather unpleasant suggestions which have been put to you and Mr. York about each other." He turned to me. "We are now satisfied that you were in no way responsible for Major Davidson's death."

"That's big of you," I said lightly, but I was glad to hear it.

Lodge went on, "You can say what you like to the Coroner about the wire, of course, but I'd better warn you that he won't be too enthusiastic. He hates anything fancy, and you've no evidence. Don't worry if you don't agree with his verdict—I think it's sure to be accidental death—because inquests can always be reopened, if need be."

In view of this I was not disturbed when the Coroner, a heavily moustached man of fifty, listened keenly enough to my account of Bill's fall, but dealt a little brusquely with my wire theory. Lodge testified that he had accompanied me to the racecourse to look for the wire I had reported, but that there had been none there.

The man who had been riding directly behind me when Bill fell was also called. He was an amateur rider who lived in Yorkshire, and he had had to come a long way. He said, with an apologetic glance for me, that he had seen nothing suspicious at the fence, and that in his opinion it was a normal fall. Unexpected maybe, but not mysterious. He radiated common sense.

Had Mr. York, the Coroner enquired in a doubtful voice, mentioned the possible existence of wire to anyone at all on the day of the race? Mr. York had not.

The Coroner, summing up medical, police, and all other evidence, found that Major Davidson had died of injuries resulting from his horse having fallen in a steeplechase. He was not convinced, he said, that the fall was anything but an accident.

Owing to a mistake about the time, the local paper had failed to send a representative to the inquest, and from lack of detailed reporting the proceedings rated only small paragraphs in the evening and morning papers. The word "wire" was not mentioned. This omission did not worry me one way or the other, but Scilla was relieved. She said she could not yet stand questions from inquisitive friends, let alone reporters.

Bill's funeral was held quietly in the village on Friday morning, attended only by his family and close friends. Bearing one corner of his coffin on my shoulder and bidding my private good-byes, I knew for sure that I would not be satisfied until his death was avenged. I didn't know how it was to be done, and, strangely enough, I didn't feel any urgency about it. But in time, I promised him, in time, I'll do it.

Scilla's sister had come to the funeral and was to stay with her for two or three days; so, missing lunch out of deference to the light weight I was committed to ride at on the following day, I drove up to London to spend some long overdue hours in the office, arranging the details of insurance and customs duty on a series of shipments of copper.

The office staff were experts. My job was to discuss with Hughes, my second in command, the day-to-day affairs of the company, to make decisions and agree to plans made by Hughes, and to sign my name to endless documents and letters. It seldom took me more than three days a week. On Sunday it was my weekly task to write to my father. I had a feeling he skipped the filial introduction and the accounts of my racing, and fastened his sharp brain only on my report of the week's trade and my assessment of the future.

Those Sunday reports had been part of my life for ten years. School homework could wait, my father used to say. It was more important for me to know every detail about the kingdom I was to inherit; and to this end he made me study continually the papers he brought home from his office. By the time I left school I could appraise at a glance the significance of fluctuations in the world prices of raw materials, even if I had no idea when Charles I was beheaded.

On Friday evening I waited impatiently for Kate to join me for dinner. Unwrapped from the heavy overcoat and woolly boots she had worn at Plumpton, she was more ravishing than ever. She wore a glowing red dress, simple and devastating, and her dark hair fell smoothly to her shoulders. She seemed to be alight from within with her own brand of effervescence. The evening was fun and, to me at least, entirely satisfactory. We ate, we danced, we talked.

While we swayed lazily round the floor to some dreamy slow-tempo music, Kate introduced the only solemn note of the evening.

"I saw a bit about your friend's inquest in this morning's paper," she said.

I brushed my lips against her hair. It smelled sweet. "Accidental death," I murmured vaguely. "I don't think."

"Hm?" Kate looked up.

"I'll tell you about it one day, when I know the whole story," I said, enjoying the taut line of her neck as she tilted her face up to mine. It was strange, I thought, that it was possible to feel two strong emotions at once. Pleasure in surrendering to the seduction of the music with a dancing Kate balanced in my arms, and a tugging sympathy for Scilla trying to come to terms with her loneliness eighty miles away in the windy Cotswold hills.

"Tell me now," said Kate with interest. "If it wasn't accidental death, what was it?"

I hesitated. I didn't want too much reality pushing the evening's magic sideways.

"Come on, come on," she urged, smiling. "You can't stop there. I'll die of suspense."

So I told her about the wire. It shocked her enough to stop her dancing, and we stood flat-footed in the middle of the floor with the other couples flowing round and bumping into us.

"Dear heavens," she said, "how . . . how wicked."

She wanted me to explain why the inquest verdict had been what it was, and after I had told her that with the wire gone there was no evidence of anything else, she said, "I can't bear to think of anyone getting away with so disgusting a trick."

"Nor can I," I said, "and they won't, I promise you, if I can help it."

"That's good," she said seriously. She began to sway again to the music, and I took her in my arms and we drifted back into the dance. We didn't mention Bill again.

It seemed to me for long periods that evening as if my feet were not in proper contact with the floor, and the most extraordinary tremors constantly shook my knees. Kate seemed to notice nothing: she was friendly, funny, brimming over with gaiety, and utterly unsentimental.

When at length I helped her into the chauffeur-driven car which Uncle George had sent up from Sussex to take her home, I had discovered how painful it is to love. I was excited, keyed up. And also anxious; for I was sure that she did not feel as intensely about me as I about her.

I already knew I wanted to marry Kate. The thought that she might not have me was a bitter one.

THE NEXT DAY I went to Kempton Park races. Outside the weighing room I ran into Dane. We talked about the going, the weather, Pete's latest plans for us, and the horses. Usual jockey stuff. Then Dane said, "You took Kate out last night?"

"Yes."

"Where did you go?"

"The River Club," I said. "Where did you take her?"

"Didn't she tell you?" asked Dane.

"She said to ask you."

"River Club," said Dane.

"Damn it," I said. But I had to laugh.

"Honours even," said Dane.

"Did she ask you down to stay with Uncle George?" I asked suspiciously.

"I'm going today, after the races," said Dane, smiling. "And you?"

"Next Saturday," I said gloomily. "You know, Dane, she's teasing us abominably."

"I can stand it," said Dane. He tapped me on the shoulder. "Don't look so miserable, it may never happen."

"That's what I'm afraid of," I sighed. He laughed and went into the weighing room.

It was an uneventful afternoon. I rode my big black mare in a novice 'chase and Dane beat me by two lengths. At the end of the day we walked out to the car park together.

"How is Mrs. Davidson bearing up?" Dane asked.

"Fairly well, considering the bottom has dropped out of her world."

"Jockeys' wives' nightmare come true."

"Yes," I said.

"It makes you pause a bit, before you ask a girl to put up with that sort of constant worry," said Dane, thoughtfully.

"Kate?" I asked. He looked round sharply and grinned.

"I suppose so. Do you mind?"

"Yes," I said, keeping my voice light. "I mind very much."

We came to his car first, and he put his race glasses

and hat on the seat. His suitcase was in the back.

"So long, mate," he said. "I'll keep you posted."

I watched him drive off, answered his wave. I seldom felt envious of anybody, but at that moment I envied Dane sorely.

I climbed into the Lotus and pointed its low blue nose towards home.

It was on the road through Maidenhead Thicket that I saw the horse-box. It was parked in a lay-by on the near side, with tools scattered on the ground round it and the bonnet up. It was facing me as I approached, as if it had broken down on its way into Maidenhead. A man was walking a horse up and down in front of it.

The driver, standing by the bonnet scratching his head, saw me coming and gestured to me to stop. I pulled up beside him. He walked round to talk to me through the window, a middle-aged man, unremarkable, wearing a leather jacket.

"Do you know anything about engines, sir?" he asked.

"Not as much as you, I should think," I said, smiling. He had grease on his hands. If a horse-box driver couldn't find the fault in his own motor, it would be a long job for whoever did. "I'll take you back into Maidenhead, though, if you like. There's bound to be someone there who can help you."

"That's extremely kind of you, sir," he said, civilly "Thank you very much. But—er—I'm in a bit of a difficulty." He looked into the car and saw my binoculars on the seat beside me. His face lightened up. "You don't possibly know anything about horses, sir?"

"A bit, yes," I said.

"Well, it's like this, sir. I've got these two horses going to the London docks. They're being exported. Well, that one's all right." He pointed to the horse walking up and down. "But the other one, he don't seem so good. Sweating hard, he's been, the last hour or so, and biting at his stomach. He keeps trying to lie down. Looks ill.

The lad's in there with him now, and he's proper worried, I can tell you."

"It sounds as though it might be colic," I said. "If it is, he ought to be walking round, too. It's the only way to get him better. It's essential to keep them on the move when they've got colic."

The driver looked troubled. "It's a lot to ask, sir," he said, tentatively, "but would you have a look at him? Motors are my fancy, not horses, except to back 'em. And these lads are not too bright. I don't want a rocket from the boss for not looking after things properly."

"All right," I said, "I'll have a look. But I'm not a vet you know, by a long way."

He smiled in a relieved fashion. "Thank you, sir. Anyway, you'll know if I've got to get a vet at once or not, I should think."

I parked the car in the lay-by behind the horse-box. The door at the back of the horse-box opened and a hand, the stable lad's, I supposed, reached out to help me up. He took me by the wrist.

He didn't leave go.

There were three men waiting for me inside the horse-box. And no horse, sick or otherwise. After a flurried ten seconds during which my eyes were still unused to the dim light, I ended up standing with my back to the end post of one of the partition walls.

The horse-box was divided into three stalls with two partition walls between them, and there was a space across the whole width of the box at the back, usually occupied by lads travelling with their horses.

Two of the men held my arms. They stood one each side of the partition and slightly behind me, and they had an uncomfortable leverage on my shoulders. The post of the partition was padded with matting, as it always is in racehorse boxes, to save the horses hurting themselves while they travel. The matting tickled my neck.

The driver stepped up into the box and shut the door. His manner, still incredibly deferential, held a hint of triumph. It was entitled to. He had set a neat trap.

"Very sorry to have to do this, sir," he said politely. It was macabre.

"If it's money you want," I said, "you're going to be unlucky. I don't bet much and I didn't have a good day at the races today. I'm afraid you've gone to a lot of trouble for a measly eight quid."

"We don't want your money, sir," he said. "Though as you're offering it we might as well take it, at that." And still smiling pleasantly he put his hand inside my jacket and took my wallet out of the inside pocket.

I kicked his shin as hard as I could, but was hampered because of my position against the post. As soon as they felt me move the two men behind me jerked my arms painfully backwards.

"I shouldn't do that, sir, if I was you," said the friendly driver, rubbing his leg. He opened my wallet and took out the money, which he folded carefully and stowed inside his leather coat. He peered at the other things in the wallet, then stepped towards me, and put it back in my pocket. He was smiling faintly.

I stood still.

"That's better," he said, approvingly.

"What's all this about?" I asked. I had some idea that they intended to ransom me to my distant millionaire parent. Along the lines of "Cable us ten thousand pounds or we post your son back to you in small pieces." That would mean that they knew all along who I was, and had not just stopped any random motorist in a likely looking car to rob him.

"Surely you know, sir?" said the driver.

"I've no idea."

"I was asked to give you a message, Mr. York."

So he did know who I was. And he had not this minute discovered it from my wallet, which contained only money, stamps, and a cheque book in plain view. One or two things with my name on were in a flapped pocket, but he had not looked there.

"What makes you think my name is York?" I asked, trying a shot at outraged surprise. It was no good.

"Mr. Alan York, sir, was scheduled to drive along this road on his way from Kempton Park to the Cotswolds at approximately five fifteen p.m. on Saturday, February 27th, in a dark blue Lotus Elite, licence number KAB 890. I must thank you, sir, for making it easy for me to intercept you. You could go a month on the road without seeing another car like yours. I'd have had a job flagging you down if you'd been driving, say, a Ford or an Austin." His tone was still conversational.

"Get on with the message, I'm listening," I said.

"Deeds speak louder than words," said the driver mildly.

He came close and unbuttoned my jacket, looking at me steadily with wide eyes, daring me to kick him. I didn't move. He untied my tie, opened the neck of my shirt. We looked into each other's eyes. I hoped mine were as expressionless as his I let my arms go slack in the grip of the two men behind me, and felt them relax their hold slightly.

The driver stepped back and looked towards the fourth man, who had been leaning against the horse-box wall, silently. "He's all yours, Sonny. Deliver the message," he said.

Sonny was young, with sideboards. But I didn't look at his face, particularly. I looked at his hands.

He had a knife. The hilt lay in his palm, and his fingers were lightly curled round it, not gripping. The way a professional holds a knife.

There was nothing of the driver's mock deference in Sonny's manner. He was enjoying his work. He stood squarely in front of me and put the point of his short blade on my breastbone. It scarcely pricked, so light was his touch.

Oh bloody hell, I thought. My father would not be at all pleased to receive ransom messages reinforced by pleas from me for my own safety. I would never be able to live it down. And I was sure that this little melodrama was intended to soften me up into a suitably frightened state of mind. I sagged against the post, as if to shrink away from the knife. Sonny's grim mouth smiled thinly in a sneer.

Using the post as a springboard I thrust forwards and sideways as strongly as I knew how, bringing my knee up hard into Sonny's groin and tearing my arms out of the slackened grasp of the men behind me.

I leaped for the door and got it open. In the small area of the horse-box I had no chance, but I thought that if only I could get out into the thicket I might be able to deal with them. I had learned a nasty trick or two about fighting from my cousin, who lived in Kenya and had taken lessons from the Mau Mau.

But I didn't make it.

I tried to swing out with the door, but it was stiff and slow. The driver grabbed my ankle. I shook his hand off, but the vital second had gone. The two men who had held me clutched at my clothes. Through the open door I glimpsed the man who had been leading the horse up and down. He was looking enquiringly at the horse-box. I had forgotten about him.

I lashed out furiously with feet, fists, and elbows, but they were too much for me. I ended up where I began, against the matting-padded post with my arms pulled backwards. This time the two men were none too gentle. They slammed me back against the post hard and put their weight on my arms. I felt the wrench in my shoulders and down my chest to my stomach. I shut my teeth.

Sonny, clutching his abdomen, was half sitting, half kneeling in the corner. He watched with satisfaction.

"That hurt the bastard, Peaky," he said. "Do it again."

Peaky and his mate did it again.

Sonny laughed. Not a nice laugh.

A little more pressure and I should have some torn ligaments and a dislocated shoulder. There didn't seem to be much I could do about it.

The driver shut the horse-box door and picked the knife up from the floor, where it had fallen. He was not looking quite so calm as before. My fist had connected with his nose and blood was trickling out of it. But his temper was intact.

"Stop it. Stop it, Peaky," he said. "The boss said we weren't to hurt him. He made quite a point of it. You wouldn't want the boss to know you disobeyed him, would you?" There was a threat in his voice.

The tension on my arms slowly relaxed. Sonny's smile turned to a sullen scowl. It appeared I had the boss to thank for something, even if not much.

"Now, Mr. York," said the driver reproachfully, wiping his nose on a blue handkerchief, "all that was quite unnecessary. We only want to give you a message."

"I don't like listening with knives sticking into me," I said.

The driver sighed. "Yes, sir, I can see that was a mistake. It was meant for you to understand that the warning is serious, see. Take no notice of it, and you'll find you're in real trouble. I'm telling you, real trouble."

"What warning?" I said, mystified.

"You're to lay off asking questions about Major Davidson," he said.

"What?" I goggled at him. It was so unexpected. "I haven't been asking questions about Major Davidson," I said weakly.

"I don't know about that, I'm sure," said the driver, mopping away, "but that's the message, and you'd do well to take heed of it, sir. I'm telling you for your own good. The boss don't like people poking into his affairs."

"Who is the boss?" I asked.

"Now, sir, you know better than to ask questions like that. Sonny, go and tell Bert we've finished here. We'll load up the horse."

Sonny stood up with a groan and went over to the door, his hand still pressed to his groin. He yelled something out of the window.

"Stand still, Mr. York, and you'll come to no harm," said the driver, his politeness unimpaired. He mopped, and looked at his handkerchief to see if his nose was still bleeding. It was. I took his advice, and stood still. He opened the door and climbed down out of the horse-box. A little time passed during which Sonny and I exchanged glares and nobody said anything.

Then there was the noise of bolts and clips being undone, and the side of the horse-box which formed the ramp was lowered to the ground. The fifth man, Bert, led the horse up the ramp and fastened him into the nearest stall. The driver raised the ramp again and fastened it.

I used the brief period while what was left of the daylight flooded into the box, to twist my head round as far as I could and take a clear look at Peaky. I saw what I expected, but it only increased my bewilderment.

The driver climbed into the cab, shut the door, and started the engine.

Bert said, "Take him over to the door." I needed no urging.

The horse-box began to move. Bert opened the door. Peaky and his pal let go of my arms and Bert gave me a push. I hit the ground just as the accelerating horse-box pulled out of the lay-by on to the deserted road. It was as well I had had a good deal of practice at falling off horses. Instinctively, I landed on my shoulder and rolled.

I sat on the ground and looked after the speeding horse-box. The number plate was mostly obscured by thick dust, but I had time to see the registration letters. They were APX.

The Lotus still stood in the lay-by. I picked myself up, dusted the worst off my suit, and walked over to it. I intended to follow the horse-box and see where it went. But the thorough driver had seen to it that I should not. The car would not start. Opening the bonnet to see how much damage had been done, I found that three of the four sparking plugs had been taken out. They lay in a neat row on the battery. It took me ten minutes to replace them, because my hands were trembling.

By then I had no hope of catching the horse-box or of finding anyone who had noticed its direction. I got back into the car and fastened the neck of my suit. My tie was missing altogether.

I took out the A.A. book and looked up the registration letters PX. For what it was worth, the horse-box was originally registered in West Sussex. If the number plate were genuine, it might be possible to discover the present owner. For a quarter of an hour I sat and thought. Then I started the car, turned it, and drove back into Maidenhead.

The town was bright with lights, though nearly all the shops were shut. The door of the police station was open wide. I went in and asked for Inspector Lodge.

"He isn't in yet," said the policeman at the enquiry desk, glancing up at the clock. It was ten past six. "He'll be here any minute, if you care to wait, sir."

"He isn't in yet? Do you mean he is just starting work for the day?"

"Yes, sir. He's on late turn. Busy evening here, Saturdays." He grinned. "Dance halls, pubs, and car crashes." I smiled back, sat down on the bench and waited. After five minutes Lodge came in quickly, peeling off his coat.

"Evening, Small, what's new?" he said to the policeman at the enquiry desk.

"Gentleman here to see you, sir," said Small, gesturing to me. "He's only been waiting a few minutes."

Lodge turned round. I stood up. "Good evening," I said.

"Good evening, Mr. York." Lodge gave me a piercing look but showed no surprise at seeing me. His eyes fell to the neck of my shirt, and his eyebrows rose a fraction. But he said only, "What can I do for you?"

"Are you very busy?" I asked. "If you have time, I would like to tell you . . . how I lost my tie." In midsentence I flunked saying baldly that I had been manhandled. As it was, Small looked at me curiously, clearly thinking me mad to come into a police station to tell an inspector how I lost my tie.

But Lodge, whose perception was acute, said, "Come into my office, Mr. York." He led the way. He hung up his hat and coat on pegs and lit the gas fire, but its glowing bars couldn't make a cosy place of the austere, square, filing-cabineted little room.

Lodge sat behind his tidy desk, and I, as before, faced him. He offered me a cigarette and gave me a light. As the smoke went comfortingly down into my lungs, I was wondering where to begin.

I said, "Have you got any further with the Major Davidson business since the day before yesterday?"

"No, I'm afraid not. It no longer has any sort of priority with us. Yesterday we discussed it in conference and consulted your Senior Steward, Sir Creswell Stampe. In view of the verdict at the inquest, your story is considered, on the whole, to be the product of a youthful and overheated imagination. No one but you saw any wire. The grooves on the posts of the fence may or may not have been caused by wire, but there is no indication *when* they were made. I understand it is fairly common practice for groundsmen to raise a wire across a fence so that members of the riding public shall not try to jump it and make holes in the birch." He paused, then went on, "Sir Creswell says the view of the National Hunt Committee, several of whom he has talked to on the telephone, is that you made a mistake. If you saw any wire, they contend, it must have belonged to the groundsman."

"Have they asked him?" I said.

Lodge sighed. "The head guardsman says he didn't leave any wire on the course, but one of his staff is old and vague, and can't be sure that he didn't."

We looked at each other in glum silence.

"And what do you think, yourself?" I asked finally.

Lodge said, "I believe you saw the wire and that Major Davidson was brought down by it. There is one fact which I personally consider significant enough to justify this belief. It is that the attendant who gave his name as Thomas Cook did not collect the pay due to him for two days' work. In my experience there has to be a very good reason for a workman to ignore his pay packet." He smiled sardonically.

"I could give you another fact to prove that Major Davidson's fall was no accident," I said, "but you'll have to take my word for it again. No evidence."

"Go on."

"Someone has been to great pains to tell me not to ask awkward questions about it." I told him about the events in and around the horse-box, and added, "And how's that for the product of a youthful and overheated imagination?"

"When did all this happen?" asked Lodge.

"About an hour ago."

"And what were you doing between then and the time you arrived here?"

"Thinking," I said, stubbing out my cigarette.

"Oh," said Lodge. "Well, have you given any thought to the improbabilities in your story? My chief isn't going to like them when I make my report."

"Don't make it then," I said, smiling. "But I suppose

the most glaring improbability is that five men, a horse, and a horse-box should all be employed to give a warning which might much more easily have been sent by post."

"That certainly indicates an organisation of unusual size," said Lodge, with a touch of irony.

"There are at least ten of them," I said. "One or two are probably in hospital, though."

Lodge sat up straighter.

"What do you mean. How do you know?"

"The five men who stopped me today are all taxi-drivers. Either from London or Brighton, but I don't know which. I saw them at Plumpton races three days ago, fighting a pitched battle against a rival gang."

"What?" Lodge exclaimed Then he said, "Yes, I saw a paragraph about it in a newspaper. Do you recognise them positively?"

"Yes," I said. "Sonny had his knife out at Plumpton, too, but he was pinned down by a big heavy man, and didn't get much chance to use it. But I saw his face quite clearly. Peaky you couldn't mistake, with that dark widow's peak growing down his forehead. The other three were all rounded up into the same group at Plumpton. I was waiting to give someone a lift, and I had a long time to look at the taxi-drivers after the fight was over. Bert, the man with the horse, had a black eye today, and the man who held my right arm, whose name I don't know, he had some sticking plaster on his forehead. But why were they all free? The last I saw them, they were bound for the cells, I thought, for disturbing the peace."

"They may be out on bail, or else they were let off with a fine. I don't know, without seeing a report," said Lodge. "Now why, in your opinion, were so many sent to warn you?"

"Rather flattering, sending five, when you come to think of it," I grinned. "Perhaps the taxi business is in the doldrums and they hadn't anything else to do. Or else it was, as the driver said, to ram the point home."

"Which brings me," said Lodge, "to another improbability. Why, if you were faced with a knife at your chest, did you throw yourself forward? Wasn't that asking for trouble?"

"I wouldn't have been so keen if he'd held the point a bit higher up; but it was against my breastbone. You'd need a hammer to get a knife through that. I reckoned that I'd knock it out of Sonny's hand rather than into me, and that's what happened."

"Didn't it cut you at all?"

"Not much," I said.

"Let's see," said Lodge, getting up and coming round the desk.

I opened my shirt again. Between the second and third buttons there was a shallow cut an inch or so long in the skin over my breastbone. Some blood had clotted on the cut and there was a dried rusty trail down my chest where a few drops had run. My shirt was spotted here and there. Nothing. I hadn't felt it much.

Lodge sat down again. I buttoned my shirt.

"Now," he said, picking up his pen and biting the end of it. "What questions have you been asking about Major Davidson, and of whom have you asked them?"

"That is really what is most surprising about the whole affair," I said. "I've hardly asked anything of anybody. And I certainly haven't had any useful answers."

"But you must have touched a nerve somewhere," said Lodge. He took a sheet of paper out of the drawer. "Tell me the names of everyone with whom you have discussed the wire."

"With you," I said promptly. "And with Mrs. Davidson. And everyone at the inquest heard me say I'd found it."

"But I noticed that the inquest wasn't properly reported in the papers. There was no mention of wire in the press," he said. "And anyone seeing you at the inquest wouldn't have got the impression that you were hell-bent on unravelling the mystery. You took the verdict very calmly and not at all as if you disagreed with it."

"Thanks to your warning me in advance what to expect," I said.

Lodge's list looked short and unsatisfactory on the large sheet of paper.

"Anyone else?" he said.

"Oh . . . a friend . . . a Miss Ellery-Penn. I told her last night."

"Girl friend?" he asked bluntly. He wrote her down.

"Yes," I said.

"Anyone else?"

"No."

"Why not?" he asked, pushing the paper away.

"I reckoned you and Sir Creswell needed a clear field. I thought I might mess things up for you if I asked too many questions. Put people on their guard, ready with their answers—that sort of thing. But it seems, from what you've said about dropping your enquiries, that I might as well have gone ahead." I spoke a little bitterly.

Lodge looked at me carefully. "You resent being considered youthful and hot-headed," he said.

"Twenty-four isn't young," I said. "I seem to remember England once had a Prime Minister of that age. He didn't do so badly."

"That's irrelevant, and you know it," he said.

I grinned.

Lodge said, "What do you propose to do now?"

"Go home," I said, looking at my watch.

"No, I meant about Major Davidson?"

"Ask as many questions as I can think of," I said promptly.

"In spite of the warning?"

"Because of it," I said. "The very fact that five men

were sent to warn me off means that there is a good deal to find out. Bill Davidson was a good friend, you know. I can't tamely let whoever caused his death get away with it." I thought a moment. "First, I'll find out who owns the taxis which Peaky and Co. drive."

"Well, unofficially, I wish you luck," said Lodge. "But be careful."

"Sure," I said, standing up.

Lodge came to the street door of the police station and shook hands. "Let me know how you get on," he said.

"Yes, I will."

He raised his hand in a friendly gesture, and went in. I resumed my interrupted journey to the Cotswolds. My wrenched shoulders were aching abominably, but as long as I concentrated on Bill's accident I could forget them.

It struck me that both the accident and the affair of the horse-box should give some clue to the mind which had hatched them. It was reasonable to assume it was the same mind. Both events were elaborate, where some simpler plan would have been effective, and the word "devious" drifted into my thoughts and I dredged around in my memory chasing its echo. Finally I traced it to Joe Nantwich and the threatening letter that had reached him ten days late, but decided that Joe's troubles had nothing to do with Bill's.

Both the attack on Bill and the warning to me had been, I was certain, more violent in the event than in the plan. Bill had died partly by bad luck; and I would have been less roughly handled had I not tried to escape. I came to the conclusion that I was looking for someone with a fanciful imagination, someone prepared to be brutal up to a point, and whose little squibs, because of their complicated nature, were apt to go off with bigger bangs than were intended.

And it was comforting to realize that my adversary

was not a man of superhuman intelligence. He could make mistakes. His biggest so far, I thought, was to go to great lengths to deliver an unnecessary warning whose sole effect was to stir me to greater action.

FOR TWO DAYS I did nothing. There was no harm in giving the impression that the warning was being taken to heart.

I played poker with the children and lost to Henry because half my mind was occupied with his father's affairs.

Henry said, "You aren't thinking what you're doing, Alan," in a mock sorrowful tone as he rooked me of ten chips with two pairs.

"I expect he's in love," said Polly, turning on me an assessing female eye. There was that, too.

"Pooh," said Henry. He dealt the cards.

"What's in love?" said William, who was playing tiddly-winks with his chips, to Henry's annoyance.

"Soppy stuff," said Henry. "Kissing, and all that slush."

"Mummy's in love with me," said William, a cuddly child.

"Don't be silly," said Polly loftily, from her eleven years.

"In love means weddings and brides and confetti and things."

"Well, Alan," said Henry, in a scornful voice, "you'd better get out of love quick or you won't have any chips left."

William picked up his hand. His eyes and mouth opened wide. This meant he had at least two aces. They were the only cards he ever raised on. I saw Henry give him a flick of a glance, then look back at his own hand. He discarded three, and took three more, and at his turn, he pushed away his cards. I turned them over. Two queens and two tens. Henry was a realist. He knew when to give in. And William, bouncing up and down with excitement, won only four chips with three aces and a pair of fives.

Not for the first time I wondered at the quirks of heredity. Bill had been a friendly, genuine man of many solid virtues. Scilla, matching him, was compassionate and loving. Neither was at all intellectually gifted; yet they had endowed their elder son with a piercing, exceptional intelligence.

And how could I guess, as I cut the cards for Polly and helped William straighten up his leaning tower of chips, that Henry already held in his sharp eight-year-old brain the key to the puzzle of his father's death.

He didn't know it himself.

chapter 7

THE CHELTENHAM NATIONAL Hunt Festival meeting started on Tuesday, March 2nd.

Three days of superlative racing lay ahead, and the finest 'chasers in the world crowded into the racecourse stables. Ferries from Ireland brought them across by boat and plane load; dark horses from the bogs whose supernatural turn of foot was foretold in thick mysterious brogue, and golden geldings who had already taken prizes and cups galore across the Irish Sea.

Horse-boxes from Scotland, from Kent, from Devon, from everywhere, converged on Gloucestershire. Inside, they carried Grand National winners, champion hurdlers, all-conquering handicappers, splendid hunters: the aristocrats among jumpers.

With four big races in the three days reserved for them alone, every amateur jockey in the country who could beg, borrow, or buy a mount hurried to the course. A ride at Cheltenham was an honour: a win at Cheltenham an experience never to be forgotten. The amateur jockeys embraced the Festival with passionate fervour.

But one amateur jockey, Alan York, felt none of this passionate fervour as he drove into the car park. I could not explain it to myself, but for once the hum of the gathering crowd, the expectant faces, the sunshine of the cold invigorating March morning, even the prospect of riding three good horses at the meeting, stirred me not at all.

Outside the main gate I sought out the newspaper seller I had spoken to at Plumpton. He was a short, tubby little Cockney with a large moustache and a cheerful temperament. He saw me coming, and held out a paper.

"Morning Mr. York," he said. "Do you fancy your horse today?"

"You might have a bit on," I said, "but not your shirt. There's the Irishman to be reckoned with."

"You'll do him, all right."

"Well, I hope so." I waited while he sold a newspaper to an elderly man with enormous race glasses. Then I said, "Do you remember the taxi-drivers fighting at Plumpton?"

"Couldn't hardly forget it, could I?" He beamed.

"You told me one lot came from London and one from Brighton."

"Yes, that's right."

"Which lot were which?" I said. He looked mystified. I said, "Which lot came from London and which came from Brighton?"

"Oh, I see." He sold a paper to two middle-aged ladies wearing thick tweeds and ribbed woolen stockings, and gave them change. Then he turned back to me.

"Which lot was which, like? Hm. I see 'em often enough, you know, but they ain't a friendly lot. They don't talk to you. Not like the private chauffeurs, see? I'd know the Brighton lot if I could see 'em, though. Know 'em by sight, see?" He broke off to yell "Midday Special" at the top of his lungs, and as a result sold three more papers. I waited patiently.

"How do you recognize them?" I asked.

"By their faces, 'course." He thought it a foolish question.

"Yes, but which faces? Can you describe them?"

"Oh, I see. There's all sorts."

"Can't you describe just one of them?" I asked.

He narrowed his eyes, thinking, and tugged his moustache. "One of 'em. Well, there's one nasty-looking chap with sort of slitty eyes. I wouldn't like a ride in his taxi. You'd know him by his hair, I reckon. It grows nearly down to his eyebrows. Rum-looking cove. What do you want him for?"

"I don't want him," I said. "I just want to know where he comes from."

"Brighton, that's it." He beamed at me. "There's another one I see sometimes, too. A young ted with sideboards, always cleaning his nails with a knife."

"Thanks a lot," I said. I gave him a pound note and his beam grew wider. He tucked it into an inside pocket.

"Best of luck, sir," he said. I left him, with "Midday Special" ringing in my ears, and went in to the weighing room, pondering on the information that my captors with the horse-box came from Brighton. Whoever had sent them could not have imagined that I had seen them before, and could find them again.

Preoccupied, I suddenly realised that Pete Gregory was talking to me. "Had a puncture on the way, but they've got here safely, that's the main thing. Are you listening, Alan?"

"Yes, Pete. Sorry. I was thinking."

"Glad to hear you can," said Pete with a fat laugh. Tough and shrewd though he was, his sense of humour had never grown up. Schoolboy insults passed as the highest form of wit for him; but one got used to it.

"How is Palindrome?" I asked. My best horse

"He's fine. I was just telling you, they had a puncture . . ." He broke off, exasperated. He hated having to repeat things. "Oh well . . . do you want to go over to the stables and have a look at him?"

"Yes, please," I said.

We walked down to the stables. Pete had to come with me because of the tight security rules. Even owners could not visit their horses without the trainer to vouch for them, and stable boys had passes with their photographs on, to show at the stable gate. It was all designed to prevent the doping or "nobbling" of horses.

In his box I patted my beautiful 'chaser, an eight-year-old bay with black points, and gave him a lump of sugar. Pete clicked his tongue disapprovingly and said, "Not before the race," like a nanny who had caught her charge being given sweets before lunch. I grinned. Pete had a phobia on the subject.

"Sugar will give him more energy," I said, giving Palindrome another lump and making a fuss of him. "He looks well."

"He ought to win if you judge it right," said Pete. "Keep your eyes on that Irishman, Barney. He'll try to slip you all with a sudden burst as you go into the water so that he can start up the hill six lengths in front. I've seen him do it time and again. He gets everyone else chasing him like mad up the hill using up all the reserves they need for the finish. Now, either you burst with him, and go up the hill at his pace and no faster, or, if you lose him, take it easy up the hill and pile on the pressure when you're coming down again. Clear?"

"As glass," I said. Whatever one might think of Pete's jokes, his advice on how to ride races was invaluable, and I owed a great deal to it.

I gave Palindrome a final pat, and we went out into the yard. Owing to the security system, it was the quietest place on the racecourse.

"Pete, was Bill in any trouble, do you know?" I said, plunging in abruptly.

He finished shutting the door of Palindrome's box,

and turned round slowly, and stood looking at me vaguely for so long that I began to wonder if he had heard my question.

But at last he said, "That's a big word, trouble. Something happened . . ."

"What?" I said, as he lapsed into silence again.

But instead of answering, he said, "Why should you think there was any . . . trouble?"

I told him about the wire. He listened with a calm, unsurprised expression, but his grey eyes were bleak.

He said, "Why haven't we all heard about it before?"

"I told Sir Creswell Stampe and the police a week ago," I said, "but with the wire gone they've nothing tangible to go on, and they're dropping it."

"But you're not?" said Pete. "Can't say I blame you. I can't help you much, though. There's only one thing . . . Bill told me he'd had a telephone call which made him laugh. But I didn't listen properly to what he said—I was thinking about my horses, you know how it is. It was something about Admiral falling. He thought it was a huge joke and I didn't go into it with him to find out what I'd missed. I didn't think it was important. When Bill was killed I did wonder if there could possibly be anything odd about it, but I asked you, and you said you hadn't noticed anything . . ." His voice trailed off.

"Yes, I'm sorry," I said. Then I asked, "How long before his accident did Bill tell you about the telephone call?"

"The last time I spoke to him," Pete said. "It was on the Friday morning, just before I flew to Ireland. I rang him to say that all was ready for Admiral's race at Maidenhead the next day."

We began to walk back to the weighing room. On an impulse I said, "Pete, do you ever use the Brighton taxis?" He lived and trained on the Sussex Downs.

"Not often," he said. "Why?"

"There are one or two taxi-drivers there I'd like to

have a few words with," I said, not adding that I'd prefer to have the words with them one at a time in a deserted back alley.

"There are several taxi lines in Brighton, as far as I know," he said. "If you want to find one particular driver, why don't you try the railway station? That's where I've usually taken a taxi from. They line up there in droves for the London trains." His attention drifted off as an Irish horse passed us on its way into the paddock for the first race.

"That's Connemara Pal or I'm a Dutchman," said Pete enviously. "I took one of my owners over and tried to buy him, last August, but they wanted eight thousand for him. He was tucked away in a broken down hut behind some pig-styes, so my owner wouldn't pay that price. And now look at him. He won the Leopardstown novice 'chase on Boxing Day by twenty lengths and wouldn't have blown a candle out afterwards. Best young horse we'll see this year." Pete's mind was firmly back in its familiar groove, and we talked about the Irish raid until we were back in the weighing room.

I sought out Clem, who was very busy, and checked with him that my kit was all right, and that he knew the weight I was due to carry on Palindrome.

Kate had told me she was not coming to Cheltenham, so I went in search of the next best thing: news of her.

Dane's peg and section of bench were in the smaller of the two changing rooms, and he was sitting only one place away from the roaring stove, a sure sign of his rise in the jockeys' world. Champions get the warmest places by unwritten right. Beginners shiver beside the draughty doors.

He was clad in his shirt and pants, and was pulling on his nylon stockings. There was a hole in each foot and both his big toes were sticking comically out of them. He had long narrow feet, and long, narrow delicately strong hands to match.

"It's all very well for you to laugh," said Dane, pulling the tops of the stockings over his knees. "They don't seem to make nylons for size eleven shoes . . ."

"Get Walter to get you some stretching ones," I suggested. "Have you a busy day?"

"Three, including the Champion Hurdle," said Dane. "Pete has entered half the stable here." He grinned at me. "I might just find time to tell you about the Penn household, though, if that's what you're after. Shall I start with Uncle George, or Aunt Deb, or . . ." He broke off to pull on his silk breeches and his riding boots. His valet, Walter, gave him his under-jersey and some particularly vile pink and orange colours. Whoever had chosen them had paid no regard to their effect against a manly complexion. "Or do you want to hear about Kate?" finished Dane, covering up the sickening jersey with a windproof jacket.

The changing room was filling up, packed with the extra Irish jockeys who had come over for the meeting and were in high spirits and robust voice. Dane and I went out into the crowded weighing room, where at least one could hear oneself speak.

"Uncle George," he said, "is a gem. And I'm not going to spoil him for you by telling you about him. Aunt Deb is the Honourable Mrs. Penn to you and me, mate, and Aunt Deb to Kate alone. She has a chilly sort of charm that lets you know she would be downright rude if she were not so well bred. She disapproved of me, for a start. I think she disapproves on principle of everything to do with racing, including Heavens Above and Uncle George's idea of a birthday present."

"Go on," I urged, anxious for him to come to the most interesting part of the chronicle before someone else buttonholed him.

"Ah yes. Kate. Gorgeous, heavenly Kate. Strictly, you know, her name is Kate Ellery, not Penn at all. Uncle George added the hyphen and the Penn to her name when he took her in. He said it would be easier for her to have the same surname as him—save a lot of explanations. I suppose it does," said Dane, musingly, knowing full well how he was tantalising me. He relented, and grinned. "She sent you her love."

I felt a warm glow inside. The Cheltenham Festival meeting suddenly seemed not a bad place to be, after all.

"Thanks," I said, trying not to smile fatuously and scarcely succeeding. Dane looked at me speculatively; but I changed the subject back to racing, and presently I asked him if he had ever heard Bill Davidson spoken of in connection with any sort of odd happenings.

"No, I never did," he said positively. I told him about the wire. His reaction was typical.

"Poor Bill," he said with anger. "Poor old Bill. What a bloody shame."

"So if you hear anything which might have even the faintest significance . . ."

"I'll pass it on to you," he promised.

At that moment Joe Nantwich walked straight into Dane as if he hadn't seen him. He stopped without apology, took a step back, and then went on his way to the changing room. His eyes were wide, unfocused, staring.

"He's drunk," said Dane, incredulously. "His breath smells like a distillery."

"He has his troubles," I said.

"He'll have more still before the afternoon's much older. Just wait till one of the Stewards catches that alcoholic blast."

Joe reappeared at our side. It was true that one could smell his approach a good yard away. Without preamble he spoke directly to me.

"I've had another one." He took a paper out of his pocket. It had been screwed up and straightened out again, so that it was wrinkled in a hundred fine lines, but its ball-pointed message was still abundantly clear.

"BOLINGBROKE THIS WEEK," it said.

"When did you get it?" I asked.

"It was here when I arrived, waiting for me in the letter rack."

"You've tanked up pretty quickly, then," I said.

"I'm not drunk," said Joe indignantly. "I only had a couple of quick ones in the bar opposite the weighing room."

Dane and I raised our eyebrows in unison. The bar opposite the weighing room had no front wall, and anyone drinking there was in full view of every trainer, owner, and Steward who walked out of the weighing room. There might be a surer way for a jockey to commit professional suicide than to have "a couple of quick ones" at that bar before the first race, but I couldn't think of it off-hand. Joe hiccuped.

"Double quick ones, I imagine," said Dane with a smile, taking the paper out of my hand and reading it. "What does it mean, 'Bolingbroke. This week?' Why are you so steamed up about it?"

Joe snatched the paper away and stuffed it back into his pocket. He seemed for the first time to be aware that Dane was listening.

"It's none of your business," he said rudely.

I felt a great impulse to assure him it was none of mine, either. But he turned back to me and said, "What shall I do?" in a voice full of whining self-pity.

"Are you riding today?" I asked.

"I'm in the fourth and the last. Those bloody amateurs have got two races all to themselves today. A bit thick, isn't it, leaving us only four races to earn our living in? Why don't the fat-arsed gentlemen riders stick to the point-to-points where they belong? That's all they're— well fit for," he added, alliteratively.

There was a small silence. Dane laughed. Joe was after all not too drunk to realise he was riding his hobby horse in front of the wrong man. He said weakly, in his smarmiest voice, "Well, Alan, of course I didn't mean you personally."

"If you still want my advice, in view of your opinion of amateur jockeys," I said, keeping a straight face, "you should drink three cups of strong black coffee and stay out of sight as long as you can."

"I mean, what shall I do about this note?" Joe had a thicker skin than a coach-hide cabin trunk.

"Pay it no attention at all," I said. "I should think that whoever wrote it is playing with you. Perhaps he knows you like to drown your sorrows in whisky and is relying on you to destroy yourself without his having to do anything but send you frightening letters A neat, bloodless, and effective revenge."

The sullen pout on Joe's babyish face slowly changed into a mulish determination which was only slightly less repellent.

"No one's going to do that to me," he said, with an aggressiveness which I guessed would diminish with the alcohol level in his blood. He weaved off out of the weighing room door, presumably in search of black coffee. Before Dane could ask me what was going on, he received a hearty slap on the back from Sandy Mason, who was staring after Joe with dislike.

"What's up with that stupid little clot?" he asked, but he didn't wait for an answer. He said, "Look, Dane, be a pal and gen me up on this horse of Gregory's I'm riding in the first. I've never seen it before, as far as I know. It seems the owner likes my red hair or something." Sandy's infectious laugh made several people look round with answering smiles.

"Sure," said Dane. They launched into a technical discussion and I turned away from them. But Dane touched my arm.

He said, "Is it all right for me to tell people, say Sandy for instance, about the wire and Bill?"

"Yes, do. You might strike oil with someone I

wouldn't have thought of asking about it. But be careful." I thought of telling him about the warning in the horse-box, but it was a long story and it seemed enough to say, "Remember that you're stirring up people who can kill, even if by mistake."

He looked startled. "Yes, you're right. I'll be careful."

We turned back to Sandy together.

"What are you two so solemn about? Has someone swiped that luscious brunette you're both so keen on?" he said.

"It's about Bill Davidson," said Dane, disregarding this.

"What about him?"

"The fall that killed him was caused by some wire being strung across the top of the fence. Alan saw it."

Sandy looked aghast. "Alan saw it," he repeated, and then, as the full meaning of what Dane had said sank in, "but that's murder."

I pointed out the reasons for supposing the murder had not been intended. Sandy's brown eyes stared at me unwinkingly until I had finished.

"I guess you're right," he said. "What are you going to do about it?"

"He's trying to find out what is behind it all," said Dane. "We thought you might be able to help. Have you heard anything that might explain it? People tell you things, you know."

Sandy ran his strong brown hands through his unruly red hair, and rubbed the nape of his neck. This brain massage produced no great thoughts, however. "Yes, but mostly they tell me about their girl friends or their bets or such like. Not Major Davidson though. We weren't exactly on a bosom pals basis, because he thought I strangled a horse belonging to a friend of his. Well," said Sandy with an engaging grin, "maybe I did, at that. Anyway, we had words, as they say, a few months ago."

"See if your bookmaker friends have heard any whispers, then," said Dane. "They usually have their ears usefully to the ground."

"O.K." said Sandy. "I'll pass the news along and see what happens. Now come on, we haven't much time before the first and I wanted to know what this sod of a horse is going to do." And as Dane hesitated, he said, "Come on, you don't have to wrap it up. Gregory only asks me to ride for him when it's such a stinker that he daren't ask any sensible man to get up on it."

"It's a mare," said Dane, "with a beastly habit of galloping into the bottoms of fences as if they weren't there. She usually ends up in the open ditch."

"Well thanks," said Sandy, apparently undaunted by this news. "I'll tan her hide for her and she'll soon change her ways. See you later, then." He went into the changing room.

Dane looked after him. "The horse isn't foaled that could frighten that blighter Sandy," he said with admiration.

"Nothing wrong with his nerve," I agreed. "But why ever is Pete running an animal like that here, of all places?"

"The owner fancies having a runner at Cheltenham. You know how it is. Snob value, and so on," he said indulgently.

We were being jostled continually, as we talked, by the throng of trainers and owners. We went outside. Dane was immediately appropriated by a pair of racing journalists who wanted his views on his mount in the Gold Cup, two days distant.

The afternoon wore on. The racing began. With the fine sunny day and the holiday mood of the crowd, the excitement was almost crackling in the air.

Sandy got the mare over the first open ditch but disappeared into the next. He came back with a broad smile, cursing hard.

Joe reappeared after the second race, looking less

drunk but more frightened. I avoided him shamelessly.

Dane, riding like a demon, won the Champion Hurdle by a head. Pete, patting his horse and sharing with the owner the congratulations of the great crowd round the unsaddling enclosure, was so delighted he could hardly speak. Large and red-faced, he stood there with his hat pushed back showing his baldness, trying to look as if this sort of thing happened every day, when it was in fact the most important winner he had trained.

He was so overcome that he forgot, as we stood some time later in the parade ring before the amateur's race, to make his customary joke about Palindrome going backwards as well as forwards. And when I, following his advice to the letter, stuck like a shadow to the Irishman when he tried to slip the field, lay a scant length behind him all the way to the last fence, and passed him with a satisfying spurt fifty yards from the winning post, Pete said his day was complete.

I could have hugged him, I was so elated. Although I had won several races back in Rhodesia and about thirty since I had been in England, this was my first win at Cheltenham. I felt as high as if I had already drunk the champagne which waited unopened in the changing room, the customary crateful of celebration for Champion Hurdle day. Palindrome was, in my eyes, the most beautiful, most intelligent, most perfect horse in the world. I walked on air to the scales to weigh in, and changed into my ordinary clothes, and had still not returned to earth when I went outside again. The gloom I had arrived in seemed a thousand years ago. I was so happy I could have turned cartwheels like a child. Such total, unqualified fulfillment comes rarely enough and unexpectedly, I wished that my father were there to share it.

The problem of Bill had receded like a dot in the distance, and it was only because I had earlier planned to do it that I directed my airy steps down to the horse-box parking ground.

It was packed. About twenty horses ran in each race that day, and almost every horse-box available must have been pressed into service to bring them. I sauntered along the rows, humming lightheartedly, looking at the number plates with half an eye and less attention.

And there it was.

APX 708.

My happiness burst like a bubble.

There was no doubt it was the same horse-box. Regulation wooden Jennings design. Elderly, with dull and battered varnish. No name or owner or trainer painted anywhere on the doors or bodywork.

There was no one in the driver's cab. I walked round to the back, opened the door, and climbed in.

The horse-box was empty except for a bucket, a hay net, and a rug, the normal traveling kit for racehorses. The floor was strewn with straw, whereas three days earlier it had been swept clean.

The rug, I thought, might give me a clue as to where the box had come from. Most trainers and some owners have their initials embroidered or sewn in tape in large letters on the corners of their horse rugs. If there were initials on this one, it would be easy.

I picked it up. It was pale fawn with a dark brown binding. I found the initials. I stood there as if turned to stone. Plainly in view, embroidered in dark brown silk, were the letters A. Y.

It was my own rug.

PETE, WHEN I ran him to earth, looked in no mood to answer any questions needing much thought. He leaned back against the weighing room wall with a glass of champagne in one hand and a cigar in the other, surrounded by a pack of friends similarly equipped. From their rosy smiling faces I gathered the celebration had already been going on for some time.

Dane thrust a glass into my hand.

"Where have you been? Well done on Palindrome. Have some bubbly. The owner's paying, God bless him." His eyes were alight with that fantastic, top-of-the-world elation that I had lately felt myself. It began to creep back into me, too. It was, after all, a great day. Mysteries could wait.

I drank a sip of champagne and said, "Well done yourself, you old son-of-a-gun. And here's to the Gold Cup."

"No such luck," said Dane, "I haven't much chance in that." And from his laughing face I gathered he didn't care, either. We emptied our glasses. "I'll get another bottle," he said, diving into the noisy, crowded changing room.

Looking around I saw Joe Nantwich backed up into a nearby corner by the enormous Mr. Tudor. The big man was doing the talking, forcefully, his dark face almost merging with the shadows. Joe, still dressed in racing colours, listened very unhappily.

Dane came back with the bubbles fizzing out of a newly opened bottle and filled our glasses. He followed my gaze.

"I don't know whether Joe was sober or not, but didn't he make a hash of the last race?" he said.

"I didn't see it."

"Brother, you sure missed something. He didn't try a yard. His horse damned nearly stopped altogether at the hurdle over on the far side, and it was second favourite, too. What you see now," he gestured with the bottle, "is, I should think, our Joe getting the well-deserved sack."

"That man owns Bolingbroke," I said.

"Yes, that's right. Same colours. What a fool Joe is. Owners with five or six goodish horses don't grow on bushes any more."

Clifford Tudor had nearly done. As he turned away from Joe in our direction we heard the tail end of his remarks.

". . . think you can make a fool of me and get away with it. The Stewards can warn you off altogether, as far as I'm concerned."

He strode past us, giving me a nod of recognition, which surprised me, and went out.

Joe leaned against the wall for support. His face was pallid and sweating. He looked ill. He took a few unsteady steps towards us and spoke without caution, as if he had forgotten that Stewards and members of the National Hunt Committee might easily overhear.

"I had a phone call this morning. The same voice as always. He just said, 'Don't win the sixth race' and rang off before I could say anything. And then that note saying 'Bolingbroke. This week' . . . I don't understand it. And I didn't win the race and now that bloody wog says he'll get another jockey . . . and the Stewards have started an enquiry about my riding . . . and I feel sick."

"Have some champagne," said Dane, encouragingly.

"Don't be so bloody helpful," said Joe, clutching his stomach and departing towards the changing room.

"What the hell's going on?" said Dane.

"I don't know," I said, perplexed and more interested in Joe's troubles than I had been before. The phone call was inconsistent, I thought, with the notes. One ordered business as usual, the other promised revenge. "I wonder if Joe always tells the truth," I said.

"Highly unlikely," said Dane, dismissing it.

One of the Stewards came and reminded us that even after the Champion Hurdle, drinking in the weighing room itself was frowned on, and would we please drift along into the changing room. Dane did that, but I finished my drink and went outside.

Pete, still attended by a posse of friends, had decided that it was time to go home. The friends were unwilling.

The racecourse bars, they were saying, were still open.

I walked purposefully up to Pete, and he made me his excuse for breaking away. We went towards the gates.

"Whew, what a day!" said Pete, mopping his brow with a white handkerchief and throwing away the stub of his cigar.

"A wonderful day," I agreed, looking at him carefully.

"You can take that anxious look off your face, Alan, my lad. I'm as sober as a judge and I'm driving myself home."

"Good. In that case you'll have no difficulty in answering one small question for me?"

"Shoot."

"In what horse-box did Palindrome come to Cheltenham?" I said.

"Eh? I hired one. I had five runners here today. The hurdler, the mare, and the black gelding came in my own box. I had to hire one for Palindrome and the novice Dane rode in the first."

"Where did you hire it from?"

"What's the matter?" asked Pete. "I know it's a bit old, and it had a puncture on the way, as I told you, but it didn't do him any harm. Can't have done, or he wouldn't have won."

"No, it's nothing like that," I said. "I just want to know where the horse-box comes from."

"It's not worth buying. If that's what you're after. Too old by half."

"Pete, I don't want to buy it. Just tell me where it comes from."

"The firm I usually hire a box from, Littlepeths of Steyning." He frowned. "Wait a minute. At first they said all their boxes were booked up, then they said they could get me a box if I didn't mind an old one."

"Who drove it here?" I asked

"Oh, one of their usual drivers. He was swearing a bit at having to drive such an old hen coop. He said the

firm had got two good horse-boxes out of action in Cheltenham week and he took a poor view of the adminis-
tration."

"Do you know him well?"

"Not exactly well. He often drives the hired boxes,
that's all. He's always grousing about something. Now,
what is all this in aid of?"

"It may have something to do with Bill's death," I
said, "but I'm not sure what. Can you find out where
the box really comes from? Ask the hire firm? And don't
mention me, if you don't mind."

"Is it important?" asked Pete.

"Yes, it is."

"I'll ring 'em tomorrow morning, then," he said.

AS SOON AS he saw me the next day, Pete said, "I asked
about that horse-box. It belongs to a farmer near Steyning. I've got his name and address here." He tucked two
fingers into his breast pocket, brought out a slip of paper,
and gave it to me. "The farmer uses the box to take his
hunters around, and his children's show jumpers in the
summer. He sometimes lets the hire firm use it, if he's
not needing it. Is that what you wanted?"

"Yes, thank you very much," I said. I put the paper
in my wallet.

By the end of the Festival meeting, I had repeated the
story of the wire to at least ten more people, in the hope
that someone might know why it had been put there.
The tale spread fast round the racecourse.

I told fat Lew Panake, the well-dressed bookmaker
who took my occasional bets. He promised to "sound
out the boys" and let me know.

I told Calvin Bone, a professional punter, whose nose
for the smell of dirty work was as unerring as a bloodhound's.

I told a sly little tout who made his living passing on

stray pieces of information to anyone who would pay for them.

I told the newspaper seller, who tugged his moustache and ignored a customer.

I told a racing journalist who could scent a doping scandal five furlongs away.

I told an army friend of Bill's; I told Clem in the weighing room; I told Pete Gregory's head traveling lad.

From all this busy sowing of the wind I learned absolutely nothing. And I would still, I supposed, have to reap the whirlwind.

chapter 8

ON SATURDAY MORNING as I sat with Scilla and the children and Joan round the large kitchen table having a solidly domestic breakfast, the telephone rang.

Scilla went to answer it, but came back saying, "It's for you, Alan. He wouldn't give his name."

I went into the drawing-room and picked up the receiver. The March sun streamed through the windows on to a big bowl of red and yellow striped crocuses which stood on the telephone table. I said, "Alan York speaking."

"Mr. York, I gave you a warning a week ago today. You have chosen to ignore it."

I felt the hairs rising on my neck. My scalp itched. It was a soft voice with a husky, whispering note to it, not savage or forceful, but almost mildly conversational.

I didn't answer. The voice said, "Mr. York? Are you still there?"

"Yes."

"Mr. York, I am not a violent man. Indeed, I dislike violence. I go out of my way to avoid it, Mr. York. But sometimes it is thrust upon me, sometimes it is the only way to achieve results. Do you understand me, Mr. York?"

"Yes," I said.

"If I were a violent man, Mr. York, I would have sent you a rougher warning last week. And I'm giving you another chance, to show you how reluctant I am to harm you. Just mind your own business and stop asking foolish questions. That's all. Just stop asking questions, and nothing will happen to you." There was a pause, then the soft voice went on, with a shade, a first tinge of menace, "Of course, if I find that violence is absolutely necessary, I always get someone else to apply it. So that I don't have to watch. So that it is not too painful to me. You do understand me, I hope, Mr. York?"

"Yes," I said again. I thought of Sonny, his vicious grin, and his knife.

"Good, then that's all. I do so hope you will be sensible. Good morning, Mr. York." There was a click as he broke the connection.

I jiggled the telephone rest to recall the operator. When she answered I asked if she could tell me where the call had come from.

"One moment, please," she said. She suffered from enlarged adenoids. She came back. "It was routed through London," she said, "but I can't trace it beyond there. So sorry."

"Never mind. Thank you very much," I said.

"Pleasure, I'm sure," said the adenoids.

I put down the receiver and went back to my breakfast.

"Who was that?" asked Henry, spreading marmalade thickly on his toast.

"Man about a dog," I said.

"Or in other words," said Polly, "ask no questions and you'll be told no thumping lies."

Henry made a face at her and bit deeply into his toast.

The marmalade oozed out of one corner of his mouth. He licked it.

"Henry always wants to know who's ringing up," said William.

"Yes, darling," said Scilla absently, rubbing some egg off his jersey. "I wish you would lean over your plate when you eat, William." She kissed the top of his blond head.

I passed my cup to Joan for more coffee.

Henry said, "Will you take us out to tea in Cheltenham, Alan? Can we have some of those squelchy cream things like last time, and ice-cream sodas with straws, and some peanuts for coming home?"

"Oh, yes," said William, blissfully.

"I'd love to," I said, "but I can't today. We'll do it next week, perhaps." The day of my visit to Kate's house had come at last. I was to stay there for two nights, and I planned to put in a day at the office on Monday.

Seeing the children's disappointed faces I explained, "Today I'm going to stay with a friend. I won't be back until Monday evening."

"What a bore," said Henry.

THE LOTUS ATE up the miles between the Cotswolds and Sussex with the deep purr of a contented cat. I covered the fifty miles of good road from Cirencester to Newbury in fifty-three minutes, not because I was in a great hurry, but out of sheer pleasure in driving my car at the speed it was designed for. And I was going towards Kate. Eventually.

Newbury slowed me to a crawl, to a halt. Then I zipped briefly down the Basingstoke road, past the American air base at Greenham Common, and from the twisty village of Kingsclere onwards drove at a sedate pace which seldom rose over sixty.

Kate lived about four miles from Burgess Hill, in Sussex.

I arrived in Burgess Hill at twenty past one, found my way to the railway station, and parked in a corner, tucked away behind a large shooting brake. I went into the station and bought a return ticket to Brighton. I didn't care to reconnoitre in Brighton by car: the Lotus had already identified me into one mess, and I hesitated to show my hand by taking it where it could be spotted by a cruising taxi driven by Peaky, Sonny, Bert, or the rest.

The journey took sixteen minutes. On the train I asked myself, for at least the hundredth time, what chance remark of mine had landed me in the horse-box hornet's nest. Whom had I alarmed by not only revealing that I knew about the wire, but more especially by saying that I intended to find out who had put it there? I could think of only two possible answers; and one of them I didn't like a bit.

I remembered saying to Clifford Tudor on the way from Plumpton to Brighton that a lot of questions would have to be answered about Bill's death; which was as good as telling him straight out that I knew the fall hadn't been an accident, and that I meant to do something about it.

And I had made the same thing quite clear to Kate. To Kate. To Kate. To Kate. The wheels of the train took up the refrain and mocked me.

Well, I hadn't sworn her to secrecy, and I hadn't seen any need to. She could have passed on what I had said to the whole of England, for all I knew. But she hadn't had much time. It had been after midnight when she left me in London, and the horse-box had been waiting for me seventeen hours later.

The train slowed into Brighton station. I walked up the platform and through the gate in a cluster of fellow passengers, but hung back as we came through the booking hall and out towards the forecourt. There were about twelve taxis parked there, their drivers standing outside

them, surveying the outpouring passengers for custom.
I looked at all the drivers carefully, face by face.

They were all strangers. None of them had been at
Plumpton.

Not unduly discouraged, I found a convenient corner
with a clear view of arriving taxis and settled myself to
wait, resolutely ignoring the cold draught blowing down
my neck. Taxis came up and went like busy bees, bringing passengers, taking them away. The trains from London attracted them like honey.

Gradually a pattern emerged. There were four distinct
groups of them. One group had a broad green line
painted down the wings, with the name Green Band on
the doors. A second group had yellow shields on the
doors, with small letters in black on the shields. A third
group were bright cobalt blue all over. Into the fourth
group I put the indeterminate taxis which did not belong
to the other lines.

I waited for nearly two hours, growing stiffer and
stiffer, and receiving more and more curious looks from
the station staff. I looked at my watch. The last train I
could catch and still arrive at Kate's at the right time
was due to leave in six minutes. I had begun to
straighten up and massage my cold neck, ready to go
and board it, when at last my patience was rewarded.

Empty taxis began to arrive and form a waiting line,
which I now knew meant that another London train was
due. The drivers got out of their cars and clustered in
little groups, talking. Three dusty black taxis arrived in
minor convoy and pulled up at the end of the line. They
had faded yellow shields painted on the doors. The drivers got out.

One of them was the polite driver of the horse-box.
A sensible, solid citizen, he looked. Middle-aged, unremarkable, calm. I did not know the others.

I had three minutes left. The black letters were tan-
talisingly small on the yellow shields. I couldn't get

close enough to read them without the polite driver seeing me, and I had no time to wait until he had gone. I went over to the ticket office, hovered impatiently while a woman argued about half fares for her teenage child, and asked a simple question.

"What is the name of the taxis with yellow shields on the doors?" The young man in the office gave me an uninterested glance.

"Marconicars, sir. Radio cabs, they are."

"Thank you," I said, and sprinted for the platform.

KATE LIVED IN a superbly proportioned Queen Anne house which generations of gothic-ruin-minded Victorians had left miraculously unspoilt. Its graceful symmetry, its creamy gravelled drive, its tidy lawns already mown in early spring, its air of solid serenity, all spoke of a social and financial security of such long standing that it was to be taken entirely for granted.

Inside, the house was charming, with just a saving touch of shabbiness about the furnishings, as if, though rich, the inhabitants saw no need to be either ostentatious or extravagant.

Kate met me at the door and took my arm, and walked me across the hall.

"Aunt Deb is waiting to give you tea," she said. "Tea is a bit of a ritual with Aunt Deb. You will be in her good graces for being punctual, thank goodness. She is very Edwardian, you'll find. The times have moved without her in many ways." She sounded anxious and apologetic, which meant to me that she loved her aunt protectively, and wished me to make allowances. I squeezed her arm reassuringly, and said, "Don't worry."

Kate opened one of the white panelled doors and we went into the drawing-room. It was a pleasant room, wood panelled and painted white, with a dark plum-coloured carpet, good Persian rugs, and flower-patterned curtains. On a sofa at right angles to a glowing log fire sat a woman of about seventy. Beside her stood a low round table bearing a tray with Crown Derby cups and saucers and a Georgian silver teapot and cream jug. A dark brown dachshund lay asleep at her feet.

Kate walked across the room and said with some formality, "Aunt Deb, may I introduce Alan York?"

Aunt Deb extended to me her hand, palm downwards. I shook it, feeling that in her younger days it would have been kissed.

"I am delighted to meet you, Mr. York," said Aunt Deb. And I saw exactly what Dane meant about her chilly, well-bred manner. She had no warmth, no genuine welcome in her voice. She was still, for all her years, or even perhaps because of them, exceedingly good-looking. Straight eyebrows, perfect nose, clearly outlined mouth. Grey hair cut and dressed by a first-class man. A slim, firm body, straight back, elegant legs crossed at the ankles. A fine silk shirt under a casual tweed suit, hand-made shoes of soft leather. She had everything. Everything except the inner fire which would make Kate at that age worth six of Aunt Deb.

She poured me some tea, and Kate handed it to me. There were pâté sandwiches and a home-made Madeira cake, and although tea was usually a meal I avoided if possible, I found my jinks in Brighton and no lunch had made me hungry. I ate and drank, and Aunt Deb talked.

"Kate tells me you are a jockey, Mr. York." She said it as if it were as dubious as a criminal record. "Of course I am sure you must find it very amusing, but when I was a gel it was not considered an acceptable occupation in acquaintances. But this is Kate's home, and she may ask whoever she likes here, as she knows."

I said mildly, "Surely Aubrey Hastings and Geoffrey Bennett were both jockeys and acceptable when you were—er—younger?"

She raised her eyebrows, surprised. "But they were gentlemen," she said.

I looked at Kate. She had stuffed the back of her hand against her mouth, but her eyes were laughing.

"Yes," I said to Aunt Deb, with a straight face. "That makes a difference, of course."

"You may realise then," she said, looking at me a little less frigidly, "that I do not altogether approve of my niece's new interests. It is one thing to own a racehorse, but quite another to make personal friends of the jockeys one employs to ride it. I am very fond of my niece. I do not wish her to make an undesirable . . . alliance. She is perhaps too young, and has led too sheltered a life, to understand what is acceptable and what is not. But I am sure you do, Mr. York?"

Kate, blushing painfully, said, "Aunt Deb!" This was apparently worse than she was prepared for.

"I understand you very well, Mrs. Penn," I said, politely.

"Good," she said. "In that case, I hope you will have an enjoyable stay with us. May I give you some more tea?"

Having firmly pointed out to me my place and having received what she took to be my acknowledgement of it, she was prepared to be a gracious hostess. She had the calm authority of one whose wishes had been law from the nursery. She began to talk pleasantly enough about the weather and her garden, and how the sunshine was bringing on the daffodils.

Then the door opened, and a man came in. I stood up.

Kate said, "Uncle George, this is Alan York."

He looked ten years younger than his wife. He had thick well-groomed grey hair and a scrubbed pink complexion with a fresh-from-the-bathroom moistness about it, and when he shook hands his palm was soft and moist also.

Aunt Deb said, without disapproval in her voice,

"George, Mr. York is one of Kate's jockey friends."

He nodded. "Yes, Kate told me you me were coming. Glad to have you here."

He watched Aunt Deb pour him a cup of tea, and took it from her, giving her a smile of remarkable fondness.

He was too fat for his height, but it was not a bloated-belly fatness. It was spread all over him as though he were padded. The total effect was of a jolly rotundity. He had a vaguely good-natured expression so often found on fat people, a certain bland, almost foolish, looseness of the facial muscles. And yet his fat-lidded eyes, appraising me over the rim of the teacup as he drank, were shrewd and unsmiling. He reminded me of so many businessmen I had met in my work, the slap-you-on-the-back, come-and-play-golf men who would ladle out the Krug '49 and caviar with one hand while they tried to take over your contracts with the other.

He put down his cup and smiled, and the impression faded.

"I am very interested to meet you, Mr. York," he said, sitting down and gesturing to me to do the same. He looked me over carefully, inch by inch, while he asked me what I thought of Heavens Above. We discussed the horse's possibilities with Kate, which meant that I did most of the talking, as Kate knew little more than she had at Plumpton, and Uncle George's total information about racing seemed to be confined to Midday Sun's having won the Derby in 1937.

"He remembers it because of Mad Dogs and Englishmen," said Kate. "He hums it all the time. I don't think he knows the name of a single other horse."

"Oh, yes I do," protested Uncle George. "Bucephalus, Pegasus, and Black Bess."

I laughed. "Then why did you give a racehorse to your niece?" I asked.

Uncle George opened his mouth and shut it again. He blinked. Then he said, "I thought she should meet more people. She has no young company here with us, and I believe we may have given her too sheltered an upbringing."

Aunt Deb, who had been bored into silence by the subject of horses, returned to the conversation at this point.

"Nonsense," she said briskly. "She has been brought up as I was, which is the right way. Gels are given too much freedom nowadays, with the result that they lose their heads and elope with fortune hunters or men-about-town of unsavoury background. Gels need strictness and guidance if they are to behave as ladies, and make suitable, well-connected marriages."

She at least had the grace to avoid looking directly at me while she spoke. She leaned over and patted the sleeping dachshund instead.

Uncle George changed the subject with an almost audible jolt, and asked me where I lived.

"Southern Rhodesia," I said.

"Indeed?" said Aunt Deb. "How interesting. Do your parents plan to settle there permanently?" It was a delicate, practised, social probe.

"They were both born there," I answered.

"And will they be coming to visit you in England?" asked Uncle George.

"My mother died when I was ten. My father might come some time if he is not too busy."

"Too busy doing what?" asked Uncle George interestedly.

"He's a trader," I said, giving my usual usefully noncommital answer to this question. "Trader" could cover anything from a rag-and-bone man to what he actually was, the head of the biggest general trading concern in the Federation. Both Uncle George and Aunt Deb looked unsatisfied by this reply, but I did not add to it. It would have embarrassed and angered Aunt Deb to have had my pedigree and prospects laid out before her after her little lecture on jockeys, and in any case for Dane's sake I could not do it. He had faced Aunt Deb's social snobbery without any of the defences I could muster if I wanted to, and I certainly felt myself no better man than he.

I made instead a remark admiring an arrangement of rose prints on the white panelled walls, which pleased Aunt Deb but brought forth a sardonic glance from Uncle George.

"We keep our ancestors in the dining-room," he said.

Kate stood up. "I'll show Alan where he's sleeping, and so on," she said.

"Did you come by car?" Uncle George asked. I nodded. He said to Kate, "Then ask Culbertson to put Mr. York's car in the garage, will you, my dear?"

"Yes, Uncle George," said Kate, smiling at him.

As we crossed the hall again for me to fetch my suitcase from the car, Kate said, "Uncle George's chauffeur's name is not really Culbertson. It's Higgins, or something like that. Uncle George began to call him Culbertson because he plays bridge, and soon we all did it. Culbertson seems quite resigned to it now. Trust Uncle George," said Kate, laughing, "to have a chauffeur who plays bridge."

"Does Uncle George play bridge?"

"No, he doesn't like cards, or games of any sort. He says there are too many rules to them. He says he doesn't like learning rules and can't be bothered to keep them. I should think bridge with all those conventions would drive him dotty. Aunt Deb can play quite respectably, but she doesn't make a thing of it."

I lifted my suitcase out of the car, and we turned back.

Kate said, "Why didn't you tell Aunt Deb you were an amateur rider and rich, and so on?"

"Why didn't you?" I asked. "Before I came."

She was taken aback. "I . . . I . . . because." She could not bring out the truthful answer, so I said it for her.

"Because of Dane?"

"Yes, because of Dane." She looked uncomfortable.

"That's quite all right by me," I said lightly. "And I like you for it." I kissed her cheek, and she laughed and turned away from me, and ran up the stairs in relief.

AFTER LUNCHEON—AUNT Deb gave the word three syllables—on Sunday I was given permission to take Kate out for a drive.

In the morning Aunt Deb had been to church with Kate and me in attendance. The church was a mile distant from the house, and Culbertson drove us there in a well-polished Daimler. I, by Aunt Deb's decree, sat beside him. She and Kate went in the back.

While we stood in the drive waiting for Aunt Deb to come out of the house, Kate explained that Uncle George never went to church.

"He spends most of his time in his study. That's the little room next to the breakfast room," she said. "He talks to all his friends on the telephone for hours, and he's writing a treatise or a monograph or something about Red Indians, I think, and he only comes out for meals and things like that."

"Rather dull for your Aunt," I said, admiring the way the March sunlight lay along the perfect line of her jaw and lit red glints in her dark eyelashes.

"Oh, he takes her up to Town once a week. She has her hair done, and he looks things up in the library of the British Museum. Then they have a jolly lunch at the Ritz or somewhere stuffy like that, and go to a matinee or an exhibition in the afternoon. A thoroughly debauched programme," said Kate, with a dazzling smile.

After lunch, Uncle George invited me into his study to see what he called his "trophies." These were a collection of objects belonging to various primitive or barbaric peoples, and, as far as I could judge, would have done credit to any small museum.

Ranks of weapons, together with some jewellery, pots, and ritual objects were labelled and mounted on shelves inside glass cases which lined three walls of the room. Among others, there were pieces from Central Africa and the Polynesian Islands, from the Viking age of Norway and from the Maoris of New Zealand. Uncle George's interest covered the globe.

"I study one people at a time," he explained. "It gives me something to do since I retired, and I find it enthralling. Did you know that in the Fiji Islands the men used to fatten women like cattle and eat them?"

His eyes gleamed, and I had a suspicion that part of the pleasure he derived from primitive peoples lay in contemplation of their primitive violences. Perhaps he needed a mental antidote to those lunches at the Ritz, and the matinees.

I said, "Which people are you studying now? Kate said something about Red Indians . . . ?"

He seemed pleased that I was taking an interest in his hobby.

"Yes I am doing a survey of all the ancient peoples of the Americas, and the North American Indians were my last subject. Their case is over here."

He showed me over to one corner. The collection of feathers, beads, knives, and arrows looked almost ridiculously like those in Western films, but I had no doubt that these were genuine. And in the centre hung a hank of black hair with a withered lump of matter dangling from it, and underneath was gummed the laconic label, "Scalp."

I turned round, and surprised Uncle George watching me with a look of secret enjoyment. He let his gaze slide past me to the case.

"Oh, yes," he said. "The scalp's a real one. It's only about a hundred years old."

"Interesting," I said noncommittally.

"I spent a year on the North American Indians because there are so many different tribes," he went on. "But I've moved on to Central America now. Next I'll do the South Americans, the Incas and the Fuegians and so on. I'm not a scholar, of course, and I don't do any field work, but I do write articles sometimes for various publications. At the moment I am engaged on a series about Indians for the *Boys' Stupendous Weekly*." His fat cheeks shook as he laughed silently at what appeared to be an immense private joke. Then he straightened his lips and the pink folds of flesh grew still, and he began to drift back towards the door.

I followed him, and paused by his big, carved, black oak desk which stood squarely in front of the window. On it, besides two telephones and a silver pen tray, lay several cardboard folders with pale blue stick-on labels marked Arapaho, Cherokee, Sioux, Navajo, and Mohawk.

Separated from these was another folder marked Mayas, and I idly stretched out my hand to open it, because I had never heard of such a tribe. Uncle George's plump fingers came down firmly on the folder, holding it shut.

"I have only just started on this nation," he said apologetically. "And there's nothing worth looking at yet."

"I've never heard of that tribe," I said.

"They were Central American Indians, not North," he said pleasantly. "They were astronomers and mathematicians, you know. Very civilised. I am finding them fascinating. They discovered that rubber bounced, and they made balls of it long before it was known in Europe. At the moment I am looking into their wars. I am trying to find out what they did with their prisoners of war. Several of their frescoes show prisoners begging for mercy." He paused, his eyes fixed on me, assessing me. "Would you like to help me correlate the references I have so far collected?" he said.

"Well . . . er . . . er . . ." I began.

Uncle George's jowls shook again. "I didn't suppose

you would," he said. "You'd rather take Kate for a drive, no doubt."

As I had been wondering how Aunt Deb would react to a similar suggestion, this was a gift. So three o'clock found Kate and me walking round to the big garage behind the house, with Aunt Deb's grudging consent to our being absent at tea-time.

"You remember me telling you, a week ago, while we were dancing, about the way Bill Davidson died?" I said casually, while I helped Kate open the garage doors.

"How could I forget?"

"Did you by any chance mention it to anyone the next morning? There wasn't any reason why you shouldn't . . . but I'd like very much to know if you did."

She wrinkled her nose. "I can't really remember, but I don't think so. Only Aunt Deb and Uncle George, of course, at breakfast. I can't think of anyone else. I didn't think there was any secret about it, though." Her voice rose at the end into a question.

"There wasn't," I said, reassuring, fastening back the door.

"What did Uncle George do before he retired and took up anthropology?"

"Retired?" she said. "Oh, that's only one of his jokes. He retired when he was about thirty, I think, as soon as he inherited a whacking great private income from his father. For decades he and Aunt Deb used to set off round the world every three years or so, collecting all those gruesome relics he was showing you in the study. What did you think of them?"

I couldn't help a look of distaste, and she laughed and said, "That's what I think, too, but I'd never let him suspect it. He's so devoted to them all."

The garage was a converted barn. There was plenty of room for the four cars standing in it in a row. The Daimler, a new cream coloured convertible, my Lotus, and after a gap, the social outcast, an old black eight-horse-power saloon. All of them, including mine, were spotless. Culbertson was conscientious.

"We use that old car for shopping in the village and so on," said Kate. "This gorgeous cream job is mine. Uncle George gave it to me a year ago when I came home from Switzerland. Isn't it absolutely rapturous?" She stroked it with love.

"Can we go out in yours, instead of mine?" I asked. "I would like that very much, if you wouldn't mind."

She was pleased. She let down the roof and tied a blue silk scarf over her head, and drove us out of the garage into the sunlight, down the drive, and on to the road towards the village.

"Where shall we go?" she said.

"I'd like to go to Steyning," I said.

"That's an odd sort of place to choose," she said. "How about the sea?"

"I want to call on a farmer in Washington, near Steyning, to ask him about his horse-box," I said. And I told her how some men in a horse-box had rather forcefully told me not to ask questions about Bill's death.

"It was a horse-box belonging to this farmer at Washington," I finished. "I want to ask him who hired it from him last Saturday."

"Good heavens," said Kate. "What a lark." And she drove a little faster. I sat sideways and enjoyed the sight of her. The beautiful profile, the blue scarf whipped by the wind, with one escaping wisp of hair blowing on her forehead, the cherry-red curving mouth. She could twist your heart.

It was ten miles to Washington. We went into the village and stopped, and I asked some children on their way home from Sunday school where farmer Lawson lived.

"Up by there," said the tallest girl, pointing.

"Up by there" turned out to be a prosperous work-manlike farm with a yellow old farmhouse and a large new Dutch barn rising behind it. Kate drove into the yard and stopped, and we walked round through a garden gate to the front of the house. Sunday afternoon was not a good time to call on a farmer, who was probably enjoying his one carefree nap of the week, but it couldn't be helped.

We rang the door bell, and after a long pause the door opened. A youngish good-looking man holding a newspaper looked at us enquiringly.

"Could I speak to Mr. Lawson, please?" I said.

"I'm Lawson," he said. He yawned.

"This is your farm?" I asked.

"Yes. What can I do for you?" He yawned again.

I said I understood he had a horse-box for hire. He rubbed his nose with his thumb while he looked us over. Then he said, "It's very old, and it depends when you want it."

"Could we see it, do you think?" I asked.

"Yes," he said. "Hang on, a moment." He went indoors and we heard his voice calling out and a girl's voice answering him. Then he came back without the newspaper.

"It's round here," he said, leading the way. The horse-box stood out in the open, sheltered only by the hay piled in the Dutch barn. APX 708. My old friend.

I told Lawson then that I didn't really want to hire his box, but I wanted to know who had hired it eight days ago. And because he thought this question decidedly queer and was showing signs of hustling us off at once, I told him why I wanted to know.

"It can't have been my box," he said at once.

"It was," I said.

"I didn't hire it to anyone, eight days ago. It was standing right here all day."

"It was in Maidenhead," I said, obstinately.

He looked at me for a full half minute. Then he said, "If you are right, it was taken without me knowing about it. I and my family were all away last week-end. We were in London."

"How many people would know you were away?" I asked.

He laughed. "About twelve million, I should think. We were on one of those family quiz shows on television on Friday night. My wife, my eldest son, my daughter, and I. The younger boy wasn't allowed on because he's only ten. He was furious about it. My wife said on the programme that we were all going to the Zoo on Saturday and to the Tower of London on Sunday, and we weren't going home until Monday."

I sighed. "And how soon before you went up to the quiz show did you know about it?"

"A couple of weeks. It was all in the local papers, that we were going. I was a bit annoyed about it, really. It doesn't do to let every tramp in the neighborhood know you'll be away. Of course, there are my cowmen about, but it's not the same."

"Could you ask them if they saw anyone borrow your box?"

"I suppose I could. It's almost milking time, they'll be in soon. But I can't help thinking you've mistaken the number plate."

"Have you a middleweight thoroughbred bay hunter, then," I said, "with a white star on his forehead, one lop ear, and a straggly tail?"

His scepticism vanished abruptly. "Yes, I have," he said. "He's in the stable over there."

He went and had a look at him. It was the horse Bert had been leading up and down, all right.

"Surely your men would have missed him when they went to give him his evening feed?" I said.

"My brother—he lives a mile away—borrows him whenever he wants. The men would just assume he'd got him. I'll ask the cowmen."

"Will you ask them at the same time if they found a

necktie in the box?" I said. "I lost one there, and I'm
rather attached to it. I'd give ten bob to have it back."

"I'll ask them," said Lawson. "Come into the house
while you wait." He took us through the back door,
along a stone-flagged hall into a comfortably battered
sitting-room, and left us. The voices of his wife and
children and clatter of teacups could be heard in the
distance. A half-finished jig-saw puzzle was scattered on
a table; some toy railway lines snaked round the floor.

At length Lawson came back. "I'm very sorry," he
said, "the cowmen thought my brother had the horse and
one of them noticed the box had gone. They said they
didn't find your tie, either. They're as blind as bats unless it's something of theirs that's missing."

I thanked him all the same for his trouble, and he
asked me to let him know, if I found out, who had taken
his box.

Kate and I drove off towards the sea.

She said, "Not a very productive bit of sleuthing, do
you think? Anyone in the world could have borrowed
the horse-box."

"It must have been someone who knew it was there,"
I pointed out. "I expect it was because it was so available
that they got the idea of using it at all. If they hadn't
known it would be easy to borrow, they'd have delivered
their message some other way. I dare say one of those
cowmen knows more than he's telling. Probably took a
quiet tenner to turn a blind eye, and threw in the horse
for local colour. Naturally he wouldn't confess it in a
hurry to Lawson this afternoon."

"Well, never mind," said Kate lightheartedly. "Perhaps it's just as well Farmer Lawson had nothing to do
with it. It would have been rather shattering if he had
turned out to be the head of the gang. You would probably have been bopped behind the ear with a gun butt
and dumped in a bag of cement out at sea and I would

have been tied up on the railway lines in the path of oncoming diesels."

I laughed. "If I'd thought he could have possibly been the leader of the gang I wouldn't have taken you there."

She glanced at me. "You be careful," she said, "or you'll grow into a cossetting old dear like Uncle George. He's never let Aunt Deb within arm's length of discomfort, let alone danger. I think that's why she's so out of touch with modern life."

"You don't think danger should be avoided, then?" I asked. "Of course not. I mean, if there's something you've got to do, then to hell with the danger." She gave an airy wave with her right hand to illustrate this carefree point of view, and a car's horn sounded vigourously just behind us. A man swept past glaring at Kate for her unintentional signal. She laughed.

She swung the car down to the sea in Worthing, and drove eastwards along the coast road. The smell of salt and seaweed was strong and refreshing. We passed the acres of new bungalows outside Worthing, the docks and the power stations of Shoreham, Southwick, and Portslade, the sedate façades of Hove, and came at length to the long promenade at Brighton. Kate turned deftly into a square in the town, and stopped the car.

"Let's go down by the sea," she said. "I love it."

We walked across the road, down some steps, and staggered across the bank of shingle on to the sand. Kate took her shoes off and poured out a stream of little stones. The sun shone warmly and the tide was out. We walked slowly along the beach for about a mile, jumping over the breakwaters, and then turned and went back. It was a heavenly afternoon.

As we strolled hand in hand up the road towards Kate's car, I saw for the first time that she had parked it only a hundred yards from the Pavilion Plaza Hotel, where I had driven Clifford Tudor from Plumpton ten days earlier.

And talk of the devil, I thought. There he was. The big man was standing on the steps of the hotel, talking to the uniformed doorman. Even at a distance there was no mistaking that size, that dark skin, that important carriage of the head. I watched him idly.

Just before we arrived at Kate's car a taxi came up from behind us, passed us, and drew up outside the Pavilion Plaza. It was a black taxi with a yellow shield on the door, and this time it was close enough for me to read the name: Marconicars. I looked quickly at the driver and saw his profile as he went past. He had a large nose and a receding chin, and I had never seen him before.

Clifford Tudor said a few last words to the doorman, strode across the pavement, and got straight into the taxi without pausing to tell the driver where he wanted to go. The taxi drove off without delay.

"What are you staring at?" said Kate, as we stood beside her car.

"Nothing much," I said. "I'll tell you about it if you'd like some tea in the Pavilion Plaza Hotel."

"That's a dull dump," she said. "Aunt Deb approves of it."

"More sleuthing," I said.

"All right, then. Got your magnifying glass and bloodhound handy?"

We went into the hotel. Kate said she would go and tidy her hair. While she was gone I asked the young girl in the reception desk if she knew where I could find Clifford Tudor. She fluttered her eyelashes at me and I grinned encouragingly back.

"You've just missed him, I'm afraid," she said. "He's gone back to his flat."

"Does he come here often?" I asked.

She looked at me in surprise. "I thought you knew. He's on the board of governors. One of the chief shareholders. In fact," she added with remarkable frankness, "he very nearly owns this place and has more say in running it than the manager." It was clear from her voice and manner that she thoroughly approved of Mr. Tudor.

"Has he got a car?" I asked.

This was a very odd question, but she prattled on without hesitation. "Yes, he's got a lovely big car with a long bonnet and lots of chromium. Real classy. But he doesn't use it, of course. Mostly it's taxis for him. Why, just this minute I rang for one of those radio cabs for him. Real useful, they are. You just ring their office and they radio a message to the taxi that's nearest here and in no time at all it's pulling up outside. All the guests use them . . ."

"Mavis!"

The talkative girl stopped dead and looked round guiltily. A severe girl in her late twenties had come into the reception desk.

"Thank you for relieving me, Mavis. You may go now," she said.

Mavis gave me a flirting smile and disappeared.

"Now, sir, can I help you?" She was polite enough, but not the type to gossip about her employers.

"Er—can we have afternoon tea here?" I asked.

She glanced at the clock. "It's a little late for tea, but go along into the lounge and the waiter will attend to you."

Kate eyed the resulting fishpaste sandwiches with disfavour. "This is one of the hazards of detecting, I suppose," she said, taking a tentative bite. "What did you find out about what?"

I said I was not altogether sure, but that I was interested in anything that had even the remotest connection with the yellow shield taxis or with Bill Davidson, and Clifford Tudor was connected in the most commonplace way with both.

"Nothing in it, I shouldn't think," said Kate, finishing the sandwich but refusing another.

I sighed. "I don't think so, either," I said.

"What next, then?"

"If I could find out who owns the yellow shield taxis . . ."

"Let's ring them up and ask," said Kate, standing up. She led the way to the telephone and looked up the number in the directory.

"I'll do it," she said. "I'll say I have a complaint to make and I want to write directly to the owner about it."

She got through to the taxi office and gave a tremendous performance, demanding the names and addresses of the owners, managers, and the company's solicitors. Finally, she put down the receiver and looked at me disgustedly.

"They wouldn't tell me a single thing," she said. "He was a really patient man, I must say. He didn't get ruffled when I was really quite rude to him. But all he would say was, 'Please write to us with the details of your complaint and we will look into it fully.' He said it was not the company's policy to disclose the names of its owners and he had no authority to do it. He wouldn't budge an inch."

"Never mind. It was a darned good try. I didn't really think they would tell you. But it gives me an idea . . ."

I rang up the Maidenhead police station and asked for Inspector Lodge. He was off duty, I was told. Would I care to leave a message? I would.

I said, "This is Alan York speaking. Will you please ask Inspector Lodge if he can find out who owns or controls the Marconicar radio taxi cabs in Brighton? He will know what it is about."

The voice in Maidenhead said he would give Inspector Lodge the message in the morning, but could not undertake to confirm that Inspector Lodge would institute the requested enquiries. Nice official jargon. I thanked him and rang off.

Kate was standing close to me in the telephone box.

She was wearing a delicate flowery scent, so faint that it was little more than a quiver in the air. I kissed her, gently. Her lips were soft and dry and sweet. She put her hands on my shoulders, and looked into my eyes, and smiled. I kissed her again.

A man opened the door of the telephone box. He laughed when he saw us. "I'm so sorry . . . I want to telephone . . ." We stepped out of the box in confusion.

I looked at my watch. It was nearly half-past six.

"What time does Aunt Deb expect us back?" I asked.

"Dinner is at eight. We've got until then," said Kate. "Let's walk through the Lanes and look at the antique shops."

We went slowly down the back pathways of Brighton, pausing before each brightly lit window to admire the contents. And stopping, too, in one or two corners in the growing dusk, to continue where we had left off in the telephone box. Kate's kisses were sweet and virginal. She was unpractised in love, and though her body trembled once or twice in my arms, there was no passion, no hunger in her response.

At the end of one of the Lanes, while we were discussing whether to go any further, some lights were suddenly switched on behind us. We turned round. The licensee of the Blue Duck was opening his doors for the evening. It looked a cozy place.

"How about a snifter before we go back?" I suggested.

"Lovely," said Kate. And in this casual inconsequential way we made the most decisive move in our afternoon's sleuthing.

We went into the Blue Duck.

chapter 9

THE BAR WAS covered with a big sheet of gleaming copper. The beer handles shone. The glasses sparkled. It was a clean, friendly little room with warm lighting and original oils of fishing villages round the walls.

Kate and I leaned on the bar and discussed sherries with the innkeeper. He was a military-looking man of about fifty with a bristly moustache waxed at the ends. I put him down as a retired sergeant-major. But he knew his stuff, and the sherry he recommended to us was excellent. We were his first customers, and we stood chatting to him. He had the friendly manner of all good innkeepers, but underlying this I saw a definite wariness. It was like the nostril cocked for danger in a springbok, uneasy, even when all appeared safe. But I didn't pay much attention, for his troubles, I thought erroneously, had nothing to do with me.

Another man and a girl came in, and Kate and I turned to take our drinks over to one of the small scattered tables. As we did so she stumbled, knocked her glass against the edge of the bar and broke it. A jagged edge cut her hand, and it began to bleed freely.

The innkeeper called his wife, a thin, small woman with bleached hair. She saw the blood welling out of Kate's hand, and exclaimed with concern, "Come and put it under the cold tap. That'll stop the bleeding. Mind you don't get it on your nice coat."

She opened a hatch in the bar to let us through, and led us into her kitchen, which was as spotless as the bar. On a table at one side were slices of bread, butter, cooked meats, and chopped salads. We had interrupted the innkeeper's wife in making sandwiches for the evening's customers. She went across to the sink, turned on the tap, and beckoned to Kate to put her hand in the running water. I stood just inside the kitchen door looking round me.

"I'm sorry to be giving you all this trouble," said Kate, as the blood dripped into the sink. "It really isn't a very bad cut. There just seems to be an awful lot of gore coming out of it."

"It's no trouble at all, dear," said the innkeeper's wife. "I'll find you a bandage." She opened a dresser drawer to look for one, giving Kate a reassuring smile.

I started to walk over from the doorway to take a closer look at the damage. Instantly there was a deadly menacing snarl, and a black alsatian dog emerged from a box beside the refrigerator. His yellow eyes were fixed on me, his mouth was slightly open with the top lip drawn back, and the razor-sharp teeth were parted. There was a collar round his neck, but he was not chained up. Another snarl rumbled deep in his throat.

I stood stock still in the center of the kitchen.

The innkeeper's wife took a heavy stick from beside the dresser and went over to the dog. She seemed flustered.

"Lie down, Prince. Lie down." She pointed with the stick to the box. The dog, after a second's hesitation, stepped back into it and sat erect, still looking at me with the utmost hostility. I didn't move.

"I'm very sorry, sir. He doesn't like strange men. He's a very good guard dog, you see. He won't hurt you now, not while I'm here." And she laid the stick on the dresser, and went over to Kate with cotton wool, disinfectant, and a bandage.

I took a step towards Kate. Muscles rippled along the dog's back, but he stayed in his box. I finished the journey to the sink. The bleeding had almost stopped, and, as Kate said, it was not a bad cut. The innkeeper's wife dabbed it with cotton wool soaked in disinfectant, dried it, and wound on a length of white gauze bandage.

I leaned against the draining board, looking at the dog and the heavy stick, and remembering the underlying edginess of the innkeeper. They added up to just one thing.

Protection.

Protection against what? Protection against Protection, said my brain, dutifully, in a refrain. Someone had been trying the protection racket on my host. Pay up or we smash up your pub . . . or you . . . or your wife. But this particular innkeeper, whether or not I was right about his sergeant-major past, looked tough enough to defy that sort of bullying. The collectors of Protection had been met, or were to be met, by an authentically lethal alsatian. They were likely to need protection themselves.

The innkeeper put his head round the door.

"All right?" he said.

"It's fine, thank you very much," said Kate.

"I've been admiring your dog," I said.

The innkeeper took a step into the room. Prince turned his head away from me for the first time and looked at his master.

"He's a fine fellow," he agreed.

Suddenly out of nowhere there floated into my mind a peach of an idea. There could not, after all, be too many gangs in Brighton, and I had wondered several times why a taxi line should employ thugs and fight pitched battles. So I said, with a regrettable lack of caution, "Marconicars."

The innkeeper's professionally friendly smile vanished, and he suddenly looked at me with appalling, vivid hate. He picked the heavy stick off the dresser and raised it to hit me. The dog was out of his box in one fluid stride, crouching ready to spring, with his ears flat and his teeth bared. I had struck oil with a vengeance.

Kate came to the rescue. She stepped to my side and said, without the slightest trace of alarm, "For heaven's sake don't hit him too hard because Aunt Deb is expecting us for roast lamb and the odd potato within half an hour or so and she is very strict about us being back on the dot."

This surprising drivel made the innkeeper hesitate long enough for me to say, "I don't belong to the Marconicars. I'm against them. Do be a good chap and put that stick down, and tell Prince his fangs are not required."

The innkeeper lowered the stick, but he left Prince where he was, on guard four feet in front of me.

Kate said to me, "Whatever have we walked into?" The bandage was trailing from her hand, and the blood was beginning to ooze through. She wound up the rest of the bandage unconcernedly and tucked in the end.

"Protection, I think?" I said to the innkeeper. "It was just a wild guess, about the taxis. I'd worked out why you need such an effective guard dog, and I've been thinking about taxi-drivers for days. The two things just clicked, that's all."

"Some of the Marconicar taxi-drivers beat him up a bit a week ago," said Kate conversationally to the innkeeper's wife. "So you can't expect him to be quite sane on the subject."

The innkeeper gave us both a long look. Then he went to his dog and put his hand round its neck and fondled it under its chin. The wicked yellow eyes closed, the lips relaxed over the sharp teeth, and the dog leaned against his master's leg in devotion. The innkeeper patted its rump, and sent it back to its box.

"A good dog, Prince," he said, with a touch of irony. "Well, now, we can't leave the bar unattended Sue, dear, will you look after the customers while I talk to these young people?"

"There's the sandwiches not made yet," protested Sue.

"I'll do them," said Kate, cheerfully. "And let's hope I don't bleed into them too much." She picked up a knife and began to butter the slices of bread. The innkeeper and his wife looked less able to deal with Kate than with the taxi-drivers; but after hesitating a moment, the wife went out to the bar.

"Now, sir," said the innkeeper.

I outlined for him the story of Bill's death and my close contact with the taxi-drivers in the horse-box. I said, "If I can find out who's at the back of Marconicars, I'll probably have the man who arranged Major Davidson's accident."

"Yes, I see that," he said. "I hope you have more luck than I've had. Trying to find out who owns Marconicars is like running head on into a brick wall. Dead end. I'll tell you all I can, though. The more people sniping at them, the sooner they'll be liquidated." He leaned over and picked up two sandwiches. He gave one to me, and bit into the other.

"Don't forget to leave room for the roast lamb," said Kate, seeing me eating. She looked at her watch. "Oh, dear, we'll be terribly late for dinner and I hate to make Aunt Deb cross." But she went on placidly with her buttering.

"I bought the Blue Duck eighteen months ago," said the innkeeper. "When I got out into civvy street."

"Sergeant-major?" I murmured.

"Regimental," he said, with justifiable pride. "Thomkins, my name is. Well, I bought the Blue Duck with my savings and my retirement pay, and dead cheap it was, too. Too cheap. I should have known there'd be a catch. We hadn't been here more than three weeks, and taking good money, too, when this chap comes in one night and says as bold as brass that if we didn't pay up like the last landlord it'd be just too bad for us. And he picked up six glasses off the bar and smashed them. He said he wanted fifty quid a week. Well, I ask you, fifty quid! No wonder the last landlord wanted to get out. I was told afterwards he'd been trying to sell the place for months, but all the locals found out they would be buying trouble and left it alone for some muggins like me straight out of the army and still wet behind the ears to come along and jump in with my big feet."

Innkeeper Thomkins chewed on his sandwich while he thought.

"Well, then, I told him to eff off. And he came back the next night with about five others and smashed the place to bits. They knocked me out with one of my own bottles and locked my wife in the heads. Then they smashed all the bottles in the bar and all the glasses, and all the chairs. When I came round I was lying on the floor in the mess, and they were standing over me in a ring. They said that was just a taste. If I didn't cough up the fifty quid a week they'd be back to smash every bottle in the storeroom and all the wine in the cellar. After that, they said, it would be my wife."

His face was furious, as he relived it.

"What happened?" I asked.

"Well, my God, after the Germans and the Japs I wasn't giving in meekly to some little runts at the English seaside. I paid up for a couple of months to give myself a bit of breathing space, but fifty quid takes a bit of finding, on top of overheads and taxes. It's a good little business, see, but at that rate I wasn't going to be left with much more than my pension. It wasn't on."

"Did you tell the police?" I asked.

A curious look of shame came into Thomkins' face. "No," he said hesitantly, "not then I didn't. I didn't know then where the men had come from, see, and they'd threatened God knows what if I went to the police. Anyway, it's not good army tactics to reengage an enemy who has defeated you once, unless you've got reinforcements. That's when I started to think about a dog. And I did go to the police later," he finished, a little defensively.

"Surely the police can close the Marconicar taxi line if it's being used for systematic crime," I said.

"Well, you'd think so," he said, "but it isn't like that. It's a real taxi service, you know. A big one. Most of the drivers are on the up and up and don't even know what's going on. I told a couple of them once that they were a front for the protection racket and they refused to believe me. The crooked ones look so plausible, see? Just like the others. They drive a taxi up to your door at closing time, say, all innocent like, and walk in and ask quietly for the money, and as like as not they'll pick up a customer in the pub and drive him home for the normal fare as respectable as you please."

"Couldn't you have a policeman in plainclothes sitting at the bar ready to arrest the taxi-driver when he came to collect the money?" suggested Kate.

The innkeeper said bitterly, "It wouldn't do no good, miss. It isn't only that they come in on different days at different times, so that a copper might have to wait a fortnight to catch one, but there aren't any grounds for arrest. They've got an I.O.U. with my signature on it for fifty pounds, and if there was any trouble with the police, all they'd have to do would be show it, and they couldn't be touched. The police'll help all right if you can give them something they can use in court, but when it's just one man's word against another, they can't do much."

"A pity you signed the I.O.U.," I sighed.

"I didn't," he said, indignantly, "but it looks like my

signature, even to me. I tried to grab it once, but the chap who showed it to me said it wouldn't matter if I tore it up, they'd soon make out another one. They must have had my signature on a letter or something, and copied it. Easy enough to do."

"You do pay them, then," I said, rather disappointed.

"Not on your nellie, I don't," said the innkeeper, his moustache bristling. "I haven't paid them a sou for a year or more. Not since I got Prince. He chewed four of them up in a month, and that discouraged them, I can tell you. But they're still around all the time. Sue and I daren't go out much, and we always go together and take Prince with us. I've had burglar alarm bells put on all the doors and windows and they go off with an awful clatter if anyone tries to break in while we're out or asleep. It's no way to live, sir. It's getting on Sue's nerves."

"What a dismal story," said Kate, licking chutney off her fingers. "Surely you can't go on like that for ever?"

"Oh, no, miss, we're beating them now. It isn't only us, see, that they got money from. They had a regular round. Ten or eleven pubs like ours—free houses. And a lot of little shops, tobacconists, souvenir shops, that sort of thing, and six or seven little cafés. None of the big places. They only pick on businesses run by the people who own them, like us. When I cottoned to that I went round to every place I thought they might be putting the screws on and asked the owners straight out if they were paying protection. It took me weeks, it's such a big area. The ones that were paying were all dead scared, of course, and wouldn't talk, but I knew who they were, just by the way they clammed up. I told them we ought to stop paying and fight. But a lot of them have kids and they wouldn't risk it, and you can't blame them."

"What did you do?" asked Kate, enthralled.

"I got Prince. A year old, he was then. I'd done a bit

of dog handling in the army, and I trained Prince to be a proper fighter."

"You did, indeed," I said, looking at the dog who now lay peacefully in his box with his chin on his paws.

"I took him round and showed him to some of the other victims of the protection racket," Thomkins went on, "and told them that if they'd get dogs, too, we'd chase off the taxi-drivers. Some of them didn't realise the taxis were mixed up in it. They were too scared to open their eyes. Anyway, in the end a lot of them did get dogs and I helped to train them, but it's difficult, the dog's only got to obey one master, see, and I had to get them to obey someone else, not me. Still, they weren't too bad. Not as good as Prince, of course."

"Of course," said Kate.

The innkeeper looked at her suspiciously, but she was demurely piling sandwiches on to a plate.

"Go on," I said.

"In the end I got some of the people with children to join in, too. They bought alsatians or bull terriers, and we arranged a system for taking all the kiddies to school by car. Those regular walks to school laid them wide open to trouble, see? I hired a judo expert and his car to do nothing but ferry the children and their mothers about. We all club together to pay him. He's expensive, of course, but nothing approaching the protection money."

"How splendid," said Kate warmly.

"We're beating them all right, but it isn't all plain sailing yet. They smashed up the Cockleshell Café a fortnight ago, just round the corner from here. But we've got a system to deal with that, too, now. Several of us went round to help clear up the mess, and we all put something into the hat to pay for new tables and chairs. They've got an alsatian bitch at that café, and she'd come into season and they'd locked her in a bedroom. I ask you! Dogs are best," said the innkeeper, seriously.

Kate gave a snort of delight.

"Have the taxi-drivers attacked any of you personally, or has it always been your property?" I asked.

"Apart from being hit on the head with my own bottle, you mean?" The innkeeper pulled up his sleeve and showed us one end of a scar on his forearm. "That's about seven inches long. Three of them jumped me one evening when I went out to post a letter. It was just after Prince had sent one of their fellows off, and silly like, I went out without him. It was only a step to the pillar box, see? A mistake though. They made a mess of me, but I got a good look at them. They told me I'd get the same again if I went to the police. But I rang the boys in blue right up, and told them the lot. It was a blond young brute who slashed my arm and my evidence got him six months," he said with satisfaction. "After that I was careful not to move a step without Prince, and they've never got near enough to have another got at me."

"How about the other victims?" I asked.

"Same as me," he said. "Three or four of them were beaten up and slashed with knives. After I'd got them dogs I persuaded some of them to tell the police. They'd had the worst of it by then, I thought, but they were still scared of giving evidence in court. The gang have never actually killed anyone, as far as I know. It wouldn't be sense, any how, would it? A man can't pay up if he's dead."

"No," I said, thoughtfully. "I suppose he can't. They might reckon that one death would bring everyone else to heel, though."

"You needn't think I haven't that in my mind all the time," he said somberly. "But there's a deal of difference between six months for assault and a life sentence or a hanging, and I expect that's what has stopped 'em. This isn't Chicago after all, though you'd wonder sometimes."

I said, "I suppose if they can't get money from their old victims, the gang try 'protecting' people who don't know about your systems and your dogs . . ."

The innkeeper interrupted, "We've got a system for that, too. We put an advertisement in the Brighton paper every week telling anyone who has been threatened with protection to write to a box number and they will get help. It works a treat, I can tell you."

Kate and I looked at him with genuine admiration.

"They should have made you a general," I said, "not a sergeant-major."

"I've planned a few incidents in my time," he said modestly. "Those young lieutenants in the war, straight out of civvy street and rushed through an officer course, they were glad enough now and then for a suggestion from a regular." He stirred, "Well, how about a drink now?"

But Kate and I thanked him and excused ourselves, as it was already eight o'clock. Thomkins and I promised to let each other know how we fared in battle, and we parted on the best of terms. But I didn't attempt to pat Prince.

Aunt Deb sat in the drawing-room tapping her foot. Kate apologised very prettily for our lateness, and Aunt Deb thawed. She and Kate were clearly deeply attached to each other.

During dinner it was to Uncle George that Kate addressed most of the account of our afternoon's adventures. She told him amusingly and lightly about the wandering horse-box and made a rude joke about the Pavilion Plaza's paste sandwiches, which drew mild reproof from Aunt Deb to the effect that the Pavilion Plaza was the most hospitable of the Brighton hotels. I gave a fleeting thought to the flighty Mavis, whom I had suspected, perhaps unjustly, of dispensing her own brand of hospitality on the upper floors.

"And then we had a drink in a darling little pub called

the Blue Duck," said Kate, leaving out the telephone
box and our walk through the Lanes. "I cut my hand
there—" she held it out complete with bandage, "—but
not very badly of course, and we went into the kitchen
to wash the blood off, and that's what made us late.
They had the most terrifying alsatian there that I'd ever
seen in my life. He snarled a couple of times at Alan
and made him shiver in his shoes like a jelly . . ." she
paused to eat a mouthful of roast lamb.

"Do you not care for dogs, Mr. York?" said Aunt Deb,
with a touch of disdain. She was devoted to her dachshund.

"It depends," I said.

Kate said, "You don't exactly fall in love with Prince.
I expect they call him Prince because he's black. The
Black Prince. Anyway, he's useful if any dog is. If I told
you two dears what the man who keeps the Blue Duck
told Alan and me about the skullduggery that goes on
in respectable little old Brighton, you wouldn't sleep
sound in your beds."

"Then please don't tell us, Kate dear," said Aunt Deb.
"I have enough trouble with insomnia as it is."

I looked at Uncle George to see how he liked being
deprived of the end of the story, and saw him push his
half-filled plate away with a gesture of revulsion, as if
he were suddenly about to vomit.

He noticed I was watching, and with a wry smile said,
"Indigestion, I'm afraid. Another of the boring nuisances
of old age. We're a couple of old crocks now, you
know."

He tried to raise a chuckle, but it was a poor affair.
There was a tinge of grey in the pink cheeks, and fine
beads of sweat had appeared on the already moist-
looking skin. Something was deeply wrong in Uncle
George's world.

Aunt Deb looked very concerned about it, and as shel-
tering her from unpleasant realities was for him so old

and ingrained a habit, he made a great effort to rally his resources. He took a sip of water and blotted his mouth on his napkin, and I saw the tremor in his chubby hands. But there was steel in the man under all that fat, and he cleared his throat and spoke normally enough.

He said, "It quite slipped my mind, Kate my dear, but while you were out Gregory rang up to talk to you about Heavens Above. I asked him how the horse was doing and he said it had something wrong with its leg and won't be able to run on Thursday at Bristol as you planned."

Kate looked disappointed. "Is he lame?" she asked.

Uncle George said, "I could swear Gregory said the horse had thrown out a splint. He hadn't broken any bones though, had he? Most peculiar." He was mystified, and so, I saw, was Kate.

"Horse's leg bones sometimes grow knobs all of a sudden, and that is what a splint is," I said. "The leg is hot and tender while the splint is forming, but it usually lasts only two or three weeks. Heavens Above will be sound again after that."

"What a pest," said Kate. "I was so looking forward to Thursday. Will you be going to Bristol, Alan, now that my horse isn't running?"

"Yes," I said. "I'm riding Palindrome there. Do try and come, Kate, it would be lovely to see you." I spoke enthusiastically, which made Aunt Deb straight her back and bend on me a look of renewed disapproval.

"It is not good for a young gel's reputation for her to be seen too often in the company of jockeys," she said.

AT ELEVEN O'CLOCK, when Uncle George had locked the study door on his collection of trophies, and when Aunt Deb had swallowed her nightly quota of sleeping pills, Kate and I went out of the house to put her car away in the garage. We had left it in the drive in our haste before dinner.

The lights of the house, muted by curtains, took the blackness out of the night, so that I could still see Kate's face as she walked beside me.

I opened the car door for her, but she paused before stepping in.

"They're getting old," she said, in a sad voice, "and I don't know what I'd do without them."

"They'll live for years yet," I said.

"I hope so . . . Aunt Deb looks very tired sometimes, and Uncle George used to have so much more bounce. I think he's worried about something now . . . and I'm afraid it's Aunt Deb's heart, though they haven't said . . . They'd never tell me if there was anything wrong with them." She shivered.

I put my arms round her and kissed her. She smiled.

"You're a kind person, Alan."

I didn't feel kind. I wanted to throw her in the car and drive off with her at once to some wild and lonely hollow on the Downs for a purpose of which the cave men would thoroughly have approved. It was an effort for me to hold her lightly, and yet essential.

"I love you, Kate," I said, and I controlled even my breathing.

"No," she said. "Don't say it. Please don't say it." She traced my eyebrows with her finger. The dim light was reflected in her eyes as she looked at me, her body leaning gently against mine, her head held back.

"Why not?"

"Because I don't know . . . I'm not sure . . . I've liked you kissing me and I like being with you. But love is so big a word. It's too important. I'm . . . I'm not . . . ready . . ."

And there it was. Kate the beautiful, the brave, the friendly, was also Kate the unawakened. She was not aware yet of the fire that I perceived in her at every turn. It had been battened down from childhood by her Edwardian aunt, and how to release it without shocking her was a puzzle.

"Love easy to learn," I said. "It's like taking a risk. You set your mind on it and refuse to be afraid, and in no time you feel terrifically exhilarated and all your inhibitions fly out of the window."

"And you're left holding the baby," said Kate, keeping her feet on the ground.

"We could get married first," I said, smiling at her.

"No. Dear Alan. No. Not yet." Then she said, almost in a whisper, "I'm so sorry."

She got into the car and drove slowly round to the barn garage. I followed behind the car and helped her shut the big garage doors, and walked back with her to the house. On the doorstep she paused and squeezed my hand, and gave me a soft, brief, sisterly kiss.

I didn't want it.

I didn't feel at all like a brother.

chapter 10

ON TUESDAY IT began to rain, cold slanting rain which lashed at the opening daffodils and covered the flowers with splashed up mud. The children went to school in shining black capes with sou'westers pulled down to their eyes and gum boots up to their knees. All that could be seen of William was his cherubic mouth with milk stains at the corners.

Scilla and I spent the day sorting out Bill's clothes and personal belongings. She was far more composed than I would have expected, and seemed to have won through to an acceptance that he was gone and that life must be lived without him. Neither of us had mentioned, since it happened, the night she had spent in my bed, and I had become convinced that when she woke the next morning she had had no memory of it. Grief and drugs had played tricks with her mind.

We sorted Bill's things into piles. The biggest section was to be saved for Henry and William, and into this pile Scilla put not only cuff links and studs and two gold watches, but dinner jackets and a morning suit and grey top hat. I teased her about it.

"It isn't silly," she said. "Henry will be needing them

in ten years, if not before. He'll be very glad to have them." And she added a hacking jacket and two new white silk shirts.

"We might just as well put everything back into the cupboards and wait for Henry and William to grow," I said.

"That's not a bad idea," said Scilla, bequeathing to the little boys their father's best riding breeches and his warmly lined white mackintosh.

We finished the clothes, went downstairs to the cosy study, and turned our attention to Bill's papers. His desk was full of them. He clearly hated to throw away old bills and letters, and in the bottom drawer we found a bundle of letters that Scilla had written to him before their marriage. She sat on the window seat reading them nostalgically while I sorted out the rest.

Bill had been methodical. The bills were clipped together in chronological order, and the letters were in boxes and files. There were some miscellaneous collections in the pigeon holes, and a pile of old, empty, used envelopes with day-to-day notes on the backs. They were reminders to himself, mostly, with messages like "Tell Simpson to mend fence in five acre field," and "Polly's birthday Tuesday." I looked through them quickly, hovering them over the heap bound for the wastepaper basket.

I stopped suddenly. On one of them, in Bill's loopy sprawling handwriting, was the name Clifford Tudor, and underneath, a telephone number and an address in Brighton.

"Do you know anyone called Clifford Tudor?" I asked Scilla.

"Never heard of him," she said without looking up.

If Tudor had asked Bill to ride for him, as he had told me when I drove him from Plumpton to Brighton, it was perfectly natural for Bill to have his name and address. I turned the envelope over. It had come from a local tradesman, whose name was printed on the top left hand corner, and the postmark was date-stamped January, which meant that Bill had only recently acquired Tudor's address.

I put the envelope in my pocket and went on sorting. After the old envelopes I started on the pigeon holes. There were old photographs and some pages the children had drawn and written on with straggly letters in their babyhood, address books, luggage labels, a birthday card, school reports, and various notebooks of different shapes and sizes.

"You'd better look through these Scilla," I said.

"You look," she said, glancing up from her letters with a smile. "You can tell me what's what, and I'll look at them presently."

Bill had had no secrets. The notebooks mainly contained his day-to-day expenses, jotted down to help his accountant at the annual reckoning. They went back some years. I found the latest, and leafed through it.

School fees, hay for the horses, a new garden hose, a repair to the Jaguar's head-lamp in Bristol, a present for Scilla, a bet on Admiral, a donation to charity. And that was the end. After that came the blank pages which were not going to be filled up.

I looked again at the last entries. A bet on Admiral. Ten pounds to win, Bill had written. And the date was the day of his death. Whatever had been said to Bill about Admiral's falling, he had taken it as a joke and had backed himself to win in spite of it. I would dearly have liked to know what the "joke" had been. He had told Pete, whose mind was with the horses. He had not told Scilla, nor any of his friends as far as I could find out. Possibly he had thought it so unimportant that after he spoke to Pete it had wholly slipped his mind.

I stacked up the notebooks and began on the last pigeon hole full of oddments. Among them were fifteen or twenty of the betting tickets issued by bookmakers at race meetings. As evidence of bets lost, they are usually torn up or thrown away by disappointed punters, not carefully preserved in a tidy desk.

"Why did Bill keep these betting tickets?" I asked Scilla.

"Henry had a craze for them not long ago, don't you remember?" she said. "And after it wore off Bill still brought some home for him. I think he kept them in case William wanted to play bookmakers in his turn."

I did remember. I had backed a lot of horses for half-pennies with Henry the bookmaker, the little shark. They never won.

The extra tickets Bill had saved for him were from several different bookmakers. It was part of Bill's plea-sure at the races to walk among the bookmakers' stands in Tattersall's and put his actual cash on at the best odds, instead of betting on credit with a bookmaker on the rails.

"Do you want to keep them for William still?" I asked.

"May as well," said Scilla.

I put them back in the desk, and finished the job. It was late in the afternoon. We went into the drawing-room, stoked up the fire, and settled into armchairs.

She said, "Alan, I want to give you something which belonged to Bill. Now, don't say anything until I've fin-ished. I've been wondering what you'd like best, and I'm sure I've chosen right."

She looked from me to the fire and held her hands out to warm them.

She said, "You are to have Admiral."

"No." I was definite.

"Why not?" She looked up, sounding disappointed.

"Dearest Scilla, it's far too much," I said. "I thought you meant something like a cigarette case, a keepsake. You can't possibly give me Admiral. He's worth thousands. You must sell him, or run him in your name if you want to keep him, but you can't give him to me. It wouldn't be fair to you or the children for me to have him."

"He might be worth thousands if I sold him—but I couldn't sell him, you know. I couldn't bear to do that. He meant so much to Bill. How could I sell him as soon as Bill's back was turned? And if I keep him and run him, I'll have to pay the bills, which might not be easy for a while with death duties hanging over me. If I give him to you, he's in hands Bill would approve of, and you can pay for his keep. I've thought it all out, so you're not to argue. Admiral is yours."

She meant it.

"Then let me lease him from you," I said.

"No, he's a gift. From Bill to you, if you like."

And on those terms I gave in, and thanked her as best I could.

THE FOLLOWING MORNING, early, I drove to Pete Gregory's stables in Sussex to jump my green young Forlorn Hope over the schooling hurdles. A drizzling rain was falling as I arrived, and only because I had come so far did we bother to take the horses out. It was not a very satisfactory session, with Forlorn Hope slipping on the wet grass as we approached the first hurdle and not taking on the others with any spirit after that.

We gave it up and went down to Pete's house. I told him Admiral was to be mine and that I would be riding him.

He said, "He's in the Foxhunters' at Liverpool, did you know?"

"So he is!" I exclaimed delightedly. I had not yet ridden round the Grand National course, and the sudden prospect of doing it a fortnight later was exciting.

"You want to have a go?"

"Yes, indeed," I said.

We talked over the plans for my other horses, Pete telling me Palindrome was in fine fettle after his Cheltenham race and a certainty for the following day at Bristol. We went out to look at him and the others, and I inspected the splint which Heavens Above was throwing out. His leg was tender, but it would right itself in time.

When I left Pete's I went back to Brighton, parking the Lotus and taking a train as before. I walked out of Brighton station with a brief glance at the three taxis standing there (no yellow shields) and walked briskly in the direction of the headquarters of the Marconicars as listed in the telephone directory.

I had no particular plan, but I was sure the core of the mystery was in Brighton, and if I wanted to discover it, I would have to dig around on the spot. My feelers on the racecourse had still brought me nothing but a husky warning on the telephone.

The Marconicars offices were on the ground floor of a converted Regency terrace house. I went straight into the narrow hall.

The stairs rose on the right, and on the left were two doors, with a third, marked Private, facing me at the far end of the passage. A neat board on the door nearest the entrance said "Enquiries." I went in.

It had once been an elegant room and even the office equipment could not entirely spoil its proportions. There were two girls sitting at desks with typewriters in front of them, and through the half-open folded dividing doors I could see into an inner office where a third girl sat in front of a switchboard. She was speaking into a microphone.

"Yes, madam, a taxi will call for you in three minutes," she said. "Thank you." She had a pleasant high voice of excellent carrying quality.

The two girls in the outer office looked at me expectantly. They wore tight sweaters and large quantities of mascara. I spoke to the one nearest the door.

"Er . . . I'm enquiring about booking some taxis . . . for a wedding. My sister's," I added, improvising and inventing the sister I never had. "Is that possible?"

"Oh, yes, I think so," she said. "I'll ask the manager. He usually deals with big bookings."

I said, "I'm only asking for an estimate . . . on behalf of my sister. She has asked me to try all the firms, to find out which will be most—er—reasonable. I can't give you a definite booking until I've consulted her again."

"I see," she said. "Well, I'll ask Mr. Fielder to see you." She went out, down the passage, and through the door marked Private.

While I waited I grinned at the other girl, who patted her hair, and I listened to the girl at the switchboard.

"Just a minute, sir. I'll see if there's a taxi in your area," she was saying. She flipped a switch and said, "Come in, any car in Hove two. Come in, any car in Hove two."

There was a silence and then a man's voice said out of the radio receiving set, "It looks as though there's no one in Hove two, Marigold. I could get there in five minutes. I've just dropped a fare in Langbury Place."

"Right, Jim." She gave him the address, flipped the switch again, and spoke into the telephone. "A taxi will be with you in five minutes, sir. I am sorry for the delay, we have no cars available who can reach you faster than that. Thank you, sir." As soon as she had finished speaking the telephone rang again. She said, "Marconicars. Can I help you?"

Down the hall came the clip clop of high heels on linoleum, and the girl came back from Mr. Fielder. She said, "The manager can see you now, sir."

"Thank you," I said. I went down the hall and through the open door at the end.

The man who rose to greet me and shake hands was

a heavy, well-tailored, urbane man in his middle forties. He wore spectacles with heavy black frames, had smooth black hair and hard blue eyes. He seemed a man of too strong a personality to be sitting in the back office of a taxi firm, too high-powered an executive for the range of his job.

I felt my heart jump absurdly, and I had a moment's panic in which I feared he knew who I was and what I was trying to do. But his gaze was calm and business-like, and he said only, "I understand you wish to make a block booking for a wedding."

"Yes," I said, and launched into fictitious details. He made notes, added up some figures, wrote out an esti-mate, and held it out to me. I took it. His writing was strong and black. It fitted him.

"Thank you," I said. "I'll give this to my sister, and let you know."

As I went out of his door and shut it behind me, I looked back at him. He was sitting behind his desk star-ing at me through his glasses with unwinking blue eyes. I could read nothing in his face.

I went back into the front office and said, "I've got the estimate I wanted. Thank you for your help." I turned to go, and had a second thought. "By the way, do you know where I can find Mr. Clifford Tudor?" I asked.

The girls, showing no surprise at my enquiry, said they did not know.

"Marigold might find out for you," said one of them. "I'll ask her."

Marigold, finishing her call, agreed to help. She pressed the switch. "All cars. Did anyone pick up Mr. Tudor today? Come in please."

A man's voice said, "I took him to the station this morning, Marigold. He caught the London train."

"Thanks, Mike," said Marigold.

"She knows all their voices," said one of the girls,

admiringly. "They never have to tell her the number of their car."

"Do you all know Mr. Tudor well?" I asked.

"Never seen him," said one girl, and the others shook their heads in agreement.

"He's one of our regulars. He takes a car whenever he wants one, and we book it here. The driver tells Marigold where he's taking him. Mr. Tudor has a monthly account, and we make it up and send it to him."

"Suppose the driver takes Mr. Tudor from place to place and fails to report it to Marigold?" I asked conversationally.

"He wouldn't be so silly. The drivers get commission on regulars. Instead of tips, do you see? We put ten per cent on the bills to save the regulars having to tip the drivers every five minutes."

"A good idea," I said. "Do you have many regulars?"

"Dozens," said one of the girls. "But Mr. Tudor is about our best client."

"And how many taxis are there?" I asked.

"Thirty-one. Some of them will be in the garage for servicing, of course, and sometimes in the winter we only have half of them on the road. There's a lot of competition from the other firms."

"Who actually owns the Marconicars?" I asked casually.

They said they didn't know and couldn't care less.

"Not Mr. Fielder?" I asked.

"Oh, no," said Marigold. "I don't think so. There's a Chairman, I believe, but we've never seen him. Mr. Fielder can't be all that high-up, because he sometimes takes over from me in the evenings and at week-ends. Though another girl comes in to relieve me on my days off, of course."

They suddenly all seemed to realise that this had nothing to do with my sister's wedding. It was time to go, and I went.

I stood outside on the pavement wondering what to do next. There was a café opposite, across the broad street, and it was nearly lunch-time. I went over and into the café, which smelled of cabbage, and because I had arrived before the rush there was a table free by the window. Through the chaste net curtains of the Olde Oake Café I had a clear view of the Marconicar office. For what it was worth.

A stout girl with wispy hair pushed a typed menu card in front of me. I looked at it, depressed. English home cooking at its very plainest. Tomato soup, choice of fried cod, sausages in batter, or steak and kidney pie, with suet pudding and custard to follow. It was all designed with no regard for an amateur rider's weight. I asked for coffee. The girl said firmly I couldn't have coffee by itself at lunch-time, they needed the tables. I offered to pay for the full lunch if I could just have the coffee, and to this she agreed, clearly thinking me highly eccentric.

The coffee, when it came, was surprisingly strong and good. I was getting the first of the brew, I reflected, idly watching the Marconicar front door. No one interesting went in or out.

On the storey above the Marconicars a big red neon sign flashed on and off, showing little more than a flicker in the daylight. I glanced up at it. Across the full width of the narrow building was the name L. C. PERTH. The taxi office had "Marconicars" written in bright yellow on black along the top of its big window, and looking up I saw that the top storey was decorated with a large blue board bearing in white letters the information "Jenkins, Wholesale Hats."

The total effect was colourful indeed, but hardly what the Regency architect had had in mind. I had a mental picture of him turning in his grave so often that he made knots in his winding sheet, and I suppose I smiled, for a voice suddenly said, "Vandalism, isn't it?"

A middle-aged woman had sat down at my table, unnoticed by me as I gazed out of the window. She had a mournful horsey face with no make-up, a hideous brown hat which added years to her age, and an earnest look in her eyes. The café was filling up, and I could no longer have a table to myself.

"It's startling, certainly," I agreed.

"It ought not to be allowed. All these old houses in this district have been carved up and turned into offices, and it's really disgraceful how they look now. I belong to the Architectural Preservation Group," she confided solemnly, "and we're getting out a petition to stop people desecrating beautiful buildings with horrible advertisements."

"Are you having success?" I asked.

She looked depressed. "Not very much, I'm afraid. People just don't seem to care as they should. Would you believe it, half the people in Brighton don't know what a Regency house looks like, when they're surrounded by them all the time? Look at that row over there, with all those boards and signs. And that neon," her voice quivered with emotion, "is the last straw. It's only been there a few months. We've petitioned to make them take it down, but they won't."

"That's very discouraging," I said, watching the Marconicar door. The two typists came out and went chattering up the road, followed by two more girls whom I supposed to have come down from the upper floors.

My table companion chatted on between spoonfuls of tomato soup. "We can't get any satisfaction from Perth's at all because no one in authority there will meet us, and the men in the office say they can't take the sign down because it doesn't belong to them, but they won't tell us who it does belong to so that we can petition him in person." I found I sympathised with Perth's invisible ruler in his disinclination to meet the Architectural Preservation Group on the warpath. "It was bad enough before, when they had their name just painted on the windows, but neon . . ." Words failed her, at last.

Marigold left for lunch. Four men followed her. No one arrived.

I drank my coffee, parted from the middle-aged lady without regret, and gave it up for the day. I took the train back to my car and drove up to London. After a long afternoon in the office, I started for home at the tail end of the rush-hour traffic. In the hold-ups at crossings and roundabouts I began, as a change from Bill's mystery, to tackle Joe Nantwich's.

I pondered his "stopping" activities, his feud with Sandy Mason, his disgrace with Tudor, his obscure threatening notes. I thought about the internal workings of the weighing room, where only valets, jockeys, and officials are allowed in the changing rooms, and trainers and owners are confined to the weighing room itself, while the press and the public may not enter at all.

If the "Bolingbroke. This week" note was to be believed, Joe would already have received his punishment, because "this week" was already last week. Yet I came to the conclusion that I would see him alive and well at Bristol on the following day, even if not in the best of spirits. For, by the time I reached home, I knew I could tell him who had written the notes, though I wasn't sure I was going to.

Sleep produces the answers to puzzles in the most amazing way. I went to bed on Wednesday night thinking I had spent a more or less fruitless morning in Brighton. But I woke on Thursday morning with a name in my mind and the knowledge that I had seen it before, and where. I went downstairs in my dressing-gown to Bill's desk, and took out the betting tickets he had saved for Henry. I shuffled through them, and found what I wanted. Three of them bore the name L. C. PERTH.

I turned them over. On their backs Bill had penciled the name of a horse, the amount of his bet, and the date. He was always methodical. I took all the tickets up to my room, and looked up the races in the form book. I remembered many casual snatches of conversation. And a lot of things became clear to me.

But not enough, not enough.

chapter 11

IT POURED WITH rain at Bristol, a cold, steady unrelenting wetness which took most of the pleasure out of racing.

Kate sent a message that she was not coming because of the weather, which sounded unlike her, and I wondered what sort of pressure Aunt Deb had used to keep her at home.

The main gossip in the weighing room concerned Joe Nantwich. The Stewards had held an enquiry into his behavior during the last race on Champion Hurdle day, and had, in the official phrase, "severely cautioned him as to his future riding." It was generally considered that he was very lucky indeed to have got off so lightly, in view of his past record.

Joe himself was almost as cocky as ever. From a distance his round pink face showed no traces of the fear or drunkenness which had made a sudden mess of him at Cheltenham. Yet I was told that he had spent the preceding Friday and Saturday and most of Sunday in the Turkish baths, scared out of his wits. He had drunk himself silly and sweated it off alternately during the whole of that time, confiding to the attendants in tears that he was safe with them, and refusing to get dressed and go home.

The authority for this story, and one who gave it its full flavour, was Sandy, who had happened, he said, to go into the Turkish baths on Sunday morning to lose a few pounds for Monday's racing.

I found Joe reading the notices. He was whistling through his teeth.

"Well, Joe," I said, "what makes you so cheerful?"

"Everything." He smirked. At close quarters I could see the fine lines round his mouth and the slightly blood-shot eyes, but his experiences had left no other signs of strain. "I didn't get suspended by the Stewards. And I got paid for losing that race."

"You what?" I exclaimed.

"I got paid. You know, I told you. The packet of money. It came this morning. A hundred quid." I stared at him. "Well, I did what I was told, didn't I?" he said aggrievedly.

"I suppose you did," I agreed, weakly.

"And another thing, those threatening notes. I fooled them you know. I stayed in the Turkish baths all over the week-end, and they couldn't harm me there. I got off scot free," said Joe, triumphantly, as if "this week" could not be altered to "next week." He did not realise either that he had already taken his punishment, that there are other agonies than physical ones. He had suffered a week of acute anxiety, followed by three days of paralysing fear, and he thought he had got off scot free.

"I'm glad you think so," I said, mildly. "Joe, answer me a question. The man who rings you up to tell you what horse not to win on, what does his voice sound like?"

"You couldn't tell who it is, not by listening to him. It might be anybody. It's a soft voice, and sort of fuzzy. Almost a whisper, sometimes, as if he were afraid of being overheard. But what does it matter?" said Joe. "As long as he delivers the lolly he can croak like a frog for all I care."

"Do you mean you'll stop another horse, if he asks you to?" I said.

"I might do. Or I might not," said Joe, belatedly deciding that he had been speaking much too freely. With a sly, sidelong look at me he edged away into the changing room. His resilience was fantastic.

Pete and Dane were discussing the day's plans not far away, and I went over to them. Pete was cursing the weather and saying it would play merry hell with the going, but that Palindrome, all the same, should be able to act on it.

"Go to the front at halfway, and nothing else will be able to come to you. They're a poor lot. As far as I can see, you're a dead cert."

"That's good," I said, automatically, and then remembered with a mental wince that Admiral had been a dead cert at Maidenhead.

Dane asked me if I had enjoyed my stay with Kate and did not look too overjoyed by my enthusiastic answer.

"Curses on your head, pal, if you have cut me out with Kate." He said it in a mock ferocious voice, but I had an uncomfortable feeling that he meant it. Could a friendship survive between two men who were in love with the same girl? Suddenly at that moment, I didn't know; for I saw in Dane's familiar handsome face a passing flash of enmity. It was as disconcerting as a rock turning to quicksand. And I went rather thoughtfully into the changing room to find Sandy.

He was standing by the window, gazing through the curtain of rain which streamed down the glass. He had changed into colours for the first race, and was looking out towards the parade ring, where two miserable-looking horses were being led round by dripping, mack-intoshed stable lads.

"We'll need windscreen wipers on our goggles in this little lot," he remarked, with unabashed good spirits. "Anyone for a mud bath? Blimey, it's enough to discourage ducks."

"How did you enjoy your Turkish bath on Sunday?" I asked, smiling.

"Oh, you heard about that, did you?"

"I think everyone has heard about it," I said.

"Good. Serve the little bastard right," said Sandy, grinning hugely.

"How did you know where to find him?" I asked.

"Asked his mother . . ." Sandy broke off in the middle of the word, and his eyes widened.

"Yes," I said. "You sent him those threatening Bolingbroke notes."

"And what," said Sandy, with good humour, "makes you think so?"

"You like practical jokes, and you dislike Joe," I said. "The first note he received was put into his jacket while it hung in the changing room at Plumpton, so it had to be a jockey or a valet or an official who did it. It couldn't have been a bookmaker or a trainer or an owner or any member of the public. So I began to think that perhaps the person who planted the note in Joe's pocket was not the person who was paying him to stop horses. That person has, strangely enough, exacted no revenge at all. But I asked myself who else would be interested in tormenting Joe, and I came to you. You knew before the race that Joe was not supposed to win on Bolingbroke. When he won you told him you'd lost a lot of money, and you'd get even with him. And I guess you have. You even tracked him down to enjoy seeing him suffer."

"Revenge is sweet, and all that. Well, it's a fair cop," said Sandy. "Though how you know such a lot beats me."

"Joe told me most of it," I said.

"What a blabbermouth. That tongue of Joe's will get him into a right mess one of these days."

"Yes, it will," I said, thinking of the incautious way Joe had spoken of his "stopping" and its rewards.

"Did you tell him I had sent him those notes?" asked Sandy, with his first show of anxiety.

"No, I didn't. It would only stir up more trouble," I said.

"Thanks for that, anyway."

"And in reward for that small service, Sandy," I said, "will you tell me how you knew in advance that Bolingbroke was not supposed to win?"

He grinned widely, rocking gently on his heels, but he didn't answer.

"Go on," I said. "It isn't much to ask, and it might even give me a lead to that other mystery, about Bill Davidson."

Sandy shook his head. "It won't help you any," he said. "Joe told me himself."

"What?" I exclaimed.

"He told me himself. In the washroom when we were changing before the race. You know how he can't help swanking? He wanted to show off, and I was handy, and besides, he knew I'd stopped a horse or two in my time."

"What did he say?" I asked.

"He said if I wanted a lesson in how to choke a horse I'd better watch him on Bolingbroke. Well, a nod's as good as a wink to Sandy Mason. I got a punter to put fifty quid on Leica, which I reckoned was bound to win with Bolingbroke not trying. And look what happened. The little sod lost his nerve and beat Leica by two lengths. I could have throttled him. Fifty quid's a ruddy fortune, mate, as far as I'm concerned."

"Why did you wait as long as ten days before you gave him that first note?" I asked.

"I didn't think of it until then," he said, frankly. "But

it was a damn good revenge, wasn't it? He nearly got his licence suspended at Cheltenham, and he sweated his guts out for three days at the week-end, all in the screaming heeby-jeebies worked up by yours truly." Sandy beamed. "You should have seen him in the Turkish baths. A sodden, whining, clutching wreck. In tears, and begging me to keep him safe. Me! What a laugh. I was nearly sick, trying not to laugh. A cracking good revenge, that was."

"And you put him over the rails at Plumpton, too," I said.

"I never did," said Sandy, indignantly. "Did he tell you that? He's a bloody liar. He fell off, I saw him. I've a good mind to frighten him again." His red hair bristled and his brown eyes sparkled. Then he relaxed. "Oh, well . . . I'll think of something, sometime. There's no rush. I'll make his life uncomfortable—ants in his pants, worms in his boots, that sort of thing, Harmless," and Sandy began to laugh. Then he said, "As you're such a roaring success as a private eye, how are you getting on with that other business?"

"Not fast enough," I said. "But I know a lot more than I did at this time last week, so I haven't lost hope. You haven't heard anything useful?" He shook his head.

"Not a squeak anywhere. You're not giving it up, then?"

"No," I said.

"Well, the best of British luck," said Sandy, grinning.

An official poked his head round the door. "Jockey's out, please," he said. It was nearly time for the first race.

Sandy put his helmet on and tied the strings. Then he took out his false teeth, the two centre incisors off the upper jaw, wrapped them in a handkerchief and tucked them into the pocket of the coat hanging on his peg. He, like most jockeys, never rode races wearing false teeth, for fear of losing them, or even swallowing them if he fell. He gave me a gap-toothed grin, sketched a farewell salute, and dived out into the rain.

It was still raining an hour later when I went out to ride Palindrome. Pete was waiting for me in the parade ring, the water dripping off the brim of his hat in a steady stream.

"Isn't this a God-awful day?" he said. "I'm glad it's you that's got to strip off and get soaked, and not me. I had a bellyful when I was riding. I hope you're good at swimming."

"Why?" I asked, mystified.

"If you are, you'll know how to keep your eyes open under water." I suspected another of Pete's rather feeble jokes, but he was serious. He pointed to the goggles slung-round my neck. "You won't need those, for a start. With all the mud that's being kicked up today, they'd be covered before you'd gone a furlong."

"I'll leave them down, then," I said.

"Take them off. They'll only get in your way," he said.

So I took them off, and as I turned my head to ease the elastic over the back of my helmet, I caught a glimpse of a man walking along outside the parade ring. There were few people standing about owing to the rain, and I had a clear view of him.

It was Bert, the man in charge of the horse in the lay-by on Maidenhead Thicket. One of the Marconicar drivers.

He was not looking at me, but the sight of him was as unpleasant as an electric shock. He was a long way from base. He might have travelled the hundred and forty miles solely to enjoy an afternoon's racing in the rain. Or he might not.

I looked at Palindrome, plodding slowly round the parade ring in his waterproof rug.

A dead cert.

I shivered.

I knew I had made some progress towards my quarry, the man who had caused Bill's death, even though he himself was as unknown to me as ever. I had disregarded his two emphatic warnings and I feared I had left a broad enough trail for him to be well aware of my pursuit. Bert would not be at Bristol alone, I thought, and I could guess that a third deterrent message was on its way.

There are times when one could do without an intuition, and this was one of them. Palindrome, the dead cert. What had been done once would be tried again, and somewhere out on the rain-swept racecourse another strand of wire could be waiting. For no logical reason, I was certain of it.

It was too late to withdraw from the race. Palindrome was an odds-on favourite, and clearly in the best of health; he showed no lameness, no broken blood-vessels, none of the permitted excuses for a last minute cancellation. And if I myself were suddenly taken ill and couldn't ride, another jockey would be quickly found to take my place. I couldn't send someone out in my colours to take a fall designed for me.

If I refused point-blank, without explanation, to let Palindrome run in the race, my permit to ride would be withdrawn, and that would be the end of my steeple-chasing.

If I said to the Stewards, "Someone is going to bring Palindrome down with wire," they might possibly send an official round the course to inspect the fences: but he wouldn't find anything. I was quite sure that if a wire were rigged, it would be, as in Bill's case, a last minute job.

If I rode in the race, but kept Palindrome reined in behind other horses the whole way, the wire might not be rigged at all. But my heart sank as I regarded the faces of the jockeys who had already ridden, and re-membered in what state they had come back from their previous races. Mud was splashed on their faces like thick khaki chicken-pox, and their jerseys were soaked and muddied to such an extent that their colors were almost unrecognizable from a few steps away, let alone the distance from one fence to the next. My own coffee and cream colours would be particularly indistinct. A man waiting with wire would not be able to tell for certain which horse was in front, but he would expect me and act accordingly.

I looked at the other jockeys in the parade ring, now reluctantly taking off their raincoats and mounting their horses. There were about ten of them. They were men who had taught me a lot, and accepted me as one of themselves, and given me a companionship I enjoyed almost as much as the racing itself. If I let one of them crash in my place, I couldn't face them again.

It was no good. I'd have to ride Palindrome out in front and hope for the best. I remembered Kate saying, "If there's something you've got to do, then to hell with the danger."

To hell with the danger. After all, I could fall any day, without the aid of wire. If I fell today, with it, that would be just too bad. But it couldn't be helped. And I might be wrong; there might be no wire at all.

Pete said, "What's the matter? You look as if you'd seen a ghost."

"I'm all right," I said, taking off my coat. Palindrome was standing beside me, and I patted him, admiring his splendid intelligent head. My chief worry from then on was that he, at least, should come out of the next ten minutes unscathed.

I swung up on to his back and looked down at Pete, and said "If . . . if Palindrome falls in this race, please will you ring up Inspector Lodge at Maidenhead police station, and tell him about it?"

"What on earth . . . ?"

"Promise," I said.

"All right. But I don't understand. You could tell him

yourself, if you want to, and anyway, you won't fall."

"No, perhaps not," I said.

"I'll meet you in the winner's enclosure," he said, slapping Palindrome's rump as we moved off.

The rain was blowing into our faces as we lined up for the start in front of the stands, with two circuits of the course to complete. The tapes went up, and we were off.

Two or three horses jumped the first fence ahead of me, but after that I took Palindrome to the front, and stayed there. He was at his best, galloping and jumping with the smooth flow of a top class 'chaser. On any other day, the feel of this power beneath me would have pleased me beyond words. As it was, I scarcely noticed it.

Remembering Bill's fall, I was watching for an attendant to walk across behind a fence as the horses approached it. He would be uncoiling the wire, raising it, fixing it . . . I planned when I saw that to try to persuade Palindrome to take off too soon before the fence, so that he would hit the wire solidly with his chest when he was already past the height of his spread. That way, I hoped he might break or pull down the wire and still stay on his feet; and if we fell, it should not be in a shattering somersault like Admiral's. But it is easier to plan than to do, and I doubted whether a natural jumper like Palindrome *could* be persuaded to take off one short stride too soon.

We completed the first circuit without incident, squelching on the sodden turf. About a mile from home, on the far side of the course, I heard hoofbeats close behind, and looked over my shoulder. Most of the field were bunched up some way back, but two of them were chasing me with determination and they were almost up to Palindrome's quarters.

I shook him up and he responded immediately, and

we widened the gap from our pursuers to about five lengths.

No attendant walked across the course.

I didn't see any wire.

But Palindrome bit it, just the same.

It wouldn't have been too bad a fall but for the horses behind me. I felt the heavy jerk on Palindrome's legs as we rose over the last fence on the far side of the course, and I shot off like a bullet, hitting the ground with my shoulder several yards ahead. Before I had stopped rolling the other horses were jumping the fence. They would have avoided a man on the ground if they possibly could, but in this case, I was told afterwards, they had to swerve round Palindrome, who was struggling to get up, and found me straight in their path.

The galloping hooves thudded into my body. One of the horses kicked my head and my helmet split so drastically that it fell off. There were six seconds of bludgeoning, battering chaos, in which I could neither think nor move, but only feel.

When it was all over I lay on the wet ground, limp and growing numb, unable to get up, unable even to stir. I was lying on my back with my feet towards the fence. The rain fell on my face and trickled through my hair, and the drops felt so heavy on my eyelids that opening them was like lifting a weight. Through a slit, from under my rain-beaded lashes, I could see a man at the fence.

He wasn't coming to help me. He was very quickly coiling up a length of wire, starting on the outside of the course and working inwards. When he reached the inner post he put his hand in his raincoat pocket, drew out a tool, and clipped the wire where it was fastened eighteen inches above the fence. This time, he had not forgotten his wire cutters. He finished his job, hooked the coil over his arm, and turned toward me.

I knew him.

He was the driver of the horse-box.

The colour was going out of everything. The world looked grey to me, like an under-exposed film. The green grass was grey, the box driver's face was grey . . .

Then I saw that there was another man at the fence, and he was walking towards me. I knew him, too, and he was not a taxi-driver. I was so glad to find I had some help against the box driver that I could have wept with relief. I tried to tell him to look at the wire, so that this time there should be a witness. But the words could get no farther than my brain. My throat and tongue refused to form them.

He came over and stood beside me, and stooped down. I tried to smile and say hello, but not a muscle twitched. He straightened up.

He said, over his shoulder, to the box driver, "He's been knocked out." He turned back to me.

He said, "You nosey bastard," and he kicked me. I heard the ribs crack, and I felt the hot stab in my side. "Perhaps that'll teach you to mind your own business." He kicked me again. My grey world grew darker. I was nearly unconscious, but even in that dire moment some part of my mind went on working, and I knew why the attendant had not walked across with the wire. He had not needed to. He and his accomplice had stood on opposite sides of the course and had raised it between them.

I saw the foot drawn back a third time. It seemed hours, in my disjointed brain, until it came towards my eyes, growing bigger and bigger until it was all that I could see.

He kicked my face, and I went out like a light.

chapter 12

HEARING CAME BACK first. It came back suddenly, as if someone had pressed a switch. At one moment no messages of any sort were getting through the swirling, distorted dreams which seemed to have been going on inside my head for a very long time, and in the next I was lying in still blackness, with every sound sharp and distinct in my ears.

A woman's voice said, "He's still unconscious."

I wanted to tell her it was not true, but could not.

The sounds went on, swishing, rustling, clattering, the murmur of distant voices, the thump and rattle of water in pipes of ancient plumbing. I listened, but without much interest.

After a while I knew I was lying on my back. My limbs, when I became aware of them, were as heavy as lead and ached persistently, and ton weights rested on my eyelids.

I wondered where I was. Then I wondered who I was. I could remember nothing at all. This seemed too much to deal with, so I went to sleep.

The next time I woke up the weights were gone from my eyes. I opened them, and found I was lying in a dim light in a room whose fuzzy lines slowly grew clear. There was a washbasin in one corner, a table with a white cloth on it, an easy chair with wooden arms, a window to my right, a door straight ahead. A bare, functional room.

The door opened and a nurse came in. She looked at me in pleased surprise and smiled. She had nice teeth.

"Hello there," she said. "So you've come back at last. How do you feel?"

"Fine," I said, but it came out as a whisper, and in any case it wasn't strictly true.

"Are you comfortable?" she asked, holding my wrist for the pulse.

"No," I said, giving up the pretence.

"I'll go and tell Dr. Mitcham you've woken up, and I expect he will come and see you. Will you be all right for a few minutes?" She wrote something on a board which lay on the table, gave me another bright smile, and swished out of the door.

So I was in hospital. But I still had no idea what had happened. Had I, I wondered, been run over by a steam roller? Or a herd of elephants?

Dr. Mitcham, when he came, would solve only half the mystery.

"Why am I here?" I asked, in a croaky whisper.

"You fell off a horse," he said.

"Who am I?"

At this question he tapped his teeth with the end of his pencil and looked at me steadily for some seconds. He was a blunt-featured young man with fluffy, already receding, fair hair, and bright intelligent pale blue eyes.

"I'd rather you remember that for yourself. You will, soon, I'm sure. Don't worry about it. Don't worry about anything. Just relax, and your memory will come back. Not all at once, don't expect that, but little by little you'll remember everything, except perhaps the fall itself."

"What is wrong with me, exactly?" I asked.

"Concussion is what has affected your memory. As to the rest of you," he surveyed me from head to foot, "you have a broken collar-bone, four cracked ribs, and multiple contusions."

"Nothing serious, thank goodness," I croaked.

He opened his mouth and gasped, and then began to laugh. He said, "No, nothing serious. You lot are all the same. Quite mad."

"Which lot?" I said.

"Never mind, you'll remember soon," he said. "Just go to sleep for a while, if you can, and you'll probably understand a great deal more when you wake up."

I took his advice, closed my eyes and drifted to sleep. I dreamed of a husky voice which came from the centre of a bowl of red and yellow crocuses, whispering menacing things until I wanted to scream and run away, and then I realised it was my own voice whispering, and the crocuses faded into a vision of deep green forests with scarlet birds darting in the shadows. Then I thought I was very high up, looking to the ground, and I was leaning farther and farther forward until I fell, and this time what I said made perfect sense.

"I fell out of the tree." I knew it had happened in my boyhood.

There was an exclamation beside me. I opened my eyes. At the foot of the bed stood Dr. Mitcham.

"What tree?" he said.

"In the forest," I said. "I hit my head, and when I woke my father was kneeling beside me."

There was an exclamation again at my right hand. I rolled my head over to look.

He sat there, sunburnt, fit, distinguished, and at forty-six looking still a young man.

"Hi, there," I said.

"Do you know who this is?" asked Dr. Mitcham.

"My father."

"And what is your name?"

"Alan York," I said at once, and my memory bounded back. I could remember everything up to the morning I was going to Bristol races. I remembered setting off, but what happened after that was still a blank.

"How did you get here?" I asked my father.

"I flew over. Mrs. Davidson rang me up to tell me you had had a fall and were in hospital. I thought I'd better take a look."

"How long . . ." I began, slowly.

"How long were you unconscious?" said Dr. Mitcham. "This is Sunday morning. Two and a half days. Not too bad, considering the crack you had. I kept your crash-helmet for you to see." He opened a locker and took out the shell which had undoubtedly saved my life. It was nearly in two pieces.

"I'll need a new one," I said.

"Quite mad. You're all quite mad," said Dr. Mitcham.

This time I knew what he meant. I grinned, but it was a lopsided affair, because I discovered that half my face was swollen as well as stiff and sore. I began to put up my left hand to explore the damage, but I changed my mind before I had raised it six inches, owing to the sudden pain which the movement caused in my shoulder. In spite of the tight bandages which arched my shoulders backward, I heard and felt the broken ends of collar-bone grate together.

As if they had been waiting for a signal, every dull separate ache in my battered body sprang to vicious, throbbing life. I drew in a deep breath, and the broken ribs sharply rebelled against it. It was a bad moment.

I shut my eyes. My father said anxiously, "Is he all right?" and Dr. Mitcham answered, "Yes, don't worry. I rather think his breakages have caught up with him. I'll give him something to ease it, shortly."

"I'll be out of bed tomorrow," I said. "I've been bruised before, and I've broken my collarbone before.

It doesn't last long." But I added ruefully to myself that *while* it lasted it was highly unpleasant.

"You will certainly not get up tomorrow," said Dr. Mitcham's voice. "You'll stay where you are for a week, to give that concussion a chance."

"I can't stay in bed for a week," I protested. "I shouldn't have the strength of a flea when I got up, and I'm going to ride Admiral at Liverpool."

"When is that?" asked Dr. Mitcham suspiciously.

"March twenty-fourth," I said.

There was a short silence while they worked it out.

"That's only a week on Thursday," said my father.

"You can put it right out of your head," said Dr. Mitcham severely.

"Promise me," said my father.

I opened my eyes and looked at him, and when I saw the anxiety in his face I understood for the first time in my life how much I meant to him. I was his only child, and for ten years, after my mother died, he had reared me himself, not delegating the job to a succession of housekeepers, boarding schools, and tutors as many a rich man would have done, but spending time playing with me and teaching me, and making sure I learned in my teens how to live happily and usefully under the burden of extreme wealth. He himself had taught me how to face all kinds of danger, yet I realised that it must seem to him that if I insisted on taking my first tilt at Liverpool when I was precariously unfit, I was risking more than I had any right to do.

"I promise," I said. "I won't ride at Liverpool this month. But I'm going on racing afterwards."

"All right. It's a deal." He relaxed, smiling, and stood up. "I'll come again this afternoon."

"Where are you staying? Where are we now?" I asked.

"This is Bristol Hospital, and I'm staying with Mrs. Davidson," he said.

I said, "Did I get this lot at Bristol races? With Palindrome?" My father nodded. "How is he? Was he hurt? What sort of fall did he have?"

"No, he wasn't hurt," he said. "He's back in Gregory's stables. No one saw how or why he fell because it was raining so hard. Pete said you had a premonition you were going to fall, and he asked me to tell you he had done what you wanted."

"I don't remember anything about it, and I don't know what it was I wanted him to do," I sighed. "It's very irritating."

Dr. Mitcham and my father went away and left me puzzling over the gap in my memory. I had an illusive feeling that I had known for a few seconds a fact of paramount significance, but grope as I would my conscious life ended on the road to Bristol races and began again in Bristol Hospital.

The rest of the day passed slowly and miserably, with each small movement I made setting up a chorus of protest in every crushed muscle and nerve. I had been kicked by horses before, but never in so many places all at once, and I knew, though I couldn't see it, that my skin must be covered with large angry crimson patches which had spread and were turning black and finally yellow as the blood underneath congealed and dispersed. My face, I knew, must be giving the same rainbow performance, and I undoubtedly had two lovely black eyes.

The pills Dr. Mitcham had sent via the nurse with pretty teeth made less difference than I would have liked, so I lay with my eyes shut and pretended I was floating on the sea in the sunshine, with my grating bones and throbbing head cushioned by a gentle swell. I filled in the scene with seagulls and white clouds and children splashing in the shallows, and it worked well each time until I moved again.

Late in the evening my headache grew worse and I slid in and out of weird troubled dreams in which I imagined that my limbs had been torn off by heavy weights, and I woke soaked in sweat to wiggle my toes and fingers in an agony of fear that they were missing. But no sooner had the feel of them against the sheets sent relief flooding over me than I was drifting away into the same nightmare all over again. The cycle of short awakenings and long dreams went on and on, until I was no longer sure what was real and what was not.

So shattering was the night passed in this fashion that when Dr. Mitcham came into my room in the morning I implored him to show me that my hands and feet were in fact still attached to me. Without a word he stripped back the bedclothes, grasped my feet firmly, and lifted them a few inches so that I could see them. I raised my hands and looked at them, and laced my fingertips together over my stomach; and felt a complete idiot to have been so terrified over nothing.

"There's no need to be embarrassed," said Mitcham. "You can't expect your brain to be in perfect working order when you've been unconscious for so long. I promise you that you have no injuries you don't know about. No internal damage, no bits missing. You'll be as good as new in three weeks." His steady pale blue eyes were reliable. "Only," he added, "you'll have a scar on your face. We stitched up a cut over your left cheekbone."

As I had not been exactly handsome before, this news did not disturb me. I thanked him for his forbearance, and he pulled the sheet and blankets over me again. His blunt face suddenly lit up with a mischievous smile, and he said, "Yesterday *you* told *me* there was nothing seriously wrong with you and you'd be out of bed today, if I remember correctly."

"Blast you," I said weakly. "I'll be out of bed tomorrow."

• • •

IN THE END it was Thursday before I made it on to my feet, and I went home to Scilla's on Saturday morning feeling more tottery than I cared to admit, but in good spirits nevertheless. My father, who was still there but planning to leave early the next week, came to fetch me.

Scilla and Polly clicked their tongues and made sympathetic remarks as I levered myself out of the Jaguar at one quarter my usual speed and walked carefully up the front steps. But young Henry, giving me a sweeping, comprehensive glance which took in my black and yellow face and the long newly healed cut across one cheek, greeted me with, "And how's the horrible monster from outer space?"

"Go and boil your head," I said, and Henry grinned delightedly.

At seven o'clock in the evening, just after the children had gone upstairs to bed, Kate rang up. Scilla and my father decided to bring some wine up from the cellar, and left me alone in the drawing-room to talk to her.

"How are the cracks?" she asked.

"Knitting nicely," I said. "Thank you for your letter, and for the flowers."

"The flowers were Uncle George's idea," she said. "I said it was too much like a funeral, sending you flowers, and he thought that was so funny that he nearly choked. It didn't seem all that funny to me, actually, when I knew from Mrs. Davidson that it very nearly was your funeral."

"It was nowhere near that," I said. "Scilla was exaggerating. And whether it was your idea or Uncle George's, thank you anyway for the flowers."

"Lilies, I expect I should have sent, not tulips," Kate teased.

"You can send me lilies next time," I said, taking pleasure in hearing her slow attractive voice.

"Good heavens, is there going to be a next time?"

"Bound to be," I said cheerfully.

"Well all right," said Kate, "I'll place a standing order with Interflora, for lilies."

"I love you, Kate," I said.

"I must say," she said happily, "it's nice hearing people say that."

"People? Who else has said it? And when?" I asked, fearing the worst.

"Well," she said, after a tiny pause, "Dane, as a matter of fact."

"Oh."

"Don't be so jealous," she said. "And Dane's just as bad as you. He glowers like a thunderstorm if he hears your name. You're both being childish."

"Yes, ma'am," I said. "When will I see you again?"

We fixed a luncheon date in London, and before she rang off I told her again that I loved her. I was about to put down my own receiver, when I heard the most unexpected sound on the telephone.

A giggle. A quickly suppressed, but definite giggle.

I knew she had disconnected; but I said into the dead mouthpiece in front of me, "Hang on a minute, Kate, I—er—want to read you something . . . in the paper. Just a minute while I get it." I put my receiver down on the table, went carefully out of the drawing-room, up the stairs, and into Scilla's bedroom.

There stood the culprits, grouped in a guilty huddle round the extension telephone. Henry, with the receiver pressed to his ear; Polly, her head close against his; and William, looking earnestly up at them with his mouth open. They were all in pyjamas and dressing-gowns.

"And just what do you think you're doing?" I asked, with a severe expression.

"Oh golly," said Henry, dropping the receiver on to the bed as if it were suddenly too hot to hold.

"Alan!" said Polly, blushing deeply.

"How long have you been listening?" I demanded.

"Actually, right from the beginning," said Polly shamefacedly.

"Henry always listens," said William, proud of his brother.

"Shut up," said Henry.

"You little beasts," I said.

William looked hurt. He said again, "But Henry always listens. He listens to everyone. He's checking up, and that's good, isn't it? Henry checks up all the time, don't you Henry?"

"Shut up William," said Henry, getting red and furious.

"So Henry checks up, does he?" I said, frowning crossly at him. Henry stared back, caught out, but apparently unrepentant.

I advanced towards them, but the homily on the sacredness of privacy that I was about to deliver suddenly flew out of my mind. I stopped and thought.

"Henry, how long have you been listening to people on the telephone?" I asked mildly.

He looked at me warily. Finally he said, "Quite some time."

"Days? Weeks? Months?"

"Ages," said Polly, taking heart again as I no longer seemed angry with them.

"Did you ever listen to your father?" I asked.

"Yes, often," said Henry.

I paused, studying this tough, intelligent little boy. He was only eight, but if he knew the answers to what I was going to ask him, he would understand their significance and be appalled by his knowledge all his life. But I pressed on.

"Did you by any chance ever hear him talking to a man with a voice like this?" I asked. Then I made my voice husky and whispering, and said, "Am I speaking to Major Davidson?"

"Yes," said Henry without hesitation.

"When was that?" I asked, trying to show nothing of the excitement I felt I was sure now that he had listened in to the telephone call which Bill had mentioned as a joke to Pete, who had not taken in what he said.

"It was that voice the last time I listened to Daddy," said Henry, matter-of-factly.

"Do you remember what the voice said?" I forced myself to speak slowly, gently.

"Oh, yes, it was a joke. It was two days before he was killed," said Henry, without distress. "Just when we were going to bed, like now. The phone rang and I scooted in here and listened as usual. That man with the funny voice was saying, 'Are you going to ride Admiral on Saturday, Major Davidson?' and Daddy said he was." Henry paused. I waited, willing him to remember.

He screwed up his eyes in concentration and went on. "Then the man with the funny voice said, 'You are not to win on Admiral, Major Davidson.' Daddy just laughed, and the man said, 'I'll pay you five hundred pounds if you promise not to win.' And Daddy said, 'Go to hell' and I nearly snorted because he was always telling me not to say that. Then the whispery man said he didn't want Daddy to win, and that Admiral would fall if Daddy didn't agree not to win, and Daddy said, 'You must be mad.' And then he put down the telephone, and I ran back to my room in case he should come up and find me listening."

"Did you say anything to your father about it?" I asked.

"No," said Henry frankly. "That's the big snag about listening. You have to be awfully careful not to know too much."

"Yes, I can see that," I said, trying not to smile.

Then I saw the flicker in Henry's eyes as the meaning of what he had heard grew clearer to him. He said jerkily, "It wasn't a joke after all, was it?"

"No, it wasn't," I said.

"But that man didn't make Admiral fall, did he? He couldn't . . . could he? Could he?" said Henry desperately, wanting me to reassure him. His eyes were stretched wide open, and he was beginning to realise that he had listened to the man who had caused his father's death. Although he would have to know one day about the strand of wire, I didn't think I ought to tell him at that moment.

"I don't really know. I don't expect so," I lied calmly. But Henry's eyes stared blindly at me as if he were looking at some inward horror.

"What's the matter?" said Polly. "I don't understand why Henry is so upset. Just because someone told Daddy they didn't want him to win is no reason for Henry to go off in a fit."

"Does he always remember so clearly what people say?" I asked Polly. "It's a month ago, now, since your father died."

"I expect Daddy and that man said a lot of things that Henry has forgotten," said Polly judiciously, "but he doesn't make things up." And I knew this was true. He was a truthful child.

He said stonily, "I don't see how he could have done it."

I was glad at least that Henry was dealing with his revelation practically and not emotionally. Perhaps I had not done him too much harm, after all, in making him understand what he had heard and disregarded.

"Come along to bed and don't worry about it, Henry," I said, holding out my hand to him. He took it, and uncharacteristically held on to it all the way along the landing and into his bedroom.

chapter 13

WHILE I WAS dressing myself at tortoise pace the following morning the front door bell rang downstairs, and presently Joan came up to say that an Inspector Lodge would like to see me, please.

"Tell him I'll be down as soon as possible," I said, struggling to get my shirt on over the thick bracing bandage round my shoulders. I did up most of the buttons, but decided I didn't need a tie.

The strapping round my ribs felt tight and itched horribly, my head ached, large areas of flesh were black still and tender, I had slept badly, and I was altogether in a foul mood. The three aspirins I had swallowed in place of breakfast had not come up to scratch.

I picked up my socks, tried to bend to put them on with my one useful arm, found how far away my feet had become, and flung them across the room in a temper. The day before, in the hospital, the nurse with nice teeth had helped me to dress. Today perverseness stopped me asking my father to come and do it for me.

The sight of my smudgy, yellow, unshaven face in the looking-glass made matters no better. Henry's "horrible monster from outer space" was not so far off the mark.

I longed to scratch the livid scar on my cheek, to relieve its irritation.

I plugged in my electric razor and took off the worst, brushed my hair sketchily, thrust my bare feet into slippers, put one arm into my hacking jacket and swung it over the other shoulder, and shuffled gingerly downstairs.

Lodge's face when he saw me was a picture.

"If you laugh at me I'll knock your block off. Next week," I said.

"I'm not laughing," said Lodge, his nostrils twitching madly as he tried to keep a straight face.

"It's not funny," I said emphatically.

"No."

I scowled at him.

My father said, glancing at me from behind his Sunday newspaper in the depths of an armchair by the fire, "You sound to me as if you need a stiff brandy."

"It's only half past ten," I said crossly.

"Emergencies can happen at any time of the day," said my father, standing up, "and this would appear to be a grave one." He opened the corner cupboard where Scilla kept a few bottles and glasses, poured out a third of a tumbler full of brandy, and splashed some soda into it. I complained that it was too strong, too early, and unnecessary.

My father handed me the glass. "Drink it and shut up," he said.

Furious, I took a large mouthful. It was strong and fiery, and bit into my throat. I rolled the second mouthful round my teeth so that the scarcely diluted spirit tingled on my gums, and when I swallowed I could feel it slide warmly down to my empty stomach.

"Did you have any breakfast?" asked my father.

"No," I said.

I took another, smaller gulp. The brandy worked fast. My bad temper began draining away, and in a minute or two I felt reasonably sane. Lodge and my father were looking at me intently as though I were a laboratory animal responding to an experiment.

"Oh very well then," I admitted grudgingly, "I feel better." I took a cigarette from the silver box on the table and lit it, and noticed the sun was shining.

"Good." My father sat down again.

It appeared that he and Lodge had introduced themselves while they waited for me, and Lodge had told him, among other things, about my adventures in the horse-box outside Maidenhead, a detail I had omitted from my letters. This I considered to be treachery of the basest sort, and said so and I told them how Kate and I had tracked down the horse-box, and that that particular line of enquiry was a dead end.

I took my cigarette and glass across the room and sat on the window seat in the sun. Scilla was in the garden, cutting flowers. I waved to her.

Lodge, dressed today not in uniform but in grey flannels, fine wool shirt, and sports jacket, opened his briefcase, which lay on the table, and pulled out some papers. He sat down beside the table and spread them out.

He said, "Mr. Smith rang me up at the station on the morning after your fall at Bristol to tell me about it."

"Why on earth did he do that?" I asked.

"You asked him to," said Lodge. He hesitated, and went on, "I understand from your father that your memory is affected."

"Yes. Most bits of that day at Bristol have come back now, but I still can't remember going out of the weighing room to ride Palindrome, or the race or the fall, or anything." My last mental picture was of Sandy walking out into the rain. "Why did I ask Pete to tell you I fell?"

"You asked him before the race. You apparently thought you were likely to fall. So, unofficially, I checked up on that crash of yours." He smiled suddenly. "You've accounted for all my free time lately, and today is really my day off. Why I bother with you I really don't know!" But I guessed that he was as addicted to detecting as an alcoholic to drink. He couldn't help doing it.

He went on, "I went down to Gregory's stables and took a look a Palindrome. He had a distinct narrow wound across his front of those two pads of flesh . . ."

"Chest," I murmured.

". . . Chest, then, and I'll give you one guess at what cut him."

"Oh, no," I said, guessing, but not believing it.

"I checked up on the attendants at the fences," he said. "One of them was new and unknown to the others. He gave his name as Thomas Butler and an address which doesn't exist, and he volunteered to stand at the farthest fence from the stands, where you fell. His offer was readily accepted because of the rain and the distance of the fence from the bookmakers. The same story as at Maidenhead. Except that this time Butler collected his earnings in the normal way. Then I got the Clerk of the Course to let me inspect the fence, and I found a groove on each post six feet, six inches from the ground."

There was a short silence.

"Well, well, well," I said blankly. "It looks as though I was luckier than Bill."

"I wish you could remember something about it . . . anything. What made you suspect you would fall?" asked Lodge.

"I don't know."

"It was something that happened while you were in the parade ring waiting to mount." He leaned forward, his dark eyes fixed intently on my face, willing my sluggish memory to come to life. But I remembered nothing, and I still felt weary from head to foot. Concentration was altogether too much of an effort.

I looked out into the peaceful spring garden. Scilla

held an armful of forsythia, golden yellow against her blue dress.

"I can't remember," I said flatly. "Perhaps it'll come back when my head stops aching."

Lodge sighed and sat back in his hard chair.

"I suppose," he said, a little bitterly, "that you do at least remember sending me a message from Brighton, asking me to do your investigating for you?"

"Yes, I do," I said. "How did you get on?"

"Not very well. No one seems to know who actually owns the Marconicar taxi line. It was taken over just after the war by a business man named Clifford Tudor . . ."

"What?" I said in astonishment.

"Clifford Tudor, respectable Brighton resident, British subject. Do you know him?"

"Yes," I said. "He owns several racehorses."

Lodge sorted out a paper from his briefcase. "Clifford Tudor born Khroupista Thasos, in Trikkala, Greece. Naturalised nineteen thirty-nine, when he was twenty-five. He started life as a cook, but owing to natural business ability, he acquired his own restaurant that same year. He sold it for a large profit after the war, went to Brighton, and bought for next to nothing an old taxi business that had wilted from wartime restrictions and lack of petrol. Four years ago he sold the taxis, again at a profit, and put his money into the Pavillion Plaza Hotel. He is unmarried."

I leaned my head back against the window and waited for these details to mean something significant, but all that happened was that my inability to think increased.

Lodge went on. "The taxi line was bought from Tudor by nominees, and that's where the fog begins. There have been so many transfers of ownership from company to company mostly, through nominees who can't be traced, that no one can discover who is the actual present owner. All business matters are settled by a Mr.

Fielder, the manager. He says he consults with a person he calls 'the Chairman' by telephone, but that 'the Chairman' rings him up every morning, and never the other way round. He says the Chairman's name is Claud Thiveridge, but he doesn't know his address or telephone number."

"It sounds very fishy to me," said my father.

"It is," said Lodge. "There is no Claud Thiveridge on the electoral register, or in any other official list, including the telephone accounts department, in the whole of Kent, Surrey, or Sussex. The operators in the telephone exchange are sure the office doesn't receive a long distance call regularly every morning, yet the morning call has been standard office routine for the last four years. As this means that the call must be a local one, it seems fairly certain that Claud Thiveridge is not the gentleman's real name."

He rubbed the palm of his hand round the back of his neck and looked at me steadily. "You know a lot more than you've told me, amnesia or not," he said. "Spill the beans, there's a good chap."

"You haven't told me what the Brighton police think of the Marconicars," I said.

Lodge hesitated. "Well, they were a little touchy on the subject, I would say. It seems they have had several complaints, but not much evidence that will stand up in court. What I have just told you is the result of their enquiries over the last few years."

"They would not seem," said my father dryly, "to have made spectacular progress. Come on, Alan, tell us what's going on."

Lodge turned his head towards him in surprise. My father smiled.

"My son is Sherlock Holmes reincarnated, didn't you know?" he said. "After he went to England I had to employ a detective to do the work he used to do in connection with frauds and swindles. As one of my head clerks put it, Mr. Alan has an unerring instinct for smelling out crooks."

"Mr. Alan's unerring instinct is no longer functioning," I said gloomily. Clouds were building up near the sun, and Scilla's back disappeared through the macrocarpa hedge by the kitchen door.

"Don't be infuriating, Alan," said my father. "Elucidate."

"Oh, all right." I stubbed out my cigarette, began to scratch my cheek, and dragged my fingers away from the scar with a strong effort of will. It went on itching.

"There's a lot I don't know," I said, "but the general gist appears to be this. The Marconicars have been in the protection racket for the last four years, intimidating small concerns like cafés and free house pubs. About a year ago, owing to the strongmindedness of one particular publican, mine host of the Blue Duck, business in the protection line began to get unexpectedly rough for the protectors. He set alsatians on them, in fact." I told my fascinated father and an aghast Lodge what Kate and I had learned in the Blue Duck's kitchen, carefully watched by the yellow-eyed Prince.

"Ex-Regimental Sergeant-Major Thomkins made such serious inroads into the illicit profits of Marconicars," I continued, "that as a racket it was more or less defunct. The legitimate side hasn't been doing too well during the winter, either, according to the typists who work in the office. There are too many taxis in Brighton for the number of fares at this time of year, I should think. Anyway, it seems to me that the Marconicar boss—the Chairman, your mysterious Claud Thiveridge—set about mending his fortunes by branching out into another form of crime. He bought, I think, the shaky bookmaking business on the floor above the Marconicars, in the same building."

I could almost smell the cabbage in the Olde Oake Café as I remembered it. "An earnest lady told me the bookmakers had been taken over by a new firm about six months ago, but that its name was still the same. L. C. PERTH, written in neon. She was very wrought up about them sticking such a garish sign on an architectural gem, and she and her old buildings society, whose name I forget, had tried to reason with the new owners to take down what they had just put up. Only they couldn't find out who the new owner was. It's too much of a coincidence to have two businesses, both shady, one above the other, both with invisible and untraceable owners. They must be owned by the same person."

"It doesn't follow, and I don't see the point," said my father.

"You will in a minute," I said. "Bill died because he wouldn't stop his horse winning a race. I know his death wasn't necessarily intended, but force was used against him. He was told not to win by a husky-voiced man on the telephone. Henry, Bill's elder son—he's eight—" I explained to Lodge, "has a habit of listening on the extension upstairs, and he heard every word. Two days before Bill died, Henry says, the voice offered him five hundred pounds to stop his horse winning, and when Bill laughed at this, the voice told him he wouldn't win because his horse would fall."

I paused, but neither Lodge nor my father said anything. Swallowing the last of the brandy, I went on. "There is a jockey called Joe Nantwich who during the last six months, ever since L. C. Perth changed hands, has regularly accepted a hundred pounds, sometimes more, to stop a horse winning. Joe gets his instructions by telephone from a husky-voiced man he has never met."

Lodge stirred on his hard, self-chosen chair.

I went on. "I, as you know, was set upon by the Marconicar drivers, and a few days later the man with the husky voice rang me up and told me to take heed of the warning I had been given in the horse-box. One doesn't have to be Sherlock Holmes to see that the crooked racing and the Marconicar protection racket were being run by the same man." I stopped.

"Finish it off, then," said my father impatiently.

"The only person who would offer a jockey a large sum to lose a race is a crooked bookmaker. If he *knows* a well-fancied horse is not going to win, he can accept any amount of money on that horse without risk."

"Enlarge," said Lodge.

"Normally bookmakers try to balance their books so that whichever horse wins they come out on the winning side," I said. "If too many people want to back one horse, they accept the bets, but they back the horse themselves with another bookmaker; then if that horse wins, they collect their winnings from the second bookmaker, and pay it out to their customers. It's a universal system known as 'laying off.' Now suppose you were a crooked bookmaker and Joe Nantwich is to ride a fancied horse. You tip Joe the wink to lose. Then however much is betted with you on that horse, you do no laying off, because you know you won't have to pay out."

"I would have thought that a hundred pounds would have been more than it was worth," said Lodge, "since bookmakers normally make a profit anyway."

"Your friend wasn't satisfied with the legitimate gains from the taxis," my father pointed out.

I sighed, and shifted my stiff shoulders against the frame of the window.

"There's a bit more to it, of course," I said. "If a bookmaker knows he hasn't got to pay out on a certain horse, he can offer better odds on it. Not enough to be suspicious, but just enough to attract a lot of extra custom. A point better than anyone else would go to—say eleven to four, when the next best offer was five to two. The money would roll in, don't you think?"

I stood up and went towards the door, saying, "I'll show you something."

The stairs seemed steeper than usual. I went up to my room and fetched the racing form book and the little bunch of bookmakers' tickets, and shuffled back to the drawing-room. I laid the tickets out on the table in front of Lodge, and my father came over to have a look.

"These," I explained, "are some tickets Bill kept for his children to play with. Three of them, as you see, were issued by L. C. Perth, and all the others are from different firms, no two alike. Bill was a methodical man. On the backs of all the tickets he wrote the date, the details of his bet, and the name of the horse he'd put his money on. He used to search around in Tattersall's for the best odds and bet in cash, instead of betting on credit with Tote Investors or one of the bookmakers on the rails—those," I added for Lodge's benefit, as I could see the question forming on his lips, "are bookmakers who stand along the railing between Tattersall's and the Club enclosures, writing down bets made by Club members and other people known to them. They send out weekly accounts, win or lose. Bill didn't bet in large amounts, and he thought credit betting wasn't exciting enough."

Lodge turned over the three Perth tickets.

Bill's loopy writing was clear and unmistakable. I picked up the first ticket, and read aloud, " 'Peripatetic. November 7th. Ten pounds staked at eleven to ten.' So he stood to win eleven pounds for his money." I opened the detailed form book and turned to November 7.

"Peripatetic," I said, "lost the two mile hurdle at Sandown that day by four lengths. He was ridden by Joe Nantwich. The starting price was eleven to ten on—that is, you have to stake eleven pounds to win ten—and had earlier been as low as eleven to eight on. L. C. Perth must have done a roaring trade at eleven to ten against."

I picked up the second card and read, " 'Sackbut. October 10th. Five pounds staked at six to one.' " I opened the form book for that day. "Sackbut was unplaced at Newbury and Joe Nantwich rode it. The best price generally offered was five to one, and the starting price was seven to two."

I put the Sackbut ticket back on the table, and read the third card where it lay. " 'Malabar. December 2nd. Eight pounds staked at fifteen to eight.' " I laid the form book beside it, opened at December 2nd. "Malabar finished fourth at Birmingham. Joe Nantwich rode him. The starting price was six to four."

Lodge and my father silently checked the book with the ticket.

"I looked up all the other cards as well," I said. "Of course, as Bill still had the tickets, all the horses lost, but on only one of them did he get better odds than you'd expect. Joe didn't ride it, and I don't think it's significant, because it was an outsider at a hundred to six."

"I wish the racing fraternity would use only whole numbers and halves," said Lodge plaintively.

"Haven't you heard," I asked, "about the keen gambler who taught his baby son to count? One, six-to-four, two . . ."

Lodge laughed, his dark eyes crinkling at the corners. "I'll have to write down these figures on the Perth tickets alongside the form book information, and get it straightened out in my mind," he said, unscrewing his pen and settling to the task.

My father sat down beside him and watched the telltale list grow. I went back to the window seat and waited.

Presently Lodge said, "I can see why your father misses you as a fraud spotter." He put his pen back in his pocket.

I smiled and said, "If you want to read a really blatant fraud, you should look up the Irish racing in that form book. It's fantastic."

"Not today. This is quite enough to be going on with," said Lodge, rubbing his hand over his face and pinching his nose between thumb and forefinger.

"All that remains, as far as I'm concerned, is for you to tell us who is organising the whole thing," said my father with a touch of mockery, which from long understanding I interpreted as approval.

"That, dear Pa, I fear I cannot do," I said.

But Lodge said seriously, "Could it be anyone you know on the racecourse? It must be someone connected with racing. How about Perth, the bookmaker?"

"It could be. I don't know him. His name won't actually be Perth of course. That name was sold with the business. I'll have a bet on with him next time I go racing and see what happens," I said.

"You will do no such thing," said my father emphatically, and I felt too listless to argue.

"How about a jockey, or a trainer, or an owner?" asked Lodge.

"You'd better include the Stewards and the National Hunt Committee," I said, ironically. "They were almost the first to know I had discovered the wire and was looking into it. The man we are after knew very early on that I was inquisitive. I didn't tell many people I suspected more than an accident, or ask many pointed questions, before that affair in the horse-box."

"People you know . . ." said Lodge, musingly. "How about Gregory?"

"No," I said.

"Why not? He lives near Brighton, near enough for the Marconicar morning telephone call."

"He wouldn't risk hurting Bill or Admiral," I said.

"How can you be sure?" asked Lodge. "People aren't always what they seem, and murderers are often fond of animals, until they get in the way. One chap I saw at the assizes lately killed a nightwatchman and showed no remorse at all. But when evidence was given that the nightwatchman's dog had had his head bashed in, too, the accused burst into tears and said he was sorry."

"Pathetic," I said. "But no dice. It isn't Pete."

"Faith or evidence?" persisted Lodge.

"Faith," I said grudgingly, because I was quite sure.

"Jockeys?" suggested Lodge, leaving it.

"None of them strikes me as being the type we're looking for," I said, "and I think you're overlooking the fact that racing came second on the programme and may even have been adopted solely because a shaky bookmaking business existed on the floor above the Marconicars. I mean, that in itself may have turned the boss of Marconicars towards racing."

"You may be right," admitted Lodge.

My father said, "It's just possible that the man who originally owned Marconicars decided to launch out into crime, and faked a sale to cover his tracks."

"Clifford Tudor, nee Thasos, do you mean?" asked Lodge with interest. My father nodded, and Lodge said to me, "How about it?"

"Tudor pops up all over the place," I said. "He knew Bill, and Bill had his address noted down on a scrap of paper." I put my hand into my jacket pocket. The old envelope was still there. I drew it out and looked at it again. "Tudor told me he had asked Bill to ride a horse for him."

"When did he tell you that?" asked Lodge.

"I gave him a lift from Plumpton races into Brighton, four days after Bill died. We talked about him on the way."

"Anything else?" asked Lodge.

"Well . . . Tudor's horses have been ridden—up until lately—by our corrupted friend Joe Nantwich. It was on Tudor's horse Bolingbroke that Joe won once when he had been instructed to lose . . . but at Cheltenham he threw away a race on a horse of Tudor's, and Tudor was very angry about it."

"Camouflage," suggested my father.

But I rested my aching head against the window, and said, "I don't think Tudor can possibly be the crook we're looking for."

"Why not?" asked Lodge. "He has the organising ability, he lives in Brighton, he owned the taxis, he employs Joe Nantwich, and he knew Major Davidson. He seems the best proposition so far."

"No," I said tiredly. "The best lead we've had is the taxis. If I hadn't recognised that the men who stopped me in the horse-box were also taxi-drivers, I'd never have found out anything at all. Whoever put them on to me can't possibly have imagined I would know them, or he wouldn't have done it. But if there's one person who knew I would recognise them, it's Clifford Tudor. He was standing near me while the taxi-drivers fought, and he knew I'd had time to look at them after the police had herded them into two groups."

"I don't rule him out altogether, even so," said Lodge, gathering his papers together and putting them back into his briefcase. "Criminals often make the stupidest mistakes."

I said, "If we ever do find your Claud Thiveridge, I think he will turn out to be someone I've never met and never heard of. A complete stranger. It's far more likely."

I wanted to believe it.

I did not want to have to face another possibility, one that I shied away from so uncomfortably that I could not bring myself even to lay it open for Lodge's inspection.

Who, besides Tudor, knew before the horse-box incident that I wanted Bill's death avenged? Kate. And to whom had she passed this on? To Uncle George. Uncle George, who I suspected, housed a lean and hungry soul in his fat body, behind his fatuous expression.

Uncle George, out of the blue, had bought a horse for his niece. Why? To widen her interests, he had said. But through her, I thought, he would learn much of what went on at the races.

And Uncle George had sent Heavens Above to be trained in the stable which housed Bill's horse. Was it a coincidence . . . or the beginning of a scheme which Bill's unexpected death had cut short?

It was nebulous, unconvincing. It was based only on supposition, not on facts, and bolstered only by memory of the shock on Uncle George's face when Kate told him we had been to the Blue Duck—shock which he had called indigestion. And perhaps it had been indigestion, after all.

And all those primitive weapons in his study, the ritual objects and the scalp . . . were they the playthings of a man who relished violence? Or who loathed it? Or did both at the same time?

Scilla came into the drawing-room, carrying a copper bowl filled with forsythia and daffodils. She put it on the low table near me, and the spring sun suddenly shone on the golden flowers, so that they seemed like a burst of light, reflecting their colour upwards on to her face as she bent over them, tweaking them into order.

She gave me a sharp glance, and turned round to the others.

"Alan looks very tired," she said. "What have you been doing?"

"Talking," I said, smiling at her.

"You'll find yourself back in the hospital if you're not careful," she scolded mildly, and without pausing offered mid-morning coffee to Lodge and my father.

I was glad for the interruption, because I had not wished to discuss with them what was to be done next in pursuit of Mr. Claud Thiveridge. Every small advance I had made in his direction had brought its retribution, it was true; yet in each of his parries I had found a clue. My faulty memory was still cheating me of the information I had paid for with the drubbing at Bristol, but it did not deter me from wanting to see the business through.

I would get closer to Thiveridge. He would hit out again, and in doing it show me the next step towards him, like the flash of a gunshot in the dark revealing the hiding place of a sniper.

chapter 14

JOE NANTWICH FOUND the sniper first.

Eight days after Lodge's visit I drove down to West Sussex races, having put in a short morning at the office. My bruises had faded and gone; the ribs and collar-bone were mended and in perfect working order, and even my stubborn headache was losing its grip. I whistled my way into the changing room and presented to Clem my brand new crash-helmet, bought that morning from Bates of Jermyn Street for three guineas.

The weighing room was empty, and distant oohs and ahs proclaimed that the first race was in progress. Clem, who was tidying up the changing room after the tornado of getting a large number of jockeys out of their ordinary clothes, into racing colours, past the scales and out to the parade ring, greeted me warmly and shook hands.

"Glad to see you back, sir," he said, taking the helmet. With a ball-point pen he wrote my name on a piece of adhesive tape and stuck it on to the shiny shell. "Let's hope you won't be needing another new one of these in a hurry." He pressed his thumb firmly on to the adhesive tape.

"I'm starting again tomorrow, Clem," I said. "Can you

bring my gear? Big saddle. There's no weight problem, I'm riding Admiral."

"Top flipping weight," said Clem, resignedly. "And a lot of lead, which Admiral isn't used to. Major Davidson hardly ever needed any." Clem gave me an assessing sideways look and added, "You've lost three or four pounds, I shouldn't wonder."

"All the better," I said cheerfully, turning to the door.

"Oh, just a minute, sir," said Clem. "Joe Nantwich asked me to let you know, if you came, that he has something to tell you."

"Oh, yes?" I said.

"He was asking for you on Saturday at Liverpool, but I told him you'd probably be coming here, as Mr. Smith mentioned last week that you'd be riding Admiral to-morrow," said Clem, absent-mindedly picking up a saddle and smoothing his hand over the leather.

"Did Joe say what it was he wanted to tell me?" I asked.

"Yes, he wants to show you a bit of brown wrapping paper with something written on it. He said you'd be interested to see it, though I can't think why—the word I saw looked like something to do with chickens. He had the paper out in the changing room at Liverpool, and folded it up flat on the bench into a neat shape, and tucked it into the inside pocket of his jacket. Giggling over it, he was. He'd had a drink or two I reckon, but then most people had, it was after the National. He said what was written on the paper was double dutch to him, but it might be a clue, you never knew. I asked him a clue to what? But he wouldn't say, and anyway, I was too busy to bother with him much."

"I'll see him, and find out what it's all about," I said. "Has he still got the paper with him, do you know?"

"Yes, he has. He patted his pocket just now when he asked me if you were here, and I heard the paper crackle."

"Thanks, Clem," I said.

I went outside. The race was over, the winner was being led towards the unsaddling enclosure in front of the weighing room, and down from the stands streamed the hundreds of chattering racegoers. I stood near the weighing-room door, waiting for Joe and catching up with the latest gossip. Liverpool, I learned, had been disappointing, fabulous, bloody, a dead loss and the tops, according to who told it. I had not been there. I had been too busy getting intensive treatment on my shoulder muscles to help my strength back.

Sandy clapped me soundly on the back as he passed, remarking that it was "Bloody good to see your old physog on the horizon again, even if you do look like an understudy for Scarface." He went on, "Have you seen Joe? The little drip's been squealing for you."

"So I hear," I said. "I'm waiting for him now."

A couple of press men asked me my riding plans, and made note about Admiral for their morning edition. Sir Creswell Stampe noticed my existence with a nod of his distinguished head and the characteristic puffing up on his top lip which passed with him for a smile.

My content at being back in my favourite environment was somewhat marred by the sight of Dane strolling across the grass, talking intently to a slender, heart-catchingly beautiful girl at his side. Her face was turned intimately towards his, and she was laughing. It was Kate.

When they saw me they quickened their steps and approached me smiling, a striking pair evenly matched in grave and dark good looks.

Kate, who had got used to my battered face over lunch some days earlier, greeted me with a brisk "Hi, there," from which all undertones of love and longing were regrettably absent. She put her hand on my arm and asked me to walk down the course with her and Dane to watch the next race from beside the water jump.

I glanced at Dane. His smile was faint, and his dark eyes looked at me inscrutably, without welcome. My own muscles had tensed uncontrollably when I saw him and Kate together; so now I knew exactly how he felt about me.

It was as much unease over the low ebb of our friendship as desire to chase Claud Thiveridge which made me say, "I can't come at this instant. I must find Joe Nantwich first. How about later on . . . if you'd like to walk down again?"

"All right, Alan," she said. "Or maybe we could have tea together?" She turned away with Dane and said, "See you later," over her shoulder with a mischievous grin, in which I read her mockery of the jealousy she could arouse in me.

Watching them go, I forgot to look out for Joe, and went in to search for him through the weighing and changing rooms again. He wasn't there.

Pete towered over me as I returned to my post outside the door and greeted me like a long-lost friend. His hat tipped back on his big head, his broad shoulders spreading apart the lapels of his coat, he gazed with good humour at my face, and said, "They've made a good job of sewing you up, you know. You were a very gory sight indeed last time I saw you. I suppose you still can't remember what happened?"

"No," I said, regretfully. "Sometimes I think . . . but I can't get hold of it . . ."

"Perhaps it's just as well," he said comfortingly, hitching the strap of his race glasses higher on to his shoulder and preparing to go into the weighing room.

"Pete," I said, "have you seen Joe anywhere? I think he's been asking for me."

"Yes," he said. "He was looking for you at Liverpool, too. He was very keen to show you something, an address I think, written on some brown paper."

"Did you see it?" I asked.

"Yes, as a matter of fact I did, but he annoys me and I didn't pay much attention. Chichester, I think the place was."

"Do you know where Joe is now?" I asked. "I've been waiting for him for some time, but there isn't a sign of him."

Pete's thin lips showed contempt. "Yes, I saw the little brute going into the bar, about ten minutes ago."

"Already!" I exclaimed.

"Drunken little sod," he said dispassionately. "I wouldn't put him up on one of my horses if he was the last jockey on earth."

"Which bar?" I pressed.

"Eh? Oh, the one at the back of Tattersall's, next to the Tote. He and another man went in with that dark fellow he rides for . . . Tudor, isn't that his name?"

I gaped at him. "But Tudor finished with Joe at Cheltenham . . . and very emphatically, too."

Pete shrugged. "Tudor went into the bar with Joe and the other chap a few steps behind him. Maybe it was only coincidence."

"Thanks, anyway," I said.

It was only a hundred yards round one corner to the bar where Joe had gone. It was a long wooden hut backing on to the high fence which divided the racecourse from the road. I wasted no time, but nonetheless when I stepped into the building and threaded my way through the overcoated, beer-drinking customers, I found that Joe was no longer there. Nor was Clifford Tudor.

I went outside again. The time for the second race was drawing near, and long impatient queues waited at the Tote next door to the bar, eyes flickering between racecards and wrist watches, money clutched ready in hopeful hands. The customers from the bar poured out, hurrying past me. Men were running across the grass towards the stands, coattails flapping. Bells rang loudly in the Tote building, and the queues squirmed with the compulsion to push their money through the little windows before the shutters came down.

I hovered indecisively. There was no sign of Joe in all this activity, and I decided to go up to the jockeys' box in the stands and look for him there. I put my head into the bar for a final check, but it was now empty except for three ageing young ladies mopping up the beer-slopped counter.

It was only because I was moving so slowly that I found Joe at all.

Owing to the curve of the road behind them, the Tote and bar buildings did not stand in a perfectly straight line. The gap between the two was narrow at the front, barely eighteen inches across; but it widened farther back until, by the high fence itself, the Tote and bar walls were four or five feet apart.

I glanced into this narrow area as I passed. And there was Joe. Only I did not know it was Joe until I got close to him.

At first I saw only a man lying on the ground in the corner made by the boundary fence and the end wall of the Tote, and thinking he might be ill, or faint, or even plain drunk, went in to see if he needed help.

He lay in shadow, but something about his shape and ragdoll relaxedness struck me with shocking recognition as I took the five or six strides across to him.

He was alive, but only just. Bright red frothy blood trickled from his nose and the corner of his mouth, and a pool of it lay under his cheek on the weedy gravel. His round young face still wore, incredibly, a look of sulky petulance, as if he did not realise that what had happened to him was more than a temporary inconvenience.

Joe had a knife in his body. Its thick black handle protruded incongruously from his yellow and white checked shirt, slanting downwards from underneath his breastbone. A small patch of blood stained the cloth round it, a mild enough indication of the damage the blade was doing inside.

His eyes were open, but vague and already glazing.

I said, urgently, "Joe!"

His eyes came round to mine and I saw them sharpen into focus and recognise me. A muscle moved in his cheek and his lips opened. He made a great effort to speak.

The scarlet blood suddenly spilled in a gush from his nostrils and welled up in a sticky, bottomless pool in his open mouth. He gave a single choking sound that was almost indecently faint, and over his immature face spread a look of profound astonishment. Then his flesh blanched and his eyes rolled up, and Joe was gone. For several seconds after he died his expression said clearly, "It's not fair." The skin settled in this crisis into the lines most accustomed to it in life.

Fighting nausea at the sweet smell of his blood, I shut the eyes with my fingers, and sat back on my heels, looking at him helplessly.

I knew it was useless, but after a moment or two I opened his coat and felt in his pockets for the brown paper he had wanted to show me. It was not there, and his death would not have made sense if it had been. The brown paper was, I thought, the wrapping from Joe's last payment for stopping a horse. It had to be. With something about it which he thought would disclose who had sent it. A postmark? An address? Something to do with chickens, Clem had said; and Pete said it was Chichester. Neither of these held any significance at all for me. According to Clem it meant nothing to Joe either, and he was simply going to show it to me because he had said he would.

He had always been too talkative for his own good. Not quick or quiet. Prudently and privately he could have telephoned to tell me his discovery as soon as he made it. But instead he had flourished the paper at Liverpool. Someone had taken drastic steps to make sure he did not show it to me.

"Poor, silly blabbermouth," I said softly, to his still body.

I got to my feet, and went back to the narrow entrance of the little area. There was no one about. The voice of the commentator boomed over the loudspeakers that the horses were approaching the second open ditch, which meant that the race was already half over and that I would have to hurry.

I ran the last fifty yards to the Clerk of the Course's office and thrust open the door. A nondescript, grey-haired man in glasses, sitting at a desk, looked up, startled, his pen in mid-air and the paper he was writing on pressed under the palm of his hand. He was the Clerk of the Course's secretary.

"Mr. Rollo isn't here?" I asked unnecessarily, glancing round the otherwise empty office.

"He's watching the race. Can I help you?" A dry voice, a dry manner. Not the sort of man one would choose to announce a murder to. But it had to be done. Suppressing all urgency from my voice I told him plainly and quietly that Joe Nantwich was lying dead between the Tote and the bar with a knife through his lungs. I suggested that he send for a canvas screen to put across the gap between the two buildings, as when the crowds began to stream towards the bar and the playing-out Tote windows after the race, someone would be certain to see him. The ground round his body would be well trodden over. Clues, if there were any, would be lost.

The eyes behind the spectacles grew round and disbelieving.

"It's not a joke," I said desperately. "The race is nearly over. Tell the police then. I'll find a screen." He still did not move. I could have shaken him, but I could not spare the time. "Hurry," I urged. But his hand had still not gone out to his telephone when I shut the door.

The ambulance room was attached to the end of the weighing-room building. I went in in a hurry, to find two motherly St. John's nurses drinking tea. I spoke to the younger one, a middle-aged soul of ample proportions.

"Put that down and come with me quickly," I said, hoping she would not argue. I picked up a stretcher which was standing against the wall, and as she put her cup down slowly, I added, "Bring a blanket. There's a man hurt. Please hurry."

The call to duty got my nurse moving without demur, and picking up a blanket she followed me across the paddock, though at under half speed.

The commentator's voice rose slightly as he described the race from the last fence, and crisply into the silence when the cheers died away came another voice announcing the winner. I reached the gap by the Tote building as he spoke the names of the second and third horses.

The final stalwart punters began to drift back towards the bar. I looked in at Joe. He had not been disturbed.

I set the stretcher up on end on its handles, to make a sort of screen across the gap. The nurse came up to me, breathing audibly. I took the blanket from her and hung it over the stretcher so that no one could see into the area at all.

"Listen," I said, trying to speak slowly. "There is a man between these two buildings. He is dead, not hurt. He has been killed with a knife. I am going to make sure that the police are coming, and I want you to stand here holding the stretcher up like this. Don't let anyone past you until I come back with a policeman. Do you understand?"

She did not answer. She twisted the stretcher a little so that she could peer through the gap. She took a long look. Then, drawing up her considerable bosom and with the light of battle in her eyes, she said firmly, "No one shall go in, I'll see to that."

I hurried back to the Clerk of the Course's office. Mr. Rollo was there himself this time, and after I had told him what had happened things at last began to move.

It is always difficult to find a place to be alone at the races. After I had taken a policeman along to where Joe lay, and seen the routine bustle begin, I needed a pause to think. I had had an idea while I crouched beside Joe's body, but it was not one to be acted upon headlong.

People thronged everywhere in the paddock and the racecourse buildings, and to get away from them I walked out on to the course and over the rough grass in the centre until the stands were some way behind. Distance, I hoped, would give me a sense of proportion as well as solitude.

I thought about Bill and Scilla, and also about what I owed to my father, now back in Rhodesia. I thought about the terrorised pub-keepers in Brighton and the bloody face of Joe Nantwich.

It was no use pretending that Joe's murder had not made a great deal of difference to the situation, for until now I had blithely pursued Mr. Claud Thiveridge in the belief that though he might arrange for people to be beaten up, he did not purposely kill. Now the boundary was crossed. The next killing would come easier, and the next easier still. The plucky, dog-owning rebels against protection were in greater danger than before, and I was probably responsible.

Joe had shown his brown paper to several people, and no one, including apparently himself, had immediately seen the meaning of what was written on it. Yet he had been killed before he could show it to me. To me, then, the words would have told their tale. Perhaps to me alone.

I watched the rising wind blowing the grass in flattening ripples across the course, and heard the distant voices of the bookmakers as they shouted the odds for the next race.

The question to be answered was simple. Was I, or was I not, going on with the chase. I'm no hero. I did not want to end up dead. And there was no doubt that the idea I had had beside Joe's body was as safe as a stick of dynamite in a bonfire.

The horses for the third race came out and cantered down to the start. Idly I watched them. The race was run, the horses returned to the paddock: and still I stood in the centre of the course, dithering on top of my mental fence.

At last I walked back to the paddock. The jockeys were already out in the parade ring for the fourth race, and as I reached the weighing room one of the racecourse officials grabbed my arm, saying the police had been looking everywhere for me. They wanted me to make a statement, he said, and I would find them in the Clerk of the Course's office.

I went along there, and opened the door.

Mr. Rollo, spare and short, leaned against the window wearing a worried frown. His grey-haired bespectacled secretary still sat at his desk, his mouth slightly open as if even yet he had not grasped the reality of what had happened.

The police inspector, who introduced himself as Wakefield, had established himself at Mr. Rollo's table, and was attended by three constables, one of them armed with shorthand notebook and pencil. The racecourse doctor was sitting on a chair by the wall, and a man I did not know stood near him.

Wakefield was displeased with me for what he called my irresponsibility in disappearing for over half an hour at such a time. Big and thick, he dominated the room. Authority exuded from his short upspringing grey hair, his narrow eyes, his strong stubby fingers. A policeman to put the fear of God into evildoers. His baleful glare

suggested that at the moment I should be included in
this category.

"If you're quite ready, Mr. York," he began sarcasti-
cally, "we'll take your statement."

I looked round the crowded little office, and said, "I
prefer to make my statement to you alone."

The inspector growled and erupted and argued; but
finally everyone left except Wakefield, myself, and the
notebook constable, to whom I agreed as a compromise.
I told Wakefield exactly what had happened. The whole
truth, and nothing but the truth.

Then I went back to the weighing room, and to every
one of the dozens who clustered round asking for an
eyewitness account, I said I had found Joe alive. Yes, I
agreed steadily, he had spoken to me before he died.
What did he say? Well, it was only two or three words,
and I preferred not to discuss it at present, if they did
not mind. I added that I had not actually mentioned it
to the police yet, but of course I would if I thought it
would be important. And I put on a puzzled, thoughtful
expression, hoping I looked as if I had a key in my hand
and was on the point of finding the right lock to put it
in.

I took Kate to tea, and Pete, catching sight of us, came
over to join us. To them, too, I told the same story,
feeling ashamed, but not caring to risk their broadcasting
the truth, that Joe had died without uttering a syllable.

Shortly before the sixth race I left the meeting. The
last thing I saw, as I glanced back from the gate, was
Wakefield and Clifford Tudor standing outside the door
of the Clerk of the Course's office, shaking hands. Tudor, who had been with Joe so soon before his death,
had apparently been "assisting the police with their investigations." Satisfactorily, it seemed.

I went through the car park to the Lotus, started up,
and drove out towards the west, and along the straight
secondary roads of the South Downs I opened up the

engine and sent the little car along at over a hundred. No Marconicars, I thought with satisfaction, could compete with that. But to make quite certain I was not being followed I stopped once at a vantage point on top of a rise, and studied the road behind me with raceglasses. It was deserted. There was nothing on my tail.

About thirty miles from the racecourse I stopped at an undistinguished roadhouse and booked a room for the night. I insisted also on a lock-up garage for the car. It was too far from Brighton to be within the normal reach of the Marconicars, but I was taking no chances. I wanted to be invisible. It is one thing to stick your neck out; but quite another to go to sleep in full view of the axe.

After a dull dinner I went to my room and wrote a letter to my father. A difficult one. I told him about Joe's death, and that I was trying to use it to entice Mr. Thiveridge out of his lair. I asked him, as lightly as I could, to forgive me. I am, I wrote, only hunting another crocodile.

I finished the letter, sealed it, went early to bed, and lay awake for a long time before I slept.

On the way back to the racecourse in the morning I stopped at a post office and air-mailed my letter. I also acquired four shillings' worth of pennies, which I stacked into a paper-wrapped roll. I took the spare pair of socks out of my overnight case and slid the roll of pennies down into the foot of one of them, knotting them there securely. I swung my little cosh experimentally on to the palm of my hand. It was heavy enough, I thought, to knock a man out. I put it in my trouser pocket and finished the journey to the course.

I asked a constable on duty in the paddock where I could find Inspector Wakefield if I wanted him. The constable said that Wakefield was at the station, he thought, and was not coming to the course that afternoon, although he had been there in the morning. I thanked him, and went into the weighing room, and asked several people in a loud voice to tell me if they saw Inspector Wakefield about, as I wanted to have a word with him about what Joe had said to me before he died.

The awareness of danger, though I had brought it on myself, had a noticeable effect on my nerves. The wrought-up, quickened pulse of a race was unduly magnified, so that I could hear my own heart beating. Every noise seemed louder, every chance remark more significant, every light brighter. But I was not so much afraid as excited.

I was careful only about what I turned my back to, having no intention of being attacked from behind. It was more likely, I thought, that someone would try to cajole me into an out of the way place as they must have done with Joe, because most of the racecourse was too public for murder.

A knife in the ribs seemed what I should be most wary of. Effective in Joe's case, it had the advantages—to its wielder—of being silent and accurate. Moreover the weapon was left with the body, so that there was no subsequent difficulty in getting rid of it. The black handle protruding from Joe had the familiar knobbed shape of the sort of French steel cooking knife on sale in any hardware shop. Too common to be a clue of any kind, I suspected, and easy to replace with another to stick into the guts of a second victim. If anyone tried that I intended to be ready. My fingers closed comfortably on the pennies in my pocket.

I hoped to be able to deliver an attacker (unconscious from a four-shilling bump behind the ear) to Inspector Wakefield, to be charged with attempted murder. I had great faith that Wakefield's bulldog personality would shake information out of the toughest criminal in those circumstances, and that with reasonable luck a firm clue to Thiveridge's identity might disclose itself. It was too much to hope that Thiveridge would appear himself. I believed his husky avowal to me on the telephone that he hated personal violence and ordered others to do his dirty work for him, out of his squeamish sight.

I changed, and weighed on the trial scales, and chatted, and went about my ordinary business, and waited.

Nothing happened.

No one asked me to step into dim corners to discuss private business. No one showed any particular interest in what Joe was supposed to have told me before he died. Naturally his murder was still the chief topic of conversation, but it lost ground as the day wore on, and the living horses became more interesting to the inmates of the weighing room than the dead jockey.

Admiral was to run in the fifth race. By the time the fourth was over my nerves had calmed down and my tense readiness had evaporated. I had expected action before this. I had been at the meeting for nearly three hours, a man with essential information inviting to have his mouth permanently shut, and no move had been made against me.

It crossed my mind, not for the first time, that cause and effect in the Thiveridge organisation never followed closely on each other. Joe's death happened two whole days after he showed his brown paper at Liverpool. The warning to me on the telephone was delivered two days after I had spread at Cheltenham the news of the wire which had killed Bill. The horse-box affair had taken at least a day to arrange. The Bristol wire was rigged to bring me down two days after my excursion into the Marconicar office.

I had begun to suspect that the whole organisation was still geared to the telephone call Thiveridge made every morning to Fielder, and that Fielder had no other way of getting urgent messages to his "Chairman," or of receiving instructions from him. Presumably Thiveridge still felt the delay in his news service was a lesser evil than providing an address or telephone number at which he could be reached and perhaps discovered.

Depressed, I was coming to believe that my carefully acted lies had not at all reached the ears for which they were meant, and felt that offering myself as bait to a predator who did not know he should be hunting me was a bit idiotic.

Trying to shake off this deflation, I went out to the parade ring to join Pete and mount Admiral. Bill's horse, now mine, looked as splendid as ever. With his intelligent head, deep chest, straight hocks, and good bone below the knee, he was a perfect example of what a top class steeplechaser should be.

"Even though he hasn't been on a racecourse since that ghastly day at Maidenhead, he's at the top of his form," said Pete, admiring him beside me. "You can't lose the race, so go along quietly for a while, getting used to him. You'll find he has plenty in reserve. You'll never get to the bottom of him. Bill used to take him to the front early on, as you know, but you don't need to. He's got a terrific turn of foot from the last."

"I'll do as you say," I said.

Pete gave me a leg-up. "Admiral's odds-on, again," he said. "If you make a mess of this race the crowd'll murder you. So will I." He grinned.

"I'll try to stay alive," I said, grinning back cheerfully.

Admiral was as superb to ride as he looked. He put himself right before every fence, making his spring at exactly the right moment and needing no help from the saddle. He had the low, flowing galloping stride of the really fast mover, and from the first fence onward I found racing on his back an almost ecstatic pleasure. Following Pete's advice I went round the whole course without forcing the pace, but riding into the last fence alongside two others, I gave Admiral a kick in the ribs and shook up the reins. He took off from just inside the wings and landed as far out on the other side, gaining two lengths in the air and shedding the other two horses like dead leaves. We came home alone, easy winners, to warm cheers from the stands.

In the winner's unsaddling enclosure, where I dismounted and undid the girths, Admiral behaved as if he had only been out for an exercise gallop, his belly hardly moving as he breathed. I patted his glossy chestnut neck, noticed that he was hardly sweating at all, and asked Pete, "What on earth can he do if he really tries?"

"The National, no less," said Pete, rocking back on his heels, and tipping his hat off his face, as he collected his due congratulations from all around.

I grinned, pulled the saddle off over my arm, and went into the weighing room to weigh-in and change. The familiar joy of winning flushed through my limbs, as warming as a hot bath, and I could have done handsprings down the changing room if I hadn't known it was the horse to whom all credit was due, not the jockey.

Pete called to me to hurry up and we'd have a celebration drink together, so I changed quickly and went outside to join him. He steered me towards the bar next to the Tote building, and we stopped at the gap, looking in to where Joe had died. There was a shoulder-high wooden fence across the entrance now, to keep sensation seekers out. A rusty brown stain on the gravel was all that was left of Joe.

"A terrible thing, that," Pete said, as we stepped into the bar. "What did he say to you before he died?"

"I'll tell you sometime," I said idly. "But just now I'm more interested in where Admiral runs next." And over our drinks we talked solely about horses.

Returning to the weighing room we found two men in belted raincoats waiting for us near the door. They wore trilby hats and large shoes, and gave off that indefinable aura of solid menace which characterises many plainclothes policemen.

One of them put his hand inside his coat, drew out a

folded warrant and flipped it in my direction.

"Mr. York?"

"Yes."

"Inspector Wakefield's compliments, and will you come down to the police station to help his enquiries, please." The "please" he tacked on as an afterthought.

"Very well," I said, and asked Pete to see Clem about my kit.

"Sure," he said.

I walked with the two men across to the gate and through the car park.

"I'll get my car and follow you to the station," I said.

"There's a police car waiting for us in the road, sir," said the larger of the two. "Inspector Wakefield did say to bring you in it, and if you don't mind, sir, I'd rather do as the Inspector says."

I grinned. If Inspector Wakefield were my boss I'd do as he said, too. "All right," I agreed.

Ahead of us the sleek black Wolseley was parked outside the gate, with a uniformed driver standing beside it and another man in a peaked cap in the front passenger's seat.

Away towards my right, in front of the ranks of parked horse-boxes, several of the runners from Admiral's race were being led up and down to get the stiffness out of their limbs before they were loaded up for the journey home. Admiral was among them, with Victor, his lad, walking proudly at his head.

I was telling the man on my right, the smaller of the two, that there was my horse and wasn't he a beauty, when I got a shock which knocked the breath out of me as thoroughly as a kick in the stomach.

To cover myself I dropped my race glasses on to the turf and bent slowly to pick them up, my escort stopping a pace ahead of me to wait. I grasped the strap and slung it over my shoulder, straightening and looking back at the same time to where we had come from. Forty yards of grass separated us from the last row of cars. There was no one about except some distant people going home. I looked at my watch. The last race was just about to begin.

I turned round unhurriedly, letting my eyes travel blankly past the man on my right and on towards Admiral, now going away from me. As usual after a race, he was belted into a rug to avoid cooling down too quickly, and he still wore his bridle. Victor would change that for a head collar when he put him in the horse-box.

Victor's great drawback was his slow wits. Endowed with an instinctive feeling for horses and an inborn skill in looking after them, he had never risen above "doing his two" in forty years of stable life, and never would. I would have to do without much help from him.

"Victor," I shouted, and when he turned round I signalled to him to bring Admiral over.

"I just want to make sure the horse's legs are all right," I explained to the two men. They nodded and waited beside me, the larger one shifting from foot to foot.

I did not dare to take a third look, and in any case I knew I was not mistaken.

The man on my right was wearing the tie I had lost in the horse-box on Maidenhead Thicket.

It was made from a piece of silk which had been specially woven and given to me on my twenty-first birthday by a textile manufacturer who wanted to do business with my father. I had two other ties like it, and a scarf, and the pattern of small red and gold steamships interlaced with the letter Y on a dark green background was unique.

How likely was it that a junior C.I.D. officer should have come honestly by my tie, I asked myself urgently. Farmer Lawson had not found it, and none of his men admitted to having seen it. It was too much of a coincidence to be innocent that it should reappear round the throat of a man who was asking me to step into a car and go for a ride with him.

Here was the attack I had been waiting for, and I had damn nearly walked meekly into the trap. Getting out of it, when it was so nearly sprung, was not going to be easy. The "police" car was parked across the gateway barely twenty paces ahead, with the driver standing by the bonnet and looking in our direction. The menacing aura of my two tough escorts now revealed itself to be something a great deal more sinister than a manner assumed to deal with crooks. One of them, perhaps, had killed Joe.

If I gave the slightest sign of doubting them, I was sure the three of them would hustle me into the car and drive off in a cloud of dust, leaving only Victor to report doubtfully what he had seen. And that, as far as I was concerned, would be that. It was to be one of those rides from which the passenger did not return.

My plan to present Wakefield with an attempted murderer was no good. One, I could have managed. But not three, and another sitting in the car.

When Victor was within fifteen paces of me I let the strap of my race glasses slip from my shoulder, down my arm and into my hand. Abruptly, with all my strength, I swung the glasses like a scythe round the legs of the larger man and overbalanced him, tripped the smaller man with the one elementary judo throw I knew, and sprinted for Admiral.

The five seconds it took them to recover from the unexpected assault were enough. As they started after me with set faces I leaped on to Admiral's back, picked up the reins which lay loosely on his neck, and turned him round sharply out of Victor's grasp.

The third man was running towards me from the car. I kicked Admiral into a canter in two strides, swerving round the advancing chauffeur, and set him toward the hedge which formed the boundary of the car park. He cleared it powerfully, landing on the grass verge of the road a few yards in front of the black car. The fourth man had the door open and was scrambling out. I looked back quickly.

Victor was standing stock-still with his mouth open. The three men were all running towards the gate with purposeful strides. They had nearly reached it. I had barely time to hope they were not carrying guns, since I presented a large and close target, when I saw the sun glint on something bright in the hand of the man who was wearing my tie. It hardly seemed the moment to stop and discover whether the glint came from a black-handled chef's knife: but I nearly found out the hard way, because he drew back his arm and threw it at me. I flung myself flat on the horse's neck and it missed, and I heard it clatter on to the road beyond.

I urged Admiral straight across the road, ignoring the squeal of brakes from a speeding lorry, and jumped him into the field opposite. The land sloped upwards, so that when I reined in about halfway up it and turned round to see what was happening, the road and the car park were spread out below like a map.

The men were making no attempt to follow. They had moved the Wolseley away from the gate and were now drawing to a halt some yards farther along on the verge. It looked as if all four were inside the car.

Victor still stood in the car park, scratching his head as he looked up towards me. I could imagine his bewilderment. I wondered how long it would be before he went to tell Pete what had happened.

Once the last race was over the car park would be buzzing with people, and cars would pour out of the now unobstructed gateway. I thought that then I would be able to return safely to the racecourse without being abducted.

At this point another black car drew up behind the

Wolseley, and then another, and several others, until a line of eight or more stretched along the side of the road. There was something rather horribly familiar about the newcomers.

They were Marconicars.

chapter 15

ALL THE DRIVERS climbed out of the taxis and walked along towards the Wolseley. With its low expensive lines and its efficient-looking aerial on top, it still looked every inch a police car, but the reinforcements it had called up dispelled any last doubts it was possible to have about the nature of the "C.I.D. officers."

The men stood in a dark group on the road, and I sat on Admiral halfway up the field watching them. They seemed to be in no hurry, but having seen their armoury of bicycle chains, knives, and assorted knuckledusters when they fought the London gang at Plumpton, and with Joe's fate constantly in mind, I had no doubt what would happen if I let them catch me.

I was in a good position. They could not drive the taxis up the field because there was no gate into it from the road, nor could they hope to reach me on foot, and I was still confident that when the race crowd flocked out I could evade the enemy and return to the course.

Two things quickly happened to change the picture.

First, the men began looking and pointing towards the side of the field I was in. Turning my head to the right I saw a car driving downhill on the farther side of the hedge, and realised that there was a road there. Twisting round, I now took note for the first time that a large house with out-buildings and gardens spread extensively across the skyline.

Three of the taxis detached themselves from the line and drove round into the road on my right, stopping at intervals along it. I now had taxi-drivers to the right and ahead, and the big house at my back, but I was still not unduly dismayed.

Then yet another Marconicar came dashing up and stopped with a jerk in front of the Wolseley. A stocky man swung open the door and raised himself out of the driver's seat. He strode across the road to the hedge, and stood there pointing up at me with his arm extended. I was still wondering why when I heard the low whine of a bullet passing at the level of my feet. There was no sound of a shot.

As I turned Admiral to gallop off across the field, a bullet hit the ground with a phut in front of me. Either the range was too far for accurate shooting with a gun fitted with a silencer, or . . . I began to sweat . . . the marksman was aiming deliberately low, not at me but at Admiral.

It was only an eight or ten acre field, nothing like big enough for safety. I used precious moments to pull the horse up and take a look at the ragged sprawling hedge on the far side of the field. It was threaded halfway up with barbed wire. Over my shoulder I could see the man with the gun running along the road parallel to the course I had just taken. He would soon be within range again.

I took Admiral back a little way, faced him towards the hedge and urged him to jump. He cleared the whole thing, wire and all, without bending so much as a twig. We landed in another field, this time occupied by a herd of cows but again small and much too open to the road. Also, I discovered, trotting along the top boundary, that barbed wire had been laid lavishly in three strong strands all round it. All pastures have a gate, however, and I came to it in the farthest corner. I opened it, guided Admiral through into the next field, and shut it behind me.

This field was fenced with posts and wire only, and it was the extent of the barbed wire which decided me then to put as much space as I could between me and my pursuers in the shortest possible time. If I let the taxi-drivers follow me slowly from field to field I might find myself in a corner that even Admiral could not jump out of.

I was glad the sun was shining, for at least I could tell in which direction I was going. Since I was already headed towards the east, and because it seemed sensible to have a definite destination to aim for, I decided to take Admiral back to his own stable in Pete's yard.

I reckoned I had about twelve miles to cover, and I racked my brains to remember what the country was like in between. I knew the patchwork farmland which I was then grappling with gave way at some point ahead to Forestry Commission plantations. Then there would be a short distance of bare downland before I reached the hollow and the small village where Pete trained. Of the roads which crossed this area I had but the vaguest idea, and on any of them I could be spotted by a cruising Marconicar.

With this thought uncomfortably in mind, I found another by-road ahead. I let myself out on to it through a gate, and was trotting down it, looking for an opening in the neglected growth on the other side, when a squat black car swept round a distant bend and sped uphill towards me. Without giving Admiral a good chance to sight himself I turned him sharply towards the overgrown hedge and kicked his ribs.

It was too high for him, and too unexpected, but he did his best. He leaped straight into the tangle of sagging

wire and beech saplings, crashed his way heavily
through, and scrambled up almost from his knees on to
the higher ground of the next field. It had been ploughed
and planted with mangolds and made heavy going, but
I urged him into a canter, hearing behind me the screech
of brakes forcefully applied. A glance showed me the
driver thrusting through the hole Admiral had made, but
he did not try to chase me and I realised thankfully that
he was not the man with the gun.

All the same, he had his radio. My whereabouts would
be known to all the Marconicars within a minute.

I put another field between us and the taxi before pulling up and dismounting to see what damage Admiral
had done himself. To my relief there were only a few
scratches and one jagged cut on his stifle from which a
thread of blood was trickling. I left it to congeal.

Patting his neck and marvelling at how he retained his
calm sensible nature in very upsetting circumstances, I
grasped the leather roller he wore round his middle, and
sprang up again on to his back. The rug he was wearing
now gaped in a right-angled tear on one side, but I decided not to take it off as it gave more purchase for my
legs than riding him completely bare-back.

Three or four fields farther on the arable land began
to give way to bracken, and ahead lay the large enclosures of the Forestry Commission.

The trees, mostly conifers, were being grown in large
orderly expanses with rough tracks between each section. These acted both as convenient roadways for the
foresters and as breaks in case of fire. They occurred
about one in each half-mile, and were crossed at intervals by tracks leading in the opposite direction.

I wanted to set a course towards the southeast, but by
consulting my watch and the sun in conjunction, found
that the tracks ran from almost due north to south, and
from east to west. Fretting at the extra mileage this was
going to cost me, I steered Admiral into an east-

bound track, took the next turning right to the south, then the next left to the east, and so on, crab-wise across the forest.

The sections of trees were of varying ages and stages of growth, and turning again to the south, I found the area on my left was planted with trees only two feet high. This did not specially alarm me until I saw, a hundred yards to my left, a red and white motor coach speeding along apparently through the middle of the plantation.

I pulled Admiral up. Looking carefully I could see the posts and the high wire fence which formed the boundary between the little trees and the road beyond. If I turned east at the next track according to schedule, I would be facing straight down to the road.

The far side of the road looked similar to the section I was in: regular rows of conifers, put there by careful design.

At some point, I knew, I would have to cross a road of some sort. If I retreated back into the part of the forest I had crossed and took no risks, I would have to stay there all night. All the same, I thought, as I cantered Admiral along the southbound track and turned into the east one, I could have wished for more cover just at that moment.

Ahead of me the wire gates to the road were open, but before going through them I stopped and took a look at the other side of the road. Not all the plantations were surrounded by high mesh wire like the one I was in, and opposite only three strands of plain wire threaded through concrete posts barred the way.

The road had to be crossed quickly because where I was I felt as sheltered as a cock pheasant on a snow field. The heads in all the passing cars turned curiously towards me. But I saw nothing which looked like a Marconicar, and waiting only for a gap in the traffic, I clicked my tongue and set Admiral towards the wire

fence opposite. His hooves clattered loudly on the tarmac, drummed on the firm verge, and he lifted into the
air like a bird. There was no track straight ahead, only
some fairly sparsely growing tall pines, and as Admiral
landed I reined him in to a gentle trot before beginning
to thread a way through them.

Coming eventually to another track I checked again
with my watch and the sun to make sure it was still
running from east to west, which it was, and set off
along it at a good pace. The going underfoot was perfect,
dry and springy with loam and pine needles, and Admiral, though he had completed a three mile race and
covered several miles of an unorthodox cross-country
course, showed no signs of flagging.

We made two more turns and the sky began to cloud
over, dulling the brilliant spring afternoon, but it was
not the fading of beauty which bothered me so much as
the fact that you cannot use a wrist watch as a compass
unless the sun is shining. I would have to be careful not
to get lost.

Just ahead, to my right, a small grass-grown hill rose
sharply to its little rounded summit, the conifer forest
flowing round its edges like sea round a rock. I had now
left the bigger trees and was cantering through sections
of young feathery pines only slightly taller than the top
of my head, and I could see the hill quite clearly. A
man, a black distant silhouetted man, was standing on
the top, waving his arms.

I did not connect him with myself at all because I
thought I had slipped my pursuers, so that what happened next had the full shock of a totally unexpected
disaster.

From a track to the right, which I had not yet reached
and could not see, a sleek black shape rolled out across
my path and stopped, blocking the whole width of the
track. It was the Wolseley.

The young pines on each side of me were too thick

and low growing to be penetrated. I flung a look over my shoulder. A squat black Marconicar was bumping up the track behind me.

I was so close to the Wolseley that I could see one of the men looking out of the rear window with a gloating grin on his face, and I decided then that even if I broke Admiral's neck and my own in trying to escape, it would be a great deal better than tamely giving in.

There was scarcely a pause between the arrival of the Wolseley and my legs squeezing tight into Admiral's sides.

I had no reason to suppose he would do it. A horse can dare just so much and no more. He had had a hard day already. He might be the best hunter-'chaser in England, but. The thoughts flickered through my brain in a second and were gone. I concentrated wholly, desperately, on getting Admiral to jump.

He scarcely faltered. He put in a short stride and a long one, gathered the immense power of his hindquarters beneath him, and thrust himself into the air. Undeterred even by the opening doors and the threatening shouts of the men scrambling out of the Wolseley, he jumped clear over its gleaming black bonnet. He did not even scratch the paint.

I nearly came off when we landed. Admiral stumbled, and I slipped off the rug on to his shoulder, clinging literally for dear life to the leather roller with one hand and Admiral's plaited mane with the other. The reins hung down, swaying perilously near his galloping feet, and I was afraid he would put his foot through them and trip. I still had one leg half across his rump, and, bumping heavily against his side, I hauled myself inch by inch on to his back. A warning twinge in my shoulder told me my newly mended collar-bone could not be relied upon for too much of this, but leaning along his neck and holding on with all my strength, I reached the reins, gathered them up, and finally succeeded in reducing Admiral to a less headlong pace.

When I got my breath back I looked to see if the Wolseley was following, but it was so far behind that I was not sure whether it was moving or not. I could not spare time to stop and find out.

I realised that I had underestimated the Marconicars, and that it was only thanks to Admiral's splendid courage that I was still free. They had had an advantage in knowing the lie of the land, and had used the little hill as a spotting point. I suspected that its summit commanded quite a large area, and that as soon as I had entered the younger pines I had been seen.

I was forced to admit that they had guessed which direction I would take and had circled round in front of me. And that being so, they probably knew I had been making for Pete's stable. If I went on I should find them in my way again, with perhaps as little warning and less chance of escape.

I had left the hill behind me, and turned right again on the next track, seeing in the distance a section of taller trees. The horse cantered along tirelessly, but he could not keep it up forever. I had to reach shelter as quickly as I could, out of sight of the man still standing on the hill-top, and out of the danger of being ambushed on another of the straight and suddenly uninviting tracks. Once we were hidden in the big trees, I promised Admiral, he should have a rest.

The light was dim under the tall pines. They had been allowed to grow close together to encourage their bare trunks to height, and the crowns of foliage far above were matted together like a roof, shutting out most of the daylight. I was glad for the obscurity. I slowed Admiral to a walk and dismounted as we entered the trees, and we went quietly and deeply into them. It was like walking through a forest of telegraph poles. Which of course, I thought fleetingly, perhaps they were destined to be.

The forest felt like home, even though it was different from those I was schooled in. It was very quiet, very dark. No birds at all. No animals. The horse and I went steadily on, silent on the thick pine needles, relying on instinct to keep us on a straight course.

I did not find our situation particularly encouraging. Whichever way I went in this extensive plantation I would have to come to a road in the end, and within three or four square miles the Marconicars knew exactly where I was. They had only to stand round the forest like hounds waiting for the fox to break cover, then it would be view tally-ho over the radio intercoms and the hunt would be on again.

There was a track ahead. A narrow one. I tied the reins round a tree and went forward alone. Standing still on the edge of the track and giving, I hoped, a good imitation of a tree trunk in my tweed suit, I slowly turned my head both ways. The daylight was much stronger on the track owing to the gap in the trees over-head, and I could see quite clearly for several hundred yards. There was no one in sight.

I went back for Admiral, made a final check, and led him across the track. There was no alarm. We walked steadily on. Admiral had begun to sweat long ago and had worked up a lather after our dash away from the Wolseley, damping large patches of the rug. Now that he was cooling down it was not good for him to keep it on, but I hadn't a dry one to give him. I decided that a damp rug was better than no rug, and trudged on.

Eventually I began to hear the hum of traffic and the occasional toot of a horn, and as soon as I could see the road in the distance. I tied Admiral to a tree and went on alone again.

The end of the plantation was marked by a fence made of only two strands of stout wire, looking as if it were designed mainly to prevent picnickers driving their cars farther in than the verge. I chose a tree as near to the fence as I could get, dropped down on to my belly behind it, and wriggled forward until I could look along the road. There was only sporadic traffic on it.

On the far side of the road there were no plantations, and no fence either. It was unorganised woodland, a mixture of trees, rhododendrons and briars. Perfect cover, if I could reach it.

A heavy lorry ground past five feet from my nose, emitting a choking cloud of diesel fumes. I put my face down into the pine needles and coughed. Two saloon cars sped by in the other direction, one trying to pass the other, followed by a single-decker country bus full of carefree people taking home their Tuesday afternoon's shopping. A pair of schoolgirls in green uniform cycled past without noticing me, and when their high twittering voices had faded into the distance and the road was empty, I put my hands under my chest to heave myself up and go back for Admiral.

At that moment two Marconicars came into sight round a bend. I dropped my face down again and lay absolutely still. They drove past my head slowly, and though I did not look at them, I guessed they must be staring keenly into the forest. I hoped wholeheartedly that I had left Admiral far enough back to be invisible, and that he would not make a noise.

The Marconicars swerved across the road and pulled up on the opposite verge barely twenty-five yards away. The drivers got out of the taxis and slammed the doors. I risked a glance at them. They were lighting cigarettes, leaning casually against the taxis, and chatting. I could hear the mumble of their voices, but not what they were saying.

They had not seen me, or Admiral. Yet. But they seemed to be in no hurry to move on. I glanced at my watch. It was six o'clock. An hour and a half since I had jumped off the racecourse. More important, there was only one hour of full daylight left. When it grew dark my mobility on Admiral would end and we should have to spend the night in the forest, as I could not get him to jump a fence if he could not see it.

There was a sudden clattering noise from one of the taxis. A driver put his hand through the window and brought out a hand microphone attached to a cord. He spoke into it distinctly, and this time I could make out what he said.

"Yeah, we got the road covered. No, he ain't crossed it yet." There was some more clattering on the taxi radio, and the driver answered, "Yeah, I'm sure. I'll let you know the second we see him." He put the microphone back in the taxi.

I began to get the glimmerings of an idea of how to use the manhunt I had caused.

But first things first, I thought; and slowly I started to slither backwards through the trees, pressing close to the ground and keeping my face down. I had left Admiral a good way inside the forest, and I was now certain that the taxi-drivers could not see him. It was uncomfortable travelling on my stomach, but I knew if I stood up the drivers would see me moving among the bare tree trunks. When finally I got to my feet my suit was a filthy peat brown, clogged with prickling pine needles. I brushed off the dirt as best I could, went over to Admiral, and untied his reins.

Out in the daylight on the road I could still catch glimpses, between the tree trunks, of the two taxis and their drivers, but knowing that they could not see me, I set off towards the west, keeping parallel with the road and at some distance from it. It was, I judged, a little more than a quarter of a mile before I saw another Marconicar parked at the side of the road. I turned back and, as I went along, began to collect an armful of small dead branches. About halfway between the parked taxis, where they were all out of my sight, I took Admiral right up to the wire fence to give him a look at it. Although extremely simple in construction, it was difficult to see in the shade of the trees. I set the dead branches up on end in a row to make it appear more solid; then jumped on to Admiral's back, and, taking him back a few paces, faced him towards the fence and waited for a heavy vehicle to come along. In still air the sound of hooves on tarmacadam would carry clearly, and I did not want the taxi-drivers round the nearby bends to hear me crossing the road. The longer they believed I was still in the pine forest, the better. But how long the taxis would *remain* parked I did not know, and the palms of my hands grew damp with tension.

A motor bike sped past, and I stayed still with an effort; but then, obligingly, a big van loaded with empty milk bottles came rattling round the bend on my right. It could not have been better. As it went past me I trotted Admiral forward. He made nothing of the dead-wood patch of fence, popped over on to the grass verge, took three loping strides over the tarmac, and in an instant was safely in the scrub on the far side. The milk lorry rattled out of sight.

I pulled up behind the first big rhododendron, dismounted, and peered round it.

I had not been a second too soon. One of the Marconicars was rolling slowly along in the wake of the milk lorry, and the driver's head was turned towards the forest I had left.

If one driver believed me still there, they all did. I walked Admiral away from the road until it was safe to mount, then jumped on to his back and broke him into a slow trot. The ground now was unevenly moulded into little hillocks and hollows and overgrown with brambles, small conifers and the brown remains of last year's bracken, so I let the horse pick his own footing to a great extent while I worked out what I was going to do.

After a little way he slowed to a walk and I left him to it, because if his limbs felt as heavy and tired as mine he was entitled to crawl.

As nearly as I could judge I travelled west, back the way I had come. If there is one thing you can be sure of in England, it is that a straight line in any direction will bring you to a road without much delay, and I had covered perhaps a mile when I came to the next one. Without going too close I followed it to the north.

I was hunting a prey myself, now. A taxi, detached from the herd.

Admiral was picking his way silently across a bare patch of leaf-moulded earth when I suddenly heard the now familiar clatter of a Marconicar radio, and the answering voice of its driver. I pulled up in two strides, dismounted, and tied Admiral to a nearby young tree. Then I climbed up into the branches.

Some way ahead I saw a white four-fingered signpost, and beside it stood a Marconicar, of which only the roof and the top half of the windows were visible. The rest was hidden from me by the rhododendrons, trees, and undergrowth which crowded the ground ahead. My old friend the pine forest rose in a dark green blur away to the right.

I climbed down from the tree and felt in my pocket for the roll of pennies. I also found two lumps of sugar, which I fed to Admiral. He blew down his nostrils and nuzzled my hand, and I patted his neck gently and blessed Scilla for giving him to me.

With so much good cover it was easy enough to approach the cross-roads without being seen, but when, from the inside of an old rhododendron I at length had a clear view of the taxi, the driver was not in it. He was a youngish sallow-faced man in a bright blue suit, and he was standing bareheaded in the middle of the cross-roads with his feet well apart, jingling some coins in his pocket. He inspected all four directions, saw nothing, and yawned.

The radio clattered again, but the driver took no notice. I had intended to creep up to his taxi and knock him out before he could broadcast that I was there; but now I waited, and cursed him, and he stood still and blew his nose.

Suddenly he began to walk purposefully in my direction.

For an instant I thought he had seen me, but he had not. He wheeled round a large patch of brambles close in front of me, turned his back towards my hiding place, and began to relieve himself. It seemed hardly fair to attack a man at such a moment, and I know I was smiling as I stepped out of the rhododendron, but it was an opportunity not to be missed. I took three quick steps and swung, and the sock-wrapped roll of pennies connected solidly with the back of his head. He collapsed without a sound.

I put my wrists under his shoulders and dragged him back to where I had left Admiral. Working as quickly as I could I ripped all the brown binding off the edge of the horse rug and tested it for strength. It seemed strong enough. Fishing my penknife out of my trouser pocket I cut the binding into four pieces and tied together the driver's ankles and knees with two of them. Then I dragged him closer to the tree and tied his wrists behind him. The fourth piece of binding knotted him securely to the trunk.

I patted his pockets. His only weapon was a spiked metal knuckleduster, which I transferred to my own jacket. He began to wake up. His gaze wandered fuzzily from me to Admiral and back again, and then his mouth opened with a gasp as he realised who I was.

He was not a big man in stature, nor, I now discovered, in courage. The sight of the horse looming so close above him seemed to worry him more than his trussed condition or the bump on the head.

"He'll tread on me," he yelled, fright drawing back his lips to show a nicotine-stained set of cheap artificial teeth

"He's very particular what he walks on," I said.

"Take him away. Take him away," he shouted. Admiral began to move restlessly at the noise.

"Be quiet and he won't harm you," I said sharply to the driver, but he took no notice and shouted again. I stuffed my handkerchief unceremoniously into his mouth until his eyes bulged.

"Now shut up," I said. "If you keep quiet he won't harm you. If you screech you'll frighten him and he might lash out at you. Do you understand?"

He nodded. I took out the handkerchief, and he began to swear vindictively, but fairly quietly.

I soothed Admiral and lengthened his tether so that he could get his head down to a patch of grass. He began munching peacefully.

"What is your name?" I asked the taxi-driver.

He spat and said nothing.

I asked him again, and he said, "What the ruddy hell has it got to do with you?"

I needed particularly to know his name and I was in a hurry.

With no feelings of compunction I took hold of Admiral's reins and turned him round so that the driver had a good close view of a massive pair of hind-quarters. My captive's new-found truculence vanished in a flash. He opened his mouth to yell.

"Don't," I said. "Remember he'll kick you if you make a noise. Now, what is your name?"

"John Smith."

"Try again," I said, backing Admiral a pace nearer.

The taxi-driver gave in completely, his mouth trembling and sweat breaking out on his forehead.

"Blake." He stumbled on the word.

"First name?"

"Corny. It's a nickname, sort of." His eyes flickered fearfully between me and Admiral's hind legs.

I asked him several questions about the working of the radio, keeping the horse handy. When I had learned all I wanted I untied the reins from the tree and fastened them to a sapling a few feet away, so that when it grew dark the horse would not accidentally tread on the taxi-driver.

Before leaving them I gave Blake a final warning. "Don't start yelling for help. For one thing there's no one to hear you, and for another, you'll upset the horse. He's a thoroughbred, which means nervous, from your point of view. If you frighten him by yelling he's strong enough to break his reins and lash out at you. Shut up and he'll stay tied up. Get it?" I knew if Admiral broke his reins he would not stop to attack the man, but luckily, Blake did not. He nodded, his body sagging with fear and frustration.

"I won't forget you're here," I said. "You won't have to stay here all night. Not that I care about you, but the horse needs to be in a stable."

Admiral had his head down to the grass. I gave his rump a pat, made sure the knots were still tight on the demoralised driver, and picked my way quickly through the bushes to the taxi.

The signpost was important, for I would have to come back and find it in the dark in miles of haphazard woodland. I wrote down all the names and mileages on all of its four arms, just to make sure. Then I got into the taxi and sat in the driver's seat.

Inside the taxi one could hear the radio as a voice and not as a clatter. The receiver was permanently tuned in so that each driver could hear all messages and replies going from taxis to base and base to taxis.

A man was saying, "Sid, here. No sign of him. I've

got a good mile and a half of the road in view from up here, nearly the whole side of that wood he's in. I'll swear he hasn't got across here. The traffic's too thick for him to do it quickly. I'm sure to see him if he tries it." Sid's voice came out of the radio small and tinny, like a voice on the telephone, and he spoke casually, as if he were looking for a lost dog.

While he spoke I started the engine, sorted out the gears, and drove off along the road going south. The daylight was just beginning to fade. Half an hour of twilight, I calculated, and perhaps another ten minutes of dusk. I put my foot down on the accelerator.

There was a short silence on the radio. Then someone said, "He has got to be found before dark."

Even though I had been half-hoping, half-expecting it, the husky timbre-less whisper made me jerk in my seat. I gripped the steering wheel tightly and the muscles round my eyes contracted. The voice was so close it seemed suddenly as if the danger it spelled for me were close as well, and I had to reassure myself by looking out sideways at the deserted heartland, and backwards in the driving mirror at the empty road astern.

"We're doing our best, sir," said a quiet voice, respectfully. "I've been driving up and down this ruddy road for nearly an hour. Two miles up and two miles back. All the parked cars in my section are still in position."

"How many of you have guns?" said the whisper.

"Four altogether, sir. We could do with more, to be sure of him."

There was a pause. Then the husky voice said, "I have one here, but you haven't time to come in for it. You'll have to manage with what you've got."

"Yes, sir."

"Pay attention, all drivers. Aim for the horse. Shoot the horse. The man is not to be found with bullets in him. Do you understand?"

There was a chorus of assent.

"Fletcher, repeat your orders."

The polite taxi-driver said, "As soon as we spot him either in the trees or breaking cover, we shoot, aiming for the horse. Call up all drivers, chase and catch the man. We are to ... er ... restrain him as necessary, place him in one of the taxis, and wait for your instructions."

Halfway through this recital of plans for my disposal, I recognised his voice. The polite tone, in the first instance, gave him away. I had heard it on the Maidenhead road, luring me with its false respectability into a waiting trap: he was the driver of the horse-box. Fletcher. I made a note of it.

Suddenly, as if someone had pressed a switch, a light flooded into my brain and I remembered the fence at Bristol. I remembered the pouring rain on my face and the greyness of everything, and now clearly I remembered the horse-box driver cutting the wire down from the fence, rolling it up, and hanging it over his arm.

There was something else, too—but before I could pin it down I came to a halt sign at a main road. I turned left from my empty by-road into a stream of traffic, and began to look for a signpost which would tell me how far away I was from Brighton. After half a mile I found one. Eleven miles. Say, twenty minutes to my destination.

I thought back to the Bristol fence, but the shade had come down again in my memory, and now I was not even sure that any gaps in it remained. My fingers wandered of their own accord to the scar on my cheek and traced along it gently, but it was a gesture I had caught myself in once or twice before, and I attached no importance to it. Besides, the immediate future needed all my thought.

All the way to Brighton I listened to the husky voice. Its tone grew both more urgent and more violent. I found it weird at first to eavesdrop on a man-hunt of which I was myself the quarry, but after a few minutes I got used to it and paid it less and less attention, and this could have been a catastrophic mistake.

"Have you anything to report, twenty-three?" said the husky whisper. There was no reply on the radio. I was only half aware of it. More sharply the voice said, "Twenty-three. Blake, have you anything to report?"

I came back to the present with a jerk. I picked up the microphone, clicked over the switch, and said "No" in as bored and nasal a tone as I could muster.

"Answer more quickly next time," said the husky voice severely. He was apparently checking that all the outlying taxis were still in position, for he went on to ask three more drivers whether they had anything to report. I thanked heaven, as I switched off the microphone, that I had not had to impersonate Blake's voice for more than one second, for any attempt at conversation would have found me out. As it was, I listened more intently than before to the exchanges on the radio.

The whispering voice began to acquire tone and characteristics as I became more familiar with it, until it formed a pattern of phrasing and emphasis which tantalised me at first because I could not remember its origin.

Then I knew. I knew for sure, at last.

You can start on a plan that you think touches the limit of what you can do; and then you have to do much, much more. Once more into the breach . . . only the breach had got bigger. Stiffen the sinews, summon up the blood . . . and bend up every spirit to his full height. There was no one like Bill Shakespeare for bounding things in a nutshell.

I drove into the outskirts of Brighton very thoughtfully indeed.

chapter 16

A TAXI-DRIVER asking the way to the main police station would be enough to arouse suspicion in a moron. I parked the taxi in a side street and hurried round the corner to ask directions in the nearest shop.

It was a tobacconist's, and busy, so I buttonholed one of the customers, an elderly man with watery eyes and a cloth cap. He told me the way quite clearly, though with frequent sniffs.

"You in trouble, mate?" he enquired inquisitively, eyeing my dirty, dishevelled appearance as I thanked him.

"Lost my dog," I said, smiling, pulling out the most unexciting reason I could think of for wanting the police.

The watery-eyed man lost interest. I walked quickly back to the taxi and found two small boys listening open-mouthed to the radio. I got into the taxi, winked at them, and said, "It's a thrilling story on children's hour, isn't it?" Their faces cleared and they grinned.

I drove off. The husky voice was saying, ". . . at all costs. I don't care how you do it. He must not get away. If you can't catch him alive you must kill him. No bullets, though."

"It would be more certain if you would let us shoot him, sir," said the polite voice of Fletcher.

Real children's hour stuff. I smiled a little sourly.

Following the watery-eyed man's instructions I found the police station without trouble. Lights shone inside it as I drove past. The daylight was going quickly.

I circled the police station until I found a quiet side turning a hundred yards away. There I stopped, close to the curb. I turned on the side-lights and shut the windows. The radio was still chattering, and the man with the husky voice could no longer keep his fury in control. For a last moment I listened to him conceding, now that time was running out, to Fletcher's plea that they should be allowed to shoot me on sight. Then with a grimace I got out of the taxi, shut the door, and walked away from it.

The Marconicars office, I reckoned, was not more than half a mile off. I half-walked, half-ran towards it, looking, as I went, for a telephone. The street lamps were suddenly turned on, the bulbs glowing palely in the fading light.

The red telephone box outside a sub-post office was lit up inside, too, and although my reason told me I was in no danger, instinct would have made me stay in darkness. The whispering voice had done my nerves no good.

Though I knew I was still out of sight of the Marconicar office, I went into the telephone box with a conscious effort. I asked enquiries for the number of the Maidenhead police station, and without delay was put through to the desk sergeant. Inspector Lodge, he told me, had left an hour earlier, but after some urging he parted with Lodge's home number. I thanked him and rang off.

Fumbling with haste, I fed more coins into the machine and gave the operator the new number. It rang and rang. My heart sank, for if I couldn't get hold of Lodge quickly I did not stand nearly so good a chance of cleaning up the Marconicars the way I wanted. But at last a voice answered. A woman's.

"Inspector Lodge? Just a minute, I'll see if I can find him."

A pause. And, finally, Lodge's voice.

"Mr. York?"

I explained briefly what had happened. I said, "I've left the taxi in Melton Close, a hundred yards back from the police station here. I want you to ring the Brighton police and get them to send someone responsible to fetch it in. Tell them to listen carefully to the radio in the taxi. Our friend with the husky voice is speaking on it, inciting all the drivers to kill me. That should settle the Marconicars once and for all, I should think. One of the drivers out looking for me is called Fletcher. He's the one who drove the horse-box at Maidenhead, and he also rigged that wire for me at Bristol. I've remembered about it. It's likely he did the same for Bill Davidson, don't you think?"

"Yes, I do. Where are you now?" asked Lodge.

"In a 'phone box," I said.

"Well, go back to the taxi and wait there while I telephone the Brighton police. I don't really understand why you didn't go straight to them and explain it at first hand yourself."

"I thought it would have more weight, coming from you. And anyway . . ." I broke off, realising just in time that I could not tell Lodge what I was going to do next. I said instead, "Don't tell the Brighton police to expect me back at the taxi. I've a few 'phone calls to make . . . er . . . I must tell Scilla I'll be late, and things like that. But you won't waste any time, will you? Mr. Claud Thiveridge won't go on talking forever, especially after it gets dark."

"I'll ring at once," promised Lodge, disconnecting. I put down the receiver and pushed out into the street.

I went on my way, totting up the time I could count on before Lodge sent the Brighton police to the Marconicar office. He had to ring them up and give them a fairly lengthy account of what was going on. Then they had to find the taxi, listen to the radio, and make a short-hand record of what they heard, to be used as proof a court would accept that the whole organisation was illegal. Very shortly after that they would come chasing round to apprehend the owner of the voice. Ten minutes altogether perhaps, if they hustled; perhaps a quarter of an hour.

When the Marconicar office was in sight I stayed close to the buildings so that I should not be seen from the Marconicar window. The street was nearly empty, and across the road the Olde Oake Café had closed its doors for the night. Through the glass I could see the plump waitress tiredly piling the old oak chairs on to the old oak tables.

A small black car was parked by the curb ahead. I glanced at it cursorily, and then with sudden recognition. I stopped. I purposely had not told Lodge whose face I had attached to the husky voice, though I knew I ought to have done. The sight of his car, parked flagrantly barely twenty yards from the Marconicar door, gave me a chance to square things with my conscience. I lifted the bonnet, unclipped the distributor lid, and took off the rocker arm, which I put in my pocket. Whatever happened now, there would be no quick getaway for Mr. Thiveridge.

There were no lights in the Marconicar office, nor in any of the floors above. The neon sign, L. C. Perth, was flashing steadily on and off at two second intervals, wasting its message on the empty road. The only gambler in sight, I reflected, was myself.

Reaching the Marconicar window I bent double below the sill and edged past as close to the wall as I could press. The street door was closed, but opened readily at a touch. I stepped very quietly into the hall, leaving the door open behind me. The silence in the house was tensely oppressive, and for a cowardly instant I was tempted to go out into the street again and wait like a sensible citizen for the police.

Stepping cautiously I went down the hall and pressed my ear to the door of Fielder's room. I could hear nothing. I opened the door gently and looked in. The room was tidy and empty. Next I tried the door on my left, which led into the back office where Marigold by day presided over her radio switchboard.

Through the thick door I could hear nothing, but when I opened it an inch a faint hum reached my ears. There was no one in the office. I went quietly in.

The hum was coming from the radio equipment. A small red brightly glowing circle in the control panel indicated that it was switched on, and through a crack in the casing the tiny light of a valve shone blue-white. The microphone lay casually on its side on its ledge.

For a sickening moment I thought that my bird had flown during the time it had taken me to ring Lodge and travel the half mile from the taxi; then I remembered the car outside, and at the same time, looking for wires leading out of the radio, saw a narrow plastic-covered cable running up the far wall and into the ceiling.

Praying that the stairs in the old house would not creak, I went up them lightly and quickly, and pressed my ear to the panels of the door of the main office of L. C. Perth. There were some large painted capital letters beside my nose. I squinted across at them while I listened. They said PLEASE ENTER.

Owing to the solidity of the regency door I could hear only a fierce hissing sound, but by this time the whisper was so familiar to me that an inch of mahogany could not disguise it.

He was there.

The hair on the back of my neck began to itch.

I judged it must have been seven or eight minutes since I spoke to Lodge. As I had to give the Brighton police time to find the taxi and record something of what they would hear on its radio, I could not risk interrupting the husky voice too soon. But neither did I intend to hover where I was until the police arrived. I made myself count one hundred slowly, and it seemed the longest three minutes of my life. Then I rubbed the palm of my hand on my trousers, and gingerly took hold of the ornate glass doorknob.

It turned silently and I eased the door open a few inches. It made no noise at all. I could see straight into the unlit room.

He was sitting at a desk with his back turned squarely towards me, and he seemed to be looking out into the street. The neon sign flashed off and on outside the window, illuminating the whole of the room and lighting up his dusky outline with a red glow. Red reflections winked on chromium ashtrays and slid along the metal edges of filing cabinets. A row of black telephones, ranked like an army on a long desk, threw curious angular shadows on the wall.

At close quarters the husky whisper lost some of its disembodied menace, even though what it was saying was now almost hysterically violent.

The open door can have stirred no current of air, for the man at the desk went on talking into his microphone, completely unaware that I was standing behind him.

"Kill him," he said. "Kill him. He's in that wood somewhere. He's an animal. Hunt him. Turn your cars towards the wood and put the headlight on. You'd better start beating through the trees. Fletcher, organise it. I want York dead, and quickly. Shoot him down. Smash him."

The man paused and drew in so sharp a breath that it gagged in his throat. His hand stretched out for a glass of water, and he drank.

Fletcher's voice came tinnily into the room through an extension loud-speaker on the desk. "We haven't seen a sign of him since he went into the wood. I think he might have got past us."

The man at the desk shook with fury. He began to whisper again with a rough burring rasp.

"If he escapes, you'll pay for it. You'll pay, I tell you. I want him dead. I want him smashed. You can do what you like with him. Use those chains to good purpose, and the spiked knuckles. Tear him to pieces. If he lives it will be the end for all of us, remember that." The whisper rose in tone to a thin sound like a strangled shriek. "Rip his guts out . . . smash . . . destroy . . ."

He went on for some time elaborating on the way I should be killed, until it was clear that his mind was very nearly unhinged.

Abruptly I had heard enough. I opened the door wide, and put my hand on the light switch, and pressed it down. The room was suddenly brilliantly flooded with light.

The man at the desk whirled round and gaped at me.

"Good evening, Uncle George," I said softly.

chapter 17

His eyes scorched with hate. The vacuous expression was torn away, the hidden personality now out in the open and as mean and savage as any crocodile. He was still Kate's amusing Uncle George in corpulent outline and country-gentleman tweeds, the Uncle George who had written for boys' magazines and taken his wife to matinees, but the face was the one which had had a knife stuck into Joe Nantwich and had urged a bloodthirsty mob to tear me to bits.

His hand snaked out across the desk and came up with a gun. It was a heavy, old-fashioned pistol, cumbersome, but deadly enough, and it was pointing straight at my chest. I resolutely looked at Uncle George's eyes, and not at the black hole in the barrel. I took a step towards him.

Then it came, the instant on which I had gambled my safety.

Uncle George hesitated.

I saw the flicker, the drawing back. For all his sin, for all the horror he had spread into the lives of others, he had never himself committed an act of violence. When he had delivered his threatening warning to me on the telephone on the very morning that I went to stay in his house, he had told me that he hated even to watch violence; and in spite of, or perhaps because of, his vicarious pleasure in the brutalities of primitive nations, I believed him. He was the sort of man, I thought, who liked to contemplate atrocities he could never inflict himself. And now, in spite of the fury he felt against me, he couldn't immediately, face to face, shoot me down.

I gave him no time to screw himself up. One fast stride and I had my hand on his wrist. He was trying to stand up. Too late he found the power to kill and squeezed the trigger, but the bullet smashed harmlessly into the wall. I bent his arm outwards with force, and twisted the gun out of his grasp. His muscles were soft and without strength, and he didn't know how to fight.

I flung him back hard into his chair, knocking the wind out of him, and then I reached over and switched off his microphone. I wasn't anxious that either the police or the taxi drivers should overhear what I was going to say.

There was a crackle as I brushed against his coat. I pulled it open. A folded piece of brown paper protruded from an inner pocket, and I tugged it out and spread it open on the desk. He was gasping for breath and didn't try to stop me. I read what was on it.

Joe's address.

I turned it over. In one corner on the other side, scribbled carelessly as if someone were not sure of the spelling and had used the nearest piece of paper to try them out on, were the words:

> Chitchen Itza
> Chitchen Itsa
> Chitsen

Not chickens, not Chichester. Chichen Itza. I had the vaguest memory of having heard it before. It was the name of an emperor I thought; and it meant nothing to me, nothing. Yet Joe had died for it.

I left the paper on the desk, and hoped that the police would find it useful.

The hysteria had drained out of Uncle George. He looked suddenly ill and old, now that his day was done. I could summon no compassion for him, all the same: but then it was not regard for Kate's uncle that had brought me into the Marconicar office, but love for Kate herself.

"The police will be here in less than a minute," I said, speaking slowly and distinctly. He shifted in his seat and made a sharp helpless gesture with his pudgy hands. I went on, "They have been listening in to what you have been saying on the radio."

Uncle George's eyes widened. "Twenty-three," he said, with a remnant of anger. "Twenty-three hasn't answered my last few calls."

I nodded. I said, "You will be charged with incitement to murder. Gaol for life, at least" I paused. "Think," I said with emphasis. "Think of your wife. You did it all for her, didn't you, so that she could go on living in the luxury she was used to?" I was guessing, but I felt sure it was true, and he didn't deny it.

"You have shielded her from reality too long," I said. "What will it do to her, if you are arrested and tried, and maybe hanged?"

Or to Kate either, I added hopelessly to myself.

Uncle George listened and stared at me, and slowly his gaze fell to the pistol I still held in my hand.

"It's quicker," I said.

There was a short silence.

Very faintly in the distance I heard an alarm bell. Uncle George heard it too. He looked up. He hated me still, but he had come to the end of the line, and he knew it.

"The police," I said. The bell grew perceptibly louder.

I took the three steps across the door, turned, and tossed the gun back into Uncle George's lap. As his stubby fingers fumbled and clutched it I went through the door, closed it, and ran down the stairs. The front door was still open. I hurried through that and pulled it shut behind me. The police alarm bells were no longer ringing.

In the shadow of the building, I slipped along into the dark porch of the next-door house, and I was only just in time. Two police cars slowed, crawled, and halted in front of the Marconicar building.

Over at the Olde Oake Café the lights were out. The plump waitress had gone home.

There had been no sound from upstairs. I shivered, struck by the horrifying thought that Uncle George, having already screwed himself once to pull the trigger, might just possibly shoot a policeman instead of himself. With the gun I had so thoughtfully given back to him.

As the doors of the police cars slammed open and the black figures poured out I took the first step towards them to warn them that their quarry was armed. But Uncle George's devotion to Aunt Deb's interests remained steadfast after all. I thought that the single crashing shot in the room behind the neon sign was the best thing he had ever done for her sake.

I WAITED FOR a few minutes in my dark doorway, and while I stood there a small crowd began to collect on the pavement, drawn by the noise of the shots and the presence of the police cars. I slipped unhurriedly among them, and after a little while walked quietly away.

Round two or three turnings I found a telephone box and stepped inside, feeling in my pocket for coins. The calls to Lodge had taken all my small change, and for a moment I looked blankly at the threepenny piece and two halfpennies which were all I could dredge from my trouser pocket. Then I remembered my cosh. I untied the sock, tipped some of the pennies out on to my hand, pushed four of them into the slot, and asked the operator for Pete's number.

He answered at the second ring.

He said, "Thank God you've rung. Where the hell have you been?"

"Touring Sussex."

"And where's Admiral?"

"Well . . . I left him tied to a tree somewhere in the heathland," I said.

Pete began to sputter, but I interrupted him.

"Can you send the horse-box to collect him? Get the driver to come down to Brighton and pick me up on the sea-front, near the main pier. And Pete . . . have you got a decent map of Sussex?"

"A map? Are you mad? Don't you know where you left him? Have you really just tied the best hunter's 'chaser in the country to a tree and forgotten where?" He sounded exasperated.

"I'll find him easily if you send a map. Don't be too long, will you? I'll tell you all about it later. It's a bit complicated."

I put down the receiver, and after some thought, rang up the Blue Duck. Ex-Regimental Sergeant-Major Thomkins answered the 'phone himself.

"The enemy is routed, sergeant-major," I said. "The Marconicars are out of business."

"A lot of people will be thankful to hear it," said the strong deep voice, with a good deal of warmth.

I went on, "However, the mopping up operations are still in progress. Would you be interested in taking charge of a prisoner and delivering him to the police?"

"I would indeed," he said.

"Meet me down at the main pier, then, at the double, and I'll gen you up."

"I'm on my way," said the sergeant-major.

He joined me by the sea wall soon after I got there myself. It was quite dark by then, and the lights along the front barely lit the ghostly grey lines of the breaking waves.

We had not long to wait for the horse-box, and when it came, Pete himself poked his big bald head out of the passenger seat and called to me. He, I and the sergeant-major got into the back and sat on a couple of straw bales, and as we swayed to the movement of the box on its way west I told them all that had happened since the day Bill died at Maidenhead. All, that is, up to my last conversation with Lodge. Of my visit to the Marconicar office and the true identity of Claud Thiveridge, I said nothing. I didn't know how English law viewed the crime of inciting to suicide, and for various reasons had decided to tell no one about it.

Parts of the story Pete already knew, and part Thomkins knew, but I had to go over the whole thing for them both to get it clear from first to last.

The horse-box driver had been given my note of the all-important signpost, and by comparing it with the map Pete had brought, he drove us back to it in remarkably short time.

Both Admiral and Corny Blake were still attached to their various trees, and we led one and frog-marched the other into the horse-box. Admiral was overjoyed to see us, but Blake's emotions seemed slightly mixed, especially when he recognised Thomkins. It appeared that it was Blake who had bashed the sergeant-major on the head with one of his own bottles.

With a grin I fished Blake's brass knuckleduster out of my pocket and handed it to Thomkins. "The prisoner's armoury," I said.

Thomkins tossed the wicked-looking weapon in his hand and tried it on for size, and Blake gave one agonised look at it and rolled off his bale of straw in a dead faint.

"We had better get round by West Sussex racecourse, if you don't mind," I said. "My car is still in the car park there; I hope."

It was there, all alone in the big field, the rising moon glinting on its low dark shape. I stepped down into the road, shook hands with Thomkins and Pete, wished them luck, and watched the red tail lights of the horse-box until they disappeared into the darkness.

Then I went over and started my car, turned my back firmly on what was doubtless my duty—the answering of interminable questions in Brighton police station— and with a purring roar set off for the Cotswolds.

Driven by an irresistible curiosity, I made a detour along the coast to Portsmouth, taking a chance that the public library would still be open there; and it was. In the reference department I hefted out a volume of an encyclopedia and looked up Chichen Itza. The first spelling on the paper was the right one.

Chichen Itza. I found, was not an emperor, it was a capital city. It was the ancient Yucatan capital of the Mayas, an Indian nation who had flourished in Central America fifteen hundred years ago.

I stared at the page until the words faded into a blur.

What happened next was partly, I suppose, delayed reaction from the abysmal fear I felt when I looked into the barrel of Uncle George's gun; and partly it was hunger and a wave of deathly tiredness, and the sudden letting up of the stresses of the past weeks. My hands, my whole body began to shake. I braced my foot against the leg of the table I was sitting at and gripped the big book hard to stop it. It went on for minutes, until I could have cried with weakness, but gradually the spasm lessened, and the tension went out of my muscles, and I was just plain cold.

Chichen Itza. I stood up stiffly and closed the book

and put it back on the shelf, and went soberly out to the car. I had set a better trap than I knew, pretending to be on the point of understanding what Joe might have said before he died.

I remembered clearly the study lined with glass cases. I could see the heavy carved oak desk, the folders devoted to Indian tribes, and the one separate folder clearly marked "Mayas." Uncle George had told me too much about the Mayas; and he'd known that Chichen Itza would lead me conclusively to him.

chapter 18

WHAT I HAD not managed to do for Kate by loving her, I had done by tearing her world apart.

She stood in front of me, rigidly controlling herself, with a look of such acrid unrelenting hatred that I tasted my misery literally as a bitterness in the mouth. The banked fires were burning fiercely at last. There was a new depth and maturity in her face, as if in two weeks she had become wholly a woman. It made her more desirable than ever.

The inquest and enquiry into the life and death of George Penn had been adjourned twice, and had just ended; and police, witnesses, and Kate and I were standing in the hall of the Brighton court building, preparing to leave.

The verdict of temporary insanity was merciful, but there had been no hiding from news-scenting journalists the extent of Uncle George's criminal activities, and L. C. Perth and Marconicars had been front-page news, on and off, for a fortnight.

My getting Uncle George to kill himself had been no help after all to Aunt Deb. It had been impossible to keep the truth from her, and shock and distress had brought on a series of heart attacks, of which the fourth was fatal. But for Kate, though she knew nothing about it, it was still the best thing. She had had to face the knowledge of his guilt, but not his trial and punishment.

But my letters of condolence had been unanswered. My telephone calls had regularly found her "out." And now I saw why. She blamed me alone for the sorrows which had come to her.

"I loathe you," she said implacably. "You nauseate me. You wormed your way into our house and accepted everything we gave you . . ." I thought of those gentle kisses, and so, from the extra flash in her eyes, did Kate . . . "and all you have done in return is to hound a poor old man to his death, and kill a defenceless old woman as a result. I have no Uncle and no Aunt. I have no one anywhere at all. I have no one." She spoke in anguish. "Why did you do it? Why couldn't you leave them alone? Why did you have to destroy my home? You knew how much I loved them. I can't bear to look at you, I loathe you so much . . ."

I swallowed, and tried to work some saliva into my dry mouth. I said, "Do you remember the children who had to be driven to school by a judo expert to keep them safe?"

But Kate stared blackly back as if she hadn't heard. "You are the most beastly person I have ever known, and although you have made it impossible for me to forget you, I shall never think of you without . . . without . . ." Her throat moved convulsively as if she were going to be sick. She turned away abruptly and walked unsteadily out through the big main door into the street.

The flash of camera bulbs met her and caught her unawares, and I saw her throw up her arm in a forlorn attempt to hide her face. The vulnerability and the loneliness in the droop of her shoulders cried out for comfort, and I who most wanted to give it, was the only person she wouldn't accept it from. I watched her walk quickly through the questioning newspapermen and get into the hired car which was waiting for her.

It drove off. I stared after it, numbly.

Presently I became aware that Lodge was standing at my elbow and had been talking for some seconds. I hadn't heard a word he said, and he appeared to be waiting for a reply.

"I beg your pardon," I said "What did you say?"

Lodge glanced out through the door where Kate had gone and sighed. "It wasn't very important. Look, she'll see things more reasonably in a little while, when she begins to think straight again. I heard a good deal of what she said . . . but you aren't to blame because her uncle took to crime."

"If I had known . . ." I stopped, on the verge of adding the give-away words "for sure": "If I had known that George Penn was Claud Thiveridge, I would have done things differently."

"Things worked out well for the Penns, I think," said Lodge. "A quick end has its mercies."

His tone was loaded with meaning, and I knew that he half guessed what part I had played in Uncle George's death. He had several times earlier remarked that my disappearance from Brighton at the moment of success was out of character, and had shown polite scepticism over my excuse that I was growing anxious about my horse. He had mentioned pointedly that the Brighton police, listening in the Marconicar taxi to Uncle George's ravings, had heard a faint murmur (indistinguishable) in the background, a single shot, and nothing more. They had not been able to account for this, apart from later finding the microphone switched off and a bullet in the wall, had come to the conclusion that Uncle George had been testing the old pistol to see if it were in working order. The shot had, however, brought them in haste to the Marconicar building, where they had arrived just in time to hear him shoot himself.

"You may be right," I said noncommittally to Lodge. His eyelids flickered, and he smiled and changed the subject.

"The Marconicar drivers come up in court again this week. You'll be there to give evidence, I suppose," he said.

"Yes," I agreed, not liking the prospect.

All the drivers who had been looking for me had been alarmed by the shot and the silence on their radios. Some had begun to drive back to Brighton, some had made for London, and one or two had left their taxis and started out on foot. But all had quickly been rounded up, as following the rather vague directions I had phoned to Lodge, the police had begun making road blocks round them while they were still listening to Uncle George. Now the drivers faced charges ranging from intimidation and grievous bodily harm to murder itself.

Records discovered in Uncle George's study, inside a folder marked with gory humour "Notes on Human Sacrifices," made it clear that Joe Nantwich had indeed been knifed by the man who had been wearing my tie.

And Uncle George's motives were now clear, too. Keeping up old standards of luxury had been too much for his income after the war, and instead of making Aunt Deb face reality, or facing it himself, he had gradually spent most of his capital. With almost the last of it he had bought Marconicars and launched into crime. He had directed everything through Fielder and had apparently never seen with his own eyes the brutal results of his orders. I doubted whether his misdeeds had seemed either more or less real to him than the primitive barbarities he spent his time studying.

The police had found neat lists, in files going back four years, of the money he had collected from the little terrorised businesses; and occasionally against the name of a café or a shop or a pub, Lodge told me, was written the single word, "Persuaded."

The racing record was shorter and contained lists of sums of money which the police did not know the purpose of; but one sheet headed "Joe Nantwich" was clear enough. It was a list of dates and amounts, of which the smallest was one hundred pounds. And underneath was drawn a thick line, with the words: "Account closed" printed in Uncle George's neat handwriting.

With Kate gone, the press men had drifted away. Their fun was over.

"Are you ready to go?" I asked Lodge. I had picked him up in Maidenhead on my way down. He nodded, and we went out to my car.

I drive fastest when I'm happy. That day I had no trouble at all in keeping within the speed limit through all the twisty Sussex villages, and Lodge endured my gloomy silence without comment half the way back to Maidenhead.

Finally he said, "Miss Ellery-Penn was very useful to her uncle. Everything you did in pursuing him went straight back to him through her. No wonder he was so well informed about your movements."

I had lived with this thought for a long time now; but hearing someone else speak it aloud had a most extraordinary effect. A tingle ran up my spine and set my brain suddenly alive, as if an alarm bell were ringing in my subconscious.

We were running through scrub and heathland. I slowed, swung the car off the road on to the peaty verge, and stopped. Lodge looked at me questioningly.

"What you said. I want to think," I said.

He waited a while in silence, and then said, "What's worrying you? The case is over. There are no more mysteries."

I shook my head. "There's someone else," I said

"What do you mean?"

"There's someone else we don't know about. Someone in Uncle George's confidence." In spite of everything, I still thought of him as Uncle George.

Lodge said, "Fielder, the manager, was rounded up. So were all the L. C. Perth operators, though they have been freed again. Only two of the clerks had any idea of what was going on, one who went to the race tracks and one in the office. They received their instructions through Fielder about which horses to accept unlimited money on."

"Joe was stopping horses for months before Uncle George gave Heavens Above to Kate, and she had never been racing before that. Someone else who goes racing must have been working for Uncle George," I said with conviction.

"Penn would need only the morning paper and a form book for choosing a horse to stop. He wouldn't need to go to the races himself. He didn't need an accomplice at the races apart from his bookmarker—Perth. You're imagining things."

"Uncle George didn't know enough about horses," I said.

"So he made out," said Lodge sceptically.

"Kate told me that for as long as she remembers he was a dead loss on the subject. He started the Marconicar Protection racket only four years ago, and the racing racket less than a year ago. Before that he had no reason to pretend. Therefore his ignorance of horses was gen- uine."

"I'll give you that," he said, "but I don't see that it proves anything."

"He *must* have had a contact on the racecourse. How else did he manage to pick on the one jockey who could most easily be corrupted?" I said.

"Perhaps he tried several, until he found a taker," sug- gested Lodge.

"No. Everyone would have talked about it, if he had."

"He tried Major Davidson," said Lodge. "That looks like a very bad mistake from your mythical adviser."

"Yes," I conceded. I changed to another tack. "There have been one or two things which have been relayed recently to Uncle George which Kate herself didn't know. How do you explain that?"

"What things?"

"Joe's bit of brown wrapping paper, for instance. He told everyone in the weighing room at Liverpool about it. Kate wasn't at the meeting. But two days later, on Uncle George's instructions, Joe was killed and the paper taken away from him."

Lodge pondered. "Someone might have rung her up on the Sunday and mentioned it in passing."

I thought fleetingly of Dane. I said, "Even then, it was surely not interesting enough for her to have told Uncle George."

"You never know," he said.

I started up and drove on in silence for some miles. I was loth to produce for his scepticism the most deep rooted of my reasons for believing an enemy still existed: the near-certainty that in the concussed gap in my memory I already knew who it was.

When at last I tentatively told him this, he treated it more seriously than I had expected. And after some minutes of thought he pierced and appalled me by saying, "Perhaps your subconscious won't let you remember who this enemy of yours is *because you like him*."

I DROPPED LODGE at Maidenhead and went on to the Cotswolds.

Entering the old stone house with the children noisily tumbling through the hall on their way to tea was like stepping into a sane world again. Scilla was coming down the stairs with her arms full of Polly's summer dresses: I went over and met her on the bottom step and kissed her cheek.

"Joan and I will have to lengthen all these," she said,

nodding at the dresses. "Polly's growing at a rate of knots."

I followed her into the drawing-room and we sat down on the hearthrug in front of a newly lit fire.

"Is it all over?" asked Scilla, pushing the dresses off her lap on to the floor.

"Yes, I think so." Too much was all over.

I told her about the inquest and the verdict. I said, "It was only because of Bill that George Penn was ever found out. Bill didn't die for nothing."

She didn't answer for a long time, and I saw the yellow flames glinting on the unshed tears in her eyes. Then she sniffed and shook her head as if to free herself from the past, and said, "Let's go and have tea with the children."

Polly wanted me to mend a puncture on her bicycle. Henry said he'd worked out some gambits in chess and would I play against him after tea. William gave me a sticky kiss and pressed an aged fruit drop into my palm as a present. I was home again.

chapter 19

THE ALMOST UNBEARABLE belief that I had lost Kate grew very little easier as the days passed. I couldn't get her out of my mind. When I woke in the morning the ache rushed in to spoil the day: when I slept I dreamed continually that she was running away down a long dark tunnel. I thought it unlikely I would ever see her again, and tried to make myself be sensible about it.

Then, a week after the inquest on Uncle George, I went to ride at Banbury races, and Kate was there. She was dressed in dark navy blue and there were big grey hollows round her eyes. Her face was pale and calm, and her expression didn't change when she saw me. She was waiting outside the weighing room, and spoke to me as soon as I drew near.

"Alan, I think I should apologise for what I said to you the other day." The words were clearly an effort.

"It's all right," I said.

"No . . . it's not. I thought about what you said . . . about those children going to school with the judo expert . . . and I realise Uncle George had got to be stopped." She paused. "It was not your fault Aunt Deb died. I'm sorry I said it was." She let out a breath as if she had performed an intolerable duty.

"Did you come all the way here especially to say that?" I asked.

"Yes. It has been worrying me that I was so unjust."

"My dear precious Kate," I said, the gloom of the past week beginning to vanish like morning mist, "I would have given anything for it not to have been Uncle George, believe me." I looked at her closely. "You look very hungry. Have you had anything to eat today?"

"No," she said, in a small voice.

"You must have some lunch," I said, and giving her no chance to refuse, took her arm and walked her briskly to the luncheon-room. There I watched her eat, pecking at first but soon with ravenous appetite, until some colour came back into her cheeks and a faint echo of her old gaiety to her manner.

She was well into her second helping of hot game pie when she said in a friendly tone. "I wish you'd eat something, too."

I said, "I'm riding."

"Yes I know, I saw in the paper. Forlorn Hope, isn't it?" she asked between forkfuls.

"Yes," I said.

"You will be careful, won't you? He's not a very good jumper, Pete says."

I looked at her with delighted astonishment, and she blushed-deeply.

"Kate!" I said.

"Well . . . I thought you'd never forgive me for being so abysmally beastly. I've spent the most vile week of my life regretting every word I said. But at least it brought me to my senses about you. I tried to tell myself I'd be delighted never to see you again and instead I got more and more miserable. I . . . I didn't think you'd come back for a second dose, after the way you looked at Brighton. So I thought if I wanted you to know I was sorry I'd have to come and tell you, and then I could see . . . how you reacted."

"How did you expect me to react?"

"I thought you'd be rather toffee-nosed and cool, and I wouldn't have blamed you." She stuffed an inelegant amount of pie-crust into her mouth.

"Will you marry me, then, Kate?" I asked.

She said, "Yes" indistinctly with her mouth full and went on uninterruptedly cutting up her food. I waited patiently while she finished the pie and made good time with a stack of cheese and biscuits.

"When did you eat last?" I asked, as she eventually put down her napkin.

"Can't remember." She looked across at me with a new joy in her face and the old sadness beneath it, and I knew from that and from her remark about Forlorn Hope—the first concern she had ever shown for my safety—that she had indeed grown up.

I said, "I want to kiss you."

"Racecourses were not designed for the convenience of newly affianced lovers," she said. "How about a horse-box?"

"We've only got ten minutes," I said. "I'm riding in the second race."

We borrowed Pete's horse-box without more ado. I took her in my arms, and found this time on Kate's lips a satisfactorily unsisterly response.

The ten minutes fled in a second, and the races wouldn't wait. We walked back, and I went into the weighing room and changed into colours, leaving Kate, who looked a bit dazed and said she felt it, sitting on a bench in the sun.

It was the first time I had been racing since Uncle George's inquest. I glanced uneasily round the changing room at the well-known faces, refusing to believe that any was the go-between who had brought death to Joe. Perhaps Lodge was right, and I didn't want to find out.

I had liked Uncle George himself, once. Did I shrink from seeing the façade stripped from another friend to reveal the crocodile underneath?

Clem handed me my lead packed weight cloth. I looked at his patient wrinkled face, and thought "Not you, not you."

It was a sort of treachery to reflect that Clem heard all that went on and that no event of any significance ever escaped his ears. "The oracle," some of the lads called him.

A hearty thump on the back cut off my speculations.

"Wotcher, me old cock sparrow, how's the sleuthing business?" bellowed Sandy, pausing and balancing his saddle on one knee while he looped up the girths. "How's Sherlock these days?"

"Retired," I said, grinning.

"No, really? After such grade A results?"

"I'll stick to steeplechasing, I think. It's less risky."

Sandy's friendly gaze strayed to the scar on my cheek.

"You're welcome to your little illusions, chum," he said. "You'll change your mind when you've broken as many bones as I have." He wound the girths round the saddle, tucked in the buckles, and with his helmet pushed far back on his head and his cheerful voice drawing heads round like a magnet, made his way out to the scales.

From across the changing room I had a good view of Dane's back solidly and deliberately turned towards me. Talking to someone by the gate, he had unfortunately seen Kate and me returning from the horse-box parking ground. He had had a good look at our radiant faces before we knew he was there, and he didn't need to have things spelled out for him. He had congratulated Kate in two clipped sentences, but to me he had still not spoken a word.

I went past his unyielding back and out to the paddock. He followed. Pete trained both the horses we were riding, and we both had to join him.

Pete jumped in with both feet.

"Alan, Kate's told me your news. Well done."

He received a fierce glower from Dane, and hastily began to assess the race. He was talking about Dane's mount, and my attention wandered.

There, ten yards away, stood the craggy Clifford Tudor, opulently rolling a cigar round his mouth and laying down the law to his trainer and jockey. Odd, I thought, how often I had come across that man. I watched him make heavy chopping motions with his dark hands to emphasise his points, and caught the young jockey, Joe's substitute, wrinkling his forehead in acute anxiety.

My gaze slid beyond him to where Sir Creswell Stampe was superintending the raising of his unamiable son David into the saddle, before going to take his judicial position in the Stewards' box. Beyond him again were other groups of owners and trainers planning their plans, hoping their hopes, giving their jockeys instructions (and counter-instructions) and calculating their last-minute bets.

So many people I knew. So many people I liked. Which of them . . . which of them was not what he seemed?

Pete gave me a leg up on to Forlorn Hope's narrow back, and I waved to Kate, who was standing by the parade ring rails, and cantered down towards the start.

On the way Dane came past briskly, turning his head in my direction as he drew level. With cold eyes he said, "Blast you," giving both words equal punch, and shook up his horse to get away from me and give me no chance to reply. I let him go. Either he would get over it or he wouldn't; and in either case there wasn't much I could do about it.

There were eleven runners in the race. We circled round while the starter's assistant tightened girths and the starter himself called the roll. Sandy asked his permission to dismount in order to straighten his saddle, which had slipped forwards on the way down to the gate. The starter nodded, looking at his wrist watch and telling Sandy not to be too long. This particular starter hated to start his races late and grew fidgety over every minor delay.

Sandy unbuckled the girths, pulled his saddle straight, and tightened it up again. I was watching him instead of concentrating wholly on Forlorn Hope, so that what happened was entirely my own fault.

An attendant flapped open under my horse's nose the white flag which it was his job to wave aloft, to signal to the stands that the horses were about to start. My green young hurdler took fright, reared up like a circus horse, twisted sideways, and threw me off. I hit the ground almost flat on my back, winding myself, and I saw Forlorn Hope kick up his heels and depart at a smart pace up the course.

For a few seconds I lay there trying to get my breath back, and Sandy walked over with his hand outstretched to help me up, laughing and making some rude remark about my sudden descent.

The most extraordinary dizziness suddenly swept over me, and my senses began to play fantastic tricks. Lying in the spring sun, I felt rain on my face. Winded but unhurt, my body was momentarily invaded by shocking pain. In my whirling brain it seemed as if past and present had become confused, and that two completely different events were somehow happening at the same time.

I stared up at Sandy's face. There was the familiar wide gap-toothed grin, the false incisors removed for safety; there were the laughing brown eyes with the reddish lashes and the bold devil-may-care expression. The sunshine bathed his face in light. And what I saw as well was the same face looming towards me in pouring rain, with cruel eyes and a grim mouth. I heard a voice say, "You nosey bastard, perhaps that'll teach you to mind your own business"; and I threw up my hand to shield my cheek against the kick which was coming . . .

My sight cleared and steadied, and Sandy and I were looking straight into each other's eyes as if a battle were being fought there. He dropped the hand outstretched to help me, and the friendliness went out of his face with the completeness of an actor shielding a role when the play is over.

I found my palm was still pressed against my cheek. I let it drop away, but the gesture had told its tale. I had remembered what had happened by the fence at Bristol, and Sandy knew it.

Strength returned to my limbs, and I stood up. The starter consulting his watch in barely concealed annoyance, asked if I was all right. I replied that I was, and apologised for holding up the race. Some way down the course someone had caught Forlorn Hope, and as I watched he was turned round to be led back to the starting gate.

Sandy, showing no haste to remount, stood his ground in front of me.

"You can't prove a thing," he said, characteristically taking the bull by the horns. "No one can connect me with Penn."

"Fletcher," I said at once.

"He'll keep his mouth shut," said Sandy, with conviction. "He's my cousin."

Uncle George's racing venture, I now saw, had not been inspired solely by the availability of a shaky book-making business. The existence of an easily recruited ally on the racecourse might have been the very factor which decided him, in the first place, to buy L. C. Perth.

I mentally reviewed the rest of the gang.

"How about Fielder?" I suggested after a short pause.

"I'm the voice on the phone to him. A voice called Smith. He doesn't know me from Adam," said Sandy.

Temporarily, I gave up. I said, "What did you do it for?"

"Money. What else?" he said scornfully, clearly thinking the question foolish.

"Why didn't you stop the horses yourself? Why let Joe collect the big fat fees for losing?"

Sandy seemed perfectly willing to explain. "I did stop a couple myself. The Stewards had me in over the second one, and I got off by the skin of my bloody teeth. I saw the red light, mate. I tipped the boss to try that little bastard Joe instead. Let him lose his licence, not me, I told him. But mind you, I was on to a bloody good percentage every time he strangled one."

"Which made you all the more angry when he won against orders on Bolingbroke," I said.

"That's right."

"Then Joe didn't tell you in the washroom he was going to pull Bolingbroke. You knew already."

"Proper little Sherlock," mocked Sandy.

"And you did put him over the rails at Plumpton, I suppose?"

"He bloody well deserved it. He lost me fifty quid on Leica as well as my bonus from the boss."

"Did he deserve to die, as well?" I asked bitterly.

The man leading Forlorn Hope back was now only a hundred yards away.

"The stupid little sod couldn't keep his mouth shut," said Sandy violently. "Waving that brown paper at Liverpool and yelling for you. I saw what was written on it, and told Fielder, that's all. I didn't know what it meant, but it was a ton to a tanner the boss wouldn't like it. Joe was asking for it."

"And after he'd got it, you rang Fielder and told him the job had been bungled, and Joe had lived long enough to talk to me?"

"Yes," said Sandy morosely. "I heard you telling every bloody body in the weighing room."

I couldn't resist it. I said, "I was lying. Joe died without saying a word."

As the full significance of this slowly dawned on him, his jaw dropped, and I saw him waver in some secret inner place as if an axe had hacked into the roots of his colossal self-confidence. He turned on his heel, strode across to where the starter's assistant held the horse, and swung abruptly into the saddle.

I went to meet Forlorn Hope, thanked the man who had brought him back, and remounted. The starter's patience had run out.

"Get into line, please," he said, and the circling horses began to straighten out across the course. I came up from behind and took a place alongside Sandy. I had one more question to ask.

"Tell me," I said, "why on earth did you get Penn to try to bribe Major Davidson? You must have known he wouldn't have stopped Admiral winning for all the money in the world."

"It was the boss's idea, not mine," said Sandy roughly. "I warned Fielder to tell him it wouldn't work, but the boss knew bee-all about horses and was pigheaded besides. Fielder said he wouldn't listen, because he thought if he fixed a cert it would be worth a fortune. He made a pocket out of it, all right. He thought up the wire himself. And I'd be a ruddy sight better off if the wire had killed you, too," he added, with a spurt of venom.

The starter's hand swept down on the lever. The tape flew up, and, five minutes later, the horses bounded forward towards the first hurdle.

I don't know exactly when Sandy decided to put me over the rails. Perhaps the thought of all the money he would not be getting overwhelmed him, and perhaps I had brought it on myself by recalling that he had done it to Joe when Joe, as he saw it, had cheated him.

In any case, as we approached the second hurdle, he

swerved his horse toward me. We were both in the group just behind the leaders, and I was on the inside, with the rails on my left.

I glanced at Sandy's face. His slitted eyes were concentrated on the jump ahead, but with every stride his horse drew nearer to mine. He wasn't leaving me much room, I thought.

Only just in time did I realise that he intended to leave me no room at all. He was aiming to crowd my horse so closely that I would be thrust into the six foot high wing leading up to the hurdles. A crash through the wings, I had been told, was one of the most dangerous of all falls. The time had clearly come for rapid evasive action if I were not to find this out for myself.

I literally hauled on the reins. Forlorn Hope lost impetus dramatically, and as soon as the quarters of Sandy's horse were past his shoulder I pulled his head unceremoniously to the right. It was only just in time. The hurdles were beneath his feet before he had time to see them, and he knocked one flat with his forelegs. The horse following us, going faster, bumped hard into the back of him, and the jockey yelled at me to mind what I was doing.

Forlorn Hope was too much of a novice to stand this sort of thing, and I decided that if I were not to ruin his nerve for good, I would have to keep him out of Sandy's way for the rest of the race.

But Sandy was not content with that. Along the straight in front of the stands he gradually worked himself back to my side. He was a better a jockey than I and his horse was more experienced. When I tried to go faster, he kept pace, and when I slowed down, he slowed too. I could not shake him off. In front of the crowds, apart from keeping pace with me, he rode fairly enough; but round the next bend lay the long curved leg out into the comparatively deserted country, and what he might do there I hated to think.

I did consider pulling up and dropping out of the race altogether, but that seemed an even more ignominious defeat than being put over the rails.

As the field swept round the bend in a bunch, Sandy tried again. He closed his horse tight up against mine and very slightly behind. On my left I was jammed against Dane. He glanced across and shouted, "Get over, Sandy. Give us some room."

Sandy did not answer. Instead I felt his knee slide along under my thigh until it was pressing fiercely on my hamstrings. Then he gave a sudden violent jerk forwards and upwards with his whole leg.

My foot flew out of the stirrup and I lost my balance completely. I swayed wildly over to the left, my head tipping down beside my horse's neck, my fingers clutching frantically at his mane. I looked down and saw the blur of hooves pounding tight-packed round the bend, and I struggled to prevent myself slipping off among them. But all my weight was too far forward, and the jolt of the horse's galloping stride tended to tip me farther forward still. I knew that in a few seconds I would be off.

It was Dane who saved me. He put his hand on my side and literally pushed me back into my saddle.

"Thanks," I gasped, feeling with my right foot for the dangling stirrup.

Not far round the bend lay the next flight of hurdles, and I fought to get myself and the horse properly balanced before we met it. As we came round the bend the sun had shone straight into our faces, but swinging out towards the country it lay on our right. Glancing to see if Sandy was still beside me I caught the sunshine full in the eyes and was for a second dazzled. He was there. He appeared to me as a black silhouette against the sun.

I remembered then that on such bright days on this course the sun shone straight into the eyes of the crowds on the stands also, and that it was difficult for them to distinguish what was happening on the far side of the course. Whatever Sandy did, he could be fairly sure the Stewards would not be able to see.

I gained a yard or two on Sandy and Dane at the next hurdle, but over my shoulder I could hear Sandy clicking with his tongue to hurry his horse, and in a few more strides he was beside me again. His shadow lay across my horse's withers.

Suddenly he swung his arm; and had I not been so acutely ready he would have had me. He swung his right arm around his body in a chop at my face, slashing with his riding whip. I ducked in a reflex, without actually seeing the whip at all. The heavy blow landed across my helmet just above the peak, and knocked it clean off my head. It bounced away on the turf.

I felt, rather than saw, Sandy draw back his arm for another try. I slipped my own whip and the reins into my left hand, and when he struck, threw up my right. More by luck than design my fingers fastened on the stick and I gripped and twisted and pulled with the strength of desperation.

I had him half out of his saddle and I almost exulted, but at the vital moment he let go of his stick and regained his balance. Rebounding, his horse swerved away from me, leaving a gap, and I looked hopefully over my shoulder for one of the other runners to come up between us. But most of them had gone on in front, and there was no one close. I threw Sandy's stick away.

The next hurdle lay ahead. I kept well away from the rails and tried to steady Forlorn Hope so that he should have a fair chance at it, but I was all too aware that Sandy was beginning to close on me again with a burst of extra speed.

My horse jumped the hurdle in reasonable style. Sandy kicked his horse into a tremendous leap, and as he landed he pulled straight across in front of me.

Forlorn Hope crashed into the rails.

By some miracle he did not fall. He bounced off, staggered, faltered, and galloped on. My leg, which had been
crushed just below the knee between his body and the
rails, was completely numb. I looked down at it, it appeared to be doing its job all right, even though I no
longer seemed to be connected to it. My silk breeches
were ripped open across the knee, and in my new extremely expensive made-to-measure racing boots flapped
a large triangular tear.

Illogically, this made me very angry.

Sandy was some lengths ahead and had not so far
managed to pull back again. Dane came up on my right,
and I was glad to see him there.

He yelled, "What the hell's going on? What the blazes
does Sandy think he's playing at?"

"He's not playing," I shouted. "He wants to get me
off."

"Why?" yelled Dane.

"He was working for George Penn. He was making a
lot of money. Now he isn't. He blames me," I shouted
in snatches, the wind picking the words out of my mouth
and blowing them back over my shoulder.

"With reason," shouted Dane.

"Yes," I agreed. I glanced at him, but now it was he
who was outlined against the sun, and I could not see
his expression clearly. If he felt badly enough about Kate
to carry on where Sandy had for the moment left off, I
should have no chance at all. He could ride rings round
me, and Sandy, too.

We raced in silence towards the next hurdle, the last
on the far side. Sandy was gradually slowing to wait for
me.

Then Dane said, "Alan?"

"Yes?" I shouted back.

"Do you want to give Sandy some of his own medi-
cine?"

"Yes." I suddenly had no reservations. It was a terrible

thing to do, and if the Stewards saw me I'd lose my permit; but I had taken just about enough from Uncle George's assorted strong-arm boys.

Dane shouted, "I'll go up on his outside. You come outside me. Then I'll get away and leave him between you and the rails. O.K.?"

I nodded. I tried to foresee the future. If I unseated Sandy he would not dare to complain to the Stewards; and I, as he said, could give no tangible evidence against him to the police. There could be an uneasy truce between us. And fall for fall, the score would be equal.

"Come on, then," Dane shouted.

He kicked his horse and began to take his place on Sandy's right. I pulled away from the rails and urged Forlorn Hope to the outside. There was nearly a mile to go to the finish, and as no one had yet begun to put on the pressure the field was still fairly closely bunched just ahead of us. There was no one behind. After the hurdle lay the long oval bend leading round into the straight. If either Sandy or I were to get the other off, it would have to be done on the bend; once we were round into the straight the Stewards would have too clear a view of our behavior.

Dane jumped the hurdle alongside Sandy with me not far behind. As soon as I was level with them both, Dane shook up his horse and sped clear away from us, leaving me, as he had promised, with Sandy between me and the rails.

I swung Forlorn Hope over roughly on to Sandy's horse, bumping him against the rails. Sandy yelled and lashed out with his fist. I hit his arm sharply with my stick.

I had got to unseat him without hurting his horse. I was being unfair enough already to the owner in trying to lose him the race by dislodging his jockey: if I could not do it without damaging the horse I must not do it at all.

Shifting the reins into my right hand, I planted my left abruptly on Sandy's body just behind his armpit, and shoved. But I was too far away to get enough force behind it. He swayed in the saddle, but kept his balance. He began to swear at me.

We were on the crown of the bend. It had to be now or never. I pushed Sandy's horse harder against the rails. He yelled again. His leg, I knew, must be being crushed, pounded, even torn by the white-painted wood. With my own leg numb from the same treatment, I had no sympathy for him. Then his foot crashed into one of the uprights with an audible snap.

He screamed.

I gritted my teeth, shot my arm, and pushed him with all my might. I knew if he had not gone then I would not have had the resolution to try again. But he began to topple, slowly, it seemed, at first, and then with an accelerating rush, as if he had been sucked away by a slipstream.

I caught a final glimpse of his face, eyes staring widely, mouth twisted with agony, as he fell into the long grass on the other side of the rails. Then I was round the bend into the straight, bruised, tattered and helmetless, but still on board.

Sandy's loose horse, relieved of his weight, spurted forward through the other runners.

Dane saw him, and turned round in his saddle and grinned at me, and jerked up his thumb.

NOW AVAILABLE IN HARDCOVER

DICK FRANCIS

SECOND WIND

PUTNAM